To: my main

I really appreciate your support and friendship.

The Write Lover

By

Brooklen Borne

Your brother and friend

Brooklen Borne

Published by Bee 5ive Production
3020 Wexford Walk Dr.
Smyrna, GA 30080

All characters and events in this book are fictitious, and any resemblance to action person, living or dead, is purely coincidental.

The cataloging-in-publication data is on file with the Library of Congress.

Library of Congress Control Number: 2011960547

ISBN - 13: 978-1469927756
ISBN - 10: 1469927756

Copyright © 2008 and 2011 by Brooklen Borne

All Rights Reserved

Printed in the United States of America

March 2012

Genre: Fiction/Suspense Romance

The Write Lover

An Urban Romance Story

By Brooklen Borne

Author of:

Savannah

Being Homeless Is Not an Option

Dedication

I dedicate this book to all that have supported me, in the earlier versions of this wonderful story. As you all know, this has been a journey.

Acknowledgements

I would like to begin by giving thanks to God for blessing me to see another day so I can work on bringing my thoughts to life. Also, giving me a sound mind to keep my creative thoughts on the forefront; one adventure after another, helping me to keep my reader's mind stimulated. I am blessed to be surrounded by true friends and family members that have prayed for me throughout my ups and downs, never leaving my side.

I would like to give a special thank you, to all who made the re-release of *"The Write Lover"* possible. Anetral Hall, Diane Johnson, NaTasha Bailey, Jackie Seaton, Joyah Seaton, Alice Walker, Bianca "Butterfly", Christina Hackett, Crystal Scott, Denise "Deeva" Ross, Beverly "Dimples" Rowley, Karl "Pathfinder" Anthony, Dena Tyson, Shaneen Martin, Savannah J, Koko McFadden, Lushanna Thompson, Katrina Gurl, Nita Bee, Katrina Burroughs, Chi-B (from Japan), Aquilla Fearson (from Germany), Wendell Shabazz (R.I.P. 1958-2011), Caressa Shepard, Louis Barrington, Rebecca Barrington, Maryann Hassan, Orlando Lunnon, Leshaun Lunnon, Gloria Pugh, James Pugh, Margaret Willis, Renae Brown, Dr. Linda Mosley, Shannon Howard, Julie Trotman, Mark Coates, Cheryl Trotman-Coates, Pat Seldon, Author Coates, Trav Lyrics, Evelyn Reed, Troy Jones, Jewel Bramwell, Teresa Rae Butler and Tina Harris.

Most of all, I would like to say thank you to the readers who have kept me inspired to write quality, entertaining stories that you love to read and tell others to go and check out. Thank you from the bottom of my heart.

To Experience Love

If you are in love or have ever been in love, you know what kind of sacrifices you've made and maybe still are making, for the sake of that beautiful connection between the two of you. You will go to the depths of hell for that special person, and you will climb to the heavens for that special person, but how far are you really willing to go for…**The Write Lover?**

Brooklen Borne

"Love is a battlefield, we all get scars."

Mary J. Blige and Ludacris

Prologue

The day Jasmine Deveraux broke her ankle in the biggest track meet of the season; she thought her life was over. She was just the tender age of 17 and had high hopes to pursue her goals of going away to college on a full track and field scholarship, but after a broken ankle, UCLA decided they would only offer her a partial scholarship in hopes she would recover and be able to run for them.

Jasmine knew there was no way her parents could afford to pay the remainder of the tuition, so she gave up on her hopes and dreams of college all together. Jasmine is a fair skinned, brown eye, beauty, who wore her hair short some weeks and long on others. Her flawless skin and exotic features didn't require her to put on any makeup. Her 5'6" package commanded attention that was noticed by both students and teachers.

Her senior year had not turned out how she planned. She was sad and depressed and didn't even want to attend the Sweethearts Ball. She was on crutches anyway, and knew she wouldn't have a good time. To make matters worse, her boyfriend of a year and a half, Eric, asked her if it would be okay, if he asked someone else to the ball, because this would be his last year to attend and he didn't want to miss the experience, since this was his senior year as well. Eric's golden brown complexion and good looks came from the combination of his Dominican mother and Haitian father. His firm build, attached to his 6'2" frame, had the young ladies at his beckoned call, and he used his assets to get what he wanted.

Reluctantly, Jasmine agreed, not knowing he would ask Brenda. Brenda favored the actress Kerri Washington, to the "tee" except for she had a bigger butt and was known for easily giving up the booty. In spite of the knowledge that many girls in the school was trying to get with Eric, Jasmine trusted him to stay loyal. He never gave her, a reason not to. They had given up their virginity to one another and even talked about getting married after they finished college. Eric was the varsity basketball captain and the best player on the team. He had already secured a full scholarship to Arizona State.

With her heavy back pack, Jasmine struggled to balance herself on the grey aluminum crutches, as she made her way across the schoolyard; trying not to be late for her first period class.

"Yo Jas, let me help you with your backpack." Malik, her homeboy yelled out, trotting towards her.

"Thanks," Jasmine said relieved, wondering where Eric was. He usually waited for her out in front of the school, but not today. It was Monday after the big Sweetheart Ball and she hadn't talk to him since Saturday night when he was getting ready for the dance.

"Is Eric going to kick my ass for helping his girl?" Malik joked.

"Please!" Jasmine laughed. "Eric knows that you and I go way back to second grade."

"That's right, I knew you first. I've been trying to get at you since the second grade and you just wouldn't give me any play." Malik joked again, pushing up his thick plastic frame glasses, on the bridge of his nose. Malik was a geek, but cute, and basically a book-smart, shy guy who was not really Jasmine's type, but they always remained good friends.

"So how was the dance? Did you have fun?" Jasmine asked Malik, with a teasing smile.

The Write Lover

"It was alright, but your man had a lot of fun. Look Jasmine, I don't want to start anything but…"

"But what?" Jasmine asked curiously.

"If you are Eric's woman, then he sure wasn't acting like it at the dance." Jasmine stopped in her tracks, resting on the crutches that were snuggled under her armpits.

"What do you mean, Malik?"

"You have to ask Eric, Jas."

"Malik don't play with me. What happened at the ball?"

"Brenda and Eric were all over each other on the dance floor and when they left the ball, a rumor has it they went and got a hotel room."

"That's a lie." Jasmine said, taking a deep breath. She never thought in a thousand years Eric would cheat on her. Even though Brenda had a big derrière, she was in no way cuter than Jasmine. Jasmine was Homecoming Queen and all the guys in the school, would had loved to have her on their arm.

"Jas, I just wanted you to know what the buzz was about, before you hear it through the grapevine." Jasmine looked up to see a few females smiling and pointing at her as she made her way to class. Just as she looked across the schoolyard, she spotted Eric standing around with his boys, laughing and next to him, big booty Brenda. She was smiling and laughing with them, like she was Eric's woman. Jasmine had never seen Brenda in their social group before. *Maybe what Malik told me is true.* Jasmine thought. She gestured for Malik to follow her, as she moved as fast as her balance would allow on the crutches, across the courtyard.

"Eric!" Jasmine yelled out. "Uh oh," someone had said aloud in the crowd where Eric had conjugated.

Brooklen Borne

"What?" Eric responded rudely. Brenda looked at Jasmine and began to chuckle at his response. At that moment, the bell rang for the first period class.

"Just tell her." Brenda said, looking at Jasmine with distain, as she walked away, swaying her hips; harder than usual.

"Tell me what?" Jasmine responded, rolling her eyes at Brenda.

"I got this," Eric told Malik, taking Jasmine's bag. Malik walked off, nodding to Jasmine.

"What's going on, Eric?"

"Look Jasmine, let me help you get to class and we can talk about this at lunchtime." "Why does it have to wait until then? I want to know what happened at the dance and I want to know now!"

"Look, I have a basketball game today. You know if I'm late for any of my classes, the coach is going to bench me. We'll talk later." Jasmine reluctantly agreed. She knew how important this upcoming game was for Eric, so she hurried as fast as she could on her crutches as Eric helped her to her journalism class. Jasmine was the editor of the school newspaper. She was a very talented writer and her teacher was trying to get her to pursue journalism in college, since her chances where slim to none for a hundred percent recovery in competing in the sport she loved so much. Eric kissed her on the cheek before rushing off to his own class.

Lunchtime could not have come fast enough. Jasmine had a spare set of keys to Eric's Cherry Red 1988 Ford Mustang, so she waited for him there before the bell rang for lunch. Everyday at lunch they would sit in the car and eat together or sometimes make out. Jasmine was very aware of the stares she got throughout the

The Write Lover

day and the gossip people seemed to be displaying around her. She waited patiently for Eric in the car, wondering what he was going to tell her. She was prepared to hear that maybe he kissed Brenda, but she knew there was no way Eric would have sex with her; even though she still had a horrible feeling in the pit of her stomach. Tears began to fill her eyes; Eric opened the door, positioning himself comfortably in the driver seat. He took a deep breath, leaning his head back on the headrest.

"Look, I'm just going to come out and say it. Brenda and I kind of fooled around in the limo after the dance and we went to a hotel with a few other people."

"Fooled around? Hotel?" Jasmine questioned.

Before she knew it, her hand rose up and slapped Eric in the face. Eric grabbed his face feeling the burning sensation. He sat in disbelief with the thought that she had slapped him. She had never hit him out of anger before. Jasmine struggled with the door handle to get out the car. Once opened, she grabbed her crutches, nearly falling out the car. Eric jumped out chasing after her.

"Hold up baby, it didn't mean anything. You know I love you. Please. Jasmine," Eric pleaded, standing in front of Jasmine.

"If you don't get out of my way, I'm gonna swing this crutch right at your lying ass head. I trusted you and you betrayed me." Jasmine yelled, as tears flowed from her eyes. "Did you have sex with her?" Eric didn't respond.

"Oh My God!" Jasmine yelled, crying harder, falling to the ground. Eric hugged her, and she wanted to push him away, but she had no strength in her body to do so. Her tears soaked into his shirt.

Brooklen Borne

"I'm sorry baby. You know my heart belongs to you. We've been together too long to let this break us up. You're the only girl for me. You know you gonna be my wife," Eric said, as he looked Jasmine in her eyes. "I'm gonna make it to the NBA and it's going to be you and me baby. You're not going to have to work or do anything, just have my kids. I know you wanted to pursue your track career, but since you can't now I'm gonna take care of us. I love you."

"You love me, huh? So why did you do, what you did?" She asked through tears of pain.

"It will never happen again. I promise you." Eric pleaded.

*****

Jasmine followed him to Arizona State, and got a part time job as a waitress; while attending a junior college. They lived in a one-bedroom apartment not far from both campuses and things seem to be working out for them. Unfortunately, Eric's basketball career was short lived. After his freshman year, he blew out his knee; in a pick-up game. He lost his scholarship and they could no longer afford to stay in Arizona without his scholarship money, so they moved back to Sacramento with their parents. Once back in Sacramento, their relationship still blossomed. Eric got a job with the electric company and Jasmine continued school part time at night, pursuing her major in journalism while working full time at a bank. Soon she became pregnant with their first son, Kyle. About six months after that, they ran off to Vegas and got married. Two years later, she was pregnant again with their second son, Kai. Jasmine finished school and landed a job at a local newspaper where she was one of three editors. On her free time, she continued to write short stories, poems and worked on her first novel; dreaming that one day it would get published. Eric was becoming very controlling and was against her outside literary endeavors. He told her she just needed to focus on their family and her job at the newspaper. Jasmine always knew one day she wanted to be a published author, and one day she would reach her goal of becoming one.

As a young mother at the tender age of twenty-four with two kids, a full-time job, and a husband, Jasmine had put her life on the back burner to be a good wife and mother. Even though, she was happily married with two beautiful sons, she was always haunted by big booty Brenda and would often have nightmares that Eric was cheating on her again. The way she expressed her anger and got over it was through her writing. It was therapeutic for her. She could create characters and make real life issues happen the way she wanted them to. The life of the track and field career she wanted became a story line for one of her characters. It was her outlet and she lived through her characters in the literary stories she created.

Jasmine had finally gotten the boys to bed, taken a shower and retired to a spare room turned into an office; to review her emails. As she checked her emails, she noticed a response from a publishing company she had submitted her manuscript to a few months back. When she opened the email and began to read, her eyes could not scan the words fast enough as she read: *We here at Baby Girl Publishing, would like to pick up your novel "Bad*

Brooklen Borne

Timing," for publication and offer you a contract, with a two thousand ($2,000.00) dollar advance. She printed out the email, rushing upstairs to Eric. He was drying off from being in the shower.

"Honey, guess what?" Jasmine spoke loud with excitement.

"What?" Eric replied, not really paying attention to her excitement.

"Baby Girl Publishing, wants to publish my book and they offered me a two thousand dollar advance." Jasmine was on cloud nine as she handed Eric the paper. He read over the printed email silently before handing it back to her.

"You don't have anything to say?" Jasmine asked, looking confused.

"You didn't tell me you submitted anything to any publisher?" he griped, searching for his pajama pants. "I told you, you don't have time for that shit right now."

"Eric, did you not just read this? They offered me two thousand dollars, upfront money."

"Tell me Jasmine, when are you supposed to make time to do book signings and shit. You have to market this thing and that means you'll be gone from the house. You can't just leave me and the boys to do that shit. We need you here at home. Besides, you need to take it easy with your heart and all. You know what the doctor said." Jasmine had suffered a cardiac arrest while giving birth to their second son, four months back. She has a weak heart, and has to take medication for the rest of her life.

"Email them back and tell them no thanks."

The Write Lover

"You're crazy!" Jasmine said defiantly resting her hands on her hips. "You know I always wanted to publish my novel."

"Your family comes first, Jasmine. You have to take it easy."

"I am taking it easy. I reduced my hours at work. I love to write and it's the only thing that relaxes me. If you're so concerned about my heart and me taking it easy, why don't you try cooking a meal every now and then, or washing the clothes and ironing your own damn shirts. That would help me take it easy!" Eric suddenly jumped up pinning Jasmine against the wall with his hand around her throat; raising her slightly off of the floor.

"I bring the majority of the money in this house, so that's your damn job!" Eric yelled. With both her hands holding on to his wrist, struggling to loosen his grip, fear and anger consumed her.

"You better get your fuckin' hand off me." She manages to warn, through clenched teeth. He loosened his grip and she fell to her knees. "If you ever put your hands on me again…"

"What you gonna do?" Eric said nonchalantly, as he cut her sentence short. Jasmine rolled her eyes at him and sucked her teeth. She began to see, that everything she wanted to do he would discourage her. But this was one battle she was not going to let him win. After five years of marriage and close to seven years of being together, since high school,

Jasmine often wondered what life would have been like if she would have never forgiven, him for screwing big booty Brenda back in high school and moved on with her life. It was too late to turn back the hands of time. Jasmine had two kids depending on her now. Even though, the thought of leaving the marriage had crossed her mind many times, she was going to hang in there for the sake of the children.

"Email the fuckin' publisher back and tell them no!" Eric spoke with menacing eyes.

"This is something I really want, Eric."

"I said no! Not right now. So email them back and tell them thanks, but no thanks." Jasmine held back her tears as she marched back to her office. She was going to pursue her writing career no matter what. So she emailed the publisher, informing them she was on board, even if she had to sneak and do it behind his back.

*****

Darius Hamilton grew up in New York and lived in the Marcy projects in Brooklyn with his mom and older brother. Darius' father was killed a few years back on his way home from work. He was a block away from home when two thugs had run up on him and demanded his wallet. Darius' father gave them the wallet with no hassle, whatsoever; still one of the thugs shot him in the chest, killing him instantly. A couple of months later the two culprits were caught by way of an anonymous tipster. When the detective asked the shooter, why he had to shot the victim, after he gave up his wallet with no resistance; he responded back with the comment, "I just wanted to know how it would feel to shoot someone."

Darius ran the streets often with his cousin Chris, who also lived in Brooklyn in the Crown Heights section. The urban streets were Darius' school and Chris was his teacher. Darius was a very good student of the game, and the curriculum consisted of how to put a cut on cocaine, burglary of commercial businesses and how to eliminate a rival without anything leading back to him. He traveled throughout the city with fear of no one, but if things got a little heated, he would call on Chris and between the two of them the problem would disappear. The two were like peas in a pod. Their relationship was very close because Darius never ran his mouth about anything no matter what circumstances were dealt. With the reputation of keeping a closed lip and outstanding fighting skills, Darius' street credibility grew.

The quick money and street life that Darius had become accustomed to changed one day for him and his cousin. He and Chris were standing on the corner of Utica Avenue and Eastern Parkway, waiting to cross the busy intersection, when they noticed an elderly lady, being robbed. Being it was the first of the month, they were probably trying to get a hold of her social security money.

"Those fools are trying to rob that old lady, in broad day light." Darius said to Chris, as both of their attention, along with other bystanders' were focused on the commotion.

"Not a damn person is doing anything," Chris replied.

"Let's help her," Darius said, tapping Chris on the shoulder, as they crossed the busy intersection, splitting their attention on the traffic and the two robbers.

"You take the one on the left and I got the one on the right," Chris said, as they made their way across Eastern Parkway to reach the woman. The two pounced on the attackers like African lions on a Gazelle. Punches were traded but Darius and Chris were getting the upper hand, when all of a sudden one of the robbers pulled out a gun and shot at Darius. He felt a hot sharp pain rip through his left shoulder. Then he pointed the gun and Chris and pulled the trigger, hitting him in the head.

The two muggers ran off, later to be caught three blocks away by New York's Finest. Chris was pronounced dead at the scene. The sight of his cousin, laying there on the concrete sidewalk, in a puddle of blood was burned in Darius' mind every time he closed his eyes to sleep. He started second guessing his actions to help the old lady, but the more he thought about it, the more he knew it was the right thing for him and Chris to do.

With the loss of his best friend and cousin, Darius turned to writing poetry and short stories while he recuperated in Kings County Hospital. During his recovery, he met a nurse assistant by the name of Patricia Tremble. She worked at the hospital for school credit and experience. She planned on majoring in nursing, at NYU; upon graduating high school, that upcoming June. Patricia would enjoy reading and listening to what Darius had written when she came to change his dressing every afternoon. Darius began looking forward to talking to her about, how he came to writing his poems and short stories. It became a daily ritual between the two. Their friendship continued to grow after he was released from the hospital. They became inseparable, even though they went to separate schools, Darius attended Stuyvesant High and Patricia attend South Shore. She continued to encourage him to write his poetry and enter them into the statewide contests. To Darius' surprise, he began to win. He knew Patricia and a few of her close friends liked his work, but for strangers to like it enough to give him awards was amazing. His name was getting around the city as one of the best lyricist in the game. He was asked to spit his words at a spoken word poetry club, located on Bowery Street

The Write Lover

in Manhattan. The manager of the club, not wanting to interfere with his school studies, told Darius he could come one night a week, only if he kept his grades up in school. Life seemed to be going well for Darius. His writing, relationship with Patricia, and home life was on point. He even began taking a big interest in helping his younger siblings with their schoolwork and showing them how to do chores around the house the correct way. This was a big help to his mother, a single parent.

Darius' SAT scores were way above average and he had applied to colleges based on their English curriculum programs. Even though he was a star wide receiver, he wanted a full academic scholarship rather than a sports scholarship. He also wanted to take his literary skills to the next level.

Darius had three months to go before graduation, when he noticed Patricia was gaining weight and her mood was out of the ordinary. The sex had slowed down, along with her feeling sick a lot. He began putting one and one together and figured out she was pregnant. One day after school, he went over to her house instead of going home first. He had a little pep, in his step, feeling good that the girl he grew to love was having his baby. He knew his mom would be upset with him, but he wasn't going to run from his responsibilities of being a father. When he knocked on her door, she immediately opened it, but Darius didn't get the usual greeting, so he knew something was wrong; but he couldn't put a finger on it. Patricia walked into the living room and sat on the couch. He sat beside her, taking her hand into his. Not wasting any time, he asked, "Baby, are you pregnant?"

"Yes, I am!" Patricia was known to be straightforward at times.

Brooklen Borne

Excited and worried at the same time, Darius promised he would do the right thing by taking care of her and the baby.

"Darius, stop talking for a minute. I have something to say." Tears escaped her eyes, traveling alongside her nose, and down her caramel cheeks.

"Go ahead baby. What is it?"

"I'm not pregnant by you."

"Yeah right, don't play with me girl, as much as I've been knocking the bottom out of that." He said, rubbing her inner thigh.

"I'm serious, Darius," she spoke loudly, getting a little agitated. Darius just looked at her in shock.

"What the hell is going on Pat?"

"I went to a party a few months ago and ran into my old boyfriend… one thing lead to another."

"So you are sure the baby that is inside you, is not mine?"

"Yes!" Patricia replied, as a steady flow of tears wet her face, along with a runny nose.

"I wasn't good enough for you? I wasn't out in the streets acting a fool. I was getting my poetry out to everyone, doing the right thing and you go to a party and have sex with an ex-boyfriend?" Darius was hurt but he didn't let out how angry he really was. His heart was so broken, he just had enough strength to get up and walk out. Patricia called out to him, just as his hand reached for the door knob, but he ignored her pleas and continued to walk out the door and out her life.

What happened between him and Patricia was too much for him to bear and started to affect his writing. He knew he couldn't go to college and write the way he had been, because Patricia was his inspiration. He needed to get far away as possible, so he decided to

The Write Lover

join the Marine Corps. A few years later, he had written a book about his past experiences with Chris and Patricia titled, "I Died Twice." But it wasn't until his four year enlistment was almost up, when Bee 5ive Publications sent him a letter, informing him, they like the manuscript and would like to publish it with a thousand dollar advance. Darius was so excited about the news, he made his mind up to write books and movie scripts for a living. He had worked in administration and had earned a Bachelor in English, so the love of writing and dealing with paper work was his passion.

Later in the same year, he was honorably discharged and found himself back in New York. He stayed at his mom's house, who now lived in Hempstead, Long Island. His mom loved having Darius home, not to mention he had earned a degree and a book deal. She was so proud and boasted about him to her friends and anyone who would listen. With the money he saved while in the service, he was financially stable until he got his own place. Darius wanted to move out as soon as possible.

A week later, he went into a realtor's office and there he met Chandra Johnson. She was a 25 year old, 5' 4", 125 pounds, long hair with caramel skin, real grey eyes. She was the number one realtor in the region, and when she saw Darius, her heart fluttered. Chandra was the type of woman that whatever she wanted, she was going to obtained it, and by the way her heart fluttered when she saw Darius; she knew she had to have him. Darius hadn't been in a serious relationship since breaking up with Patricia four years ago, but he was contemplating the idea when he saw this beautiful, single, sexy woman before him.

Within a week, Chandra had found Darius a nice affordable two-bedroom apartment in the Forest Hills section of Queens. She even helped him move into his new place. They were becoming real close, going to dinner, movies and spending quality time together, but their agendas were different. Chandra wanted him because every woman at her job, including the married ones, would give Darius the eye and show him extra attention whenever he would come in the office. She knew she had to have this fine man with chiseled features and body to boot. She wanted him as a trophy husband. She didn't care one bit about his writing career and that he may be one of the best selling authors of all times. All she cared about was the color green, the cash money green.

*****

A year later they got married. In the beginning everything seemed to be going well, the loving, the conversation, both of their careers, then one day out the blue Chandra asked Darius why doesn't he do something with his degree, instead of letting it collect dust. Darius books were doing well, but the income was not near, what Chandra was coming home with.

"Honey, I know my books are not bringing in the dollars that you're bringing in, but they soon will be."

"You'll never bring in the money with your books that I'm bringing in." Chandra said, snapping back.

"Let me throw some figures out to you, if I sell ten thousand units at fifteen dollars a book that will bring in one hundred and fifty thousand dollars. If I sell forty thousand units, that will bring in six hundred thousand dollars, and if God blesses me to sell a hundred thousand units, that will bring in one point five million dollars. This does not include the books I'm selling on the side.

It's just a matter of time baby, before the fruits of my labor pay off."

"You're good, baby, but you're no Eric Jerome Dickey."

"That's right, Chandra, I'm Darius Hamilton and I will take the literary world by storm. Just watch and see."

"I'm not going to wait too long."

"So what are you saying? You are going to walk away from this marriage? We just got married."

"Look, all I'm saying, is you need to do something else besides writing those stories."

"Do what you need to do. I believe in my product and it will pay off. I don't have time to deal with this negative vibe you are sending my way. I'll have to get my things ready for the Harlem Book Fair, which is going to be in three months. Will you come with me, to support me out there?"

"No, I have other important things to do."

"Come on Chandra, that's three months away. You can take one day off to support your man."

"Your books may not even sell and I would have spent a whole day baking in the heat when I could have sold a property."

Darius didn't say another word. He knew his books were good, and when the time arrived his books would be the hottest on the market. He just could not believe the lack of support he was getting from his wife. In the meantime, Darius was pushing his book wherever he could on his own. He didn't just rely on the publisher to sell his work. He believed in himself and in his product. *It's just a matter of time before Darius Hamilton would become a household name.* He thought to himself.

Chapter One
The Chemistry

Jasmine and Darius first encountered one another in New York City at the Harlem Book Fair. The Harlem Book Fair is an annual event located on W135th Street between 5th and 7th Avenue. The event is free and open to the public. It is one of the many literary venues that attract people from across the nation. Everybody and anybody from actors and well-known authors to avid readers, make their presence known. It's a gathering of publishers, authors, editors, and speakers promoting literacy in the African American communities. It's also a venue where they can sell their books, goods and services. This annual event is so big, C-Span televises it every year.

The two struck up a conversation, when they complained to each other, about what little space they had with the oversize beige metal frame padded table top's, in which they had to display their novels. After two cramped hours, they decided to alleviate the problem by folding up one of the tables and sharing the other. By doing so, this gave them more space and made things a lot more comfortable; but the temperature was rising; not because of the scorching city heat, but what Jasmine was wearing. She had on a form fitting yellow tank top, tight blue jean shorts that showcased her shapely legs and nice firm butt. She then rounded off her outfit with a pair of yellow Nike sneakers and a blue dungaree fabric purse.

"Jasmine, do you come every year?"

"No, this is my first time at this event."

"How about you?"

"This is my first time, as well. I wrote a book about my romantic past. It was picked up by an independent publisher, with a one thousand dollar advance. So here I am, on my grind, making this under the table money until something big happens with my book."

"Same here! I was also picked up by an indie. Who are you with?"

"I'm with Bee 5ive Publications." Darius responded, as he admired her flawless beauty; before asking her the same question.

"I'm with Baby Girl Publications." Wanting to know more about this man, that shared her passion for the literary arts, and not bad on the eyes. She continued with the questions. "Where do you live?"

"I live in Queens with my wife."

"No children?" She asked, picking up a 16 ounce green plastic bottle of Mountain Dew; taking a sip through a straw.

"No! Not yet, hopefully someday. How about you? Where do you live?"

"I'm from Sacramento, California. I'm married with two boys, three and five."

"Wow, you're a long way from home. I know the hotel is working your pockets."

"No, I'm staying at my cousin's place in Brooklyn."

The Write Lover

"Oh, okay," Darius replied, as he wiped his brow of sweat from the July heat.

"I just wished my husband would support me in my endeavor. For some reason, it seems like he doesn't want me to succeed with my writings. If I don't hold my ground against him, then I'll be a prisoner of my own doing, for the rest of my life."

"I can relate. My wife thinks my writing is a waste of time and that it will not bring in any real money. One thing she fails to realize is that this is my passion, and I'm going to make it work. Like you said, I'll be a prisoner of my own doing, if I don't keep pursuing my writing. Besides, if we didn't stick to our passion, I would've never met you."

"Aww, thank you." Jasmine replied smiling. A young couple had walked up to their table. The two cut their conversation turning their attention to them. A few hours later the event was coming to a close, and all the authors and vendors began packing up their gear. Darius and Jasmine had done well for their debut at the fair, selling fifteen books a piece. The two new friends hugged, and exchanged books and business cards, promising to stay in contact with one another.

"Have a safe trip back to the west coast."

"Thank you and you be safe during your travels, as well."

"I will. Thank you!" They waved good-bye as the crowd of people leaving the event consumed them.

*****

Jasmine and Darius kept their word and stayed in contact. They called each other at least once a week, but e-mailed one another daily. They kept each other in high spirits for their passion of writing, especially after reading each other's books. They admired each other's writing style and looked forward to working on a project together in the future. The more they talked the closer they became. One reason being, the negativity and lack of support they both received from their spouses. The other reason was they were being taken for granted in their marriage.

During the month of May there is a book fair scheduled in Dallas, Texas and they both assured each other their presence would be made. Darius and Jasmine were looking forward to seeing one another and spending time together. They had become each other's best friend and confidant.

Nine Months Later in Dallas...

"Hey, pretty lady." Smiling, Darius called out to a familiar face in a crowd of many in the lobby, where the book expo was to be held. The pretty lady looked up. It was Jasmine. Wearing a floral sun dress with red accessories and red heels, the made her looked radiant.

"Darius how are you?" She greeted with a smile and extended arms. They walked toward each other and embraced.

"You look beautiful." He complimented as he took a step back and gave her a quick look over.

"Why thank you sir and you're looking handsome." He was decked out in a blue Kango hat, white long sleeve cufflink shirt, blue jeans and blue lizard shoes.

"How long have you been here?" Darius asked looking around the huge room; as the got in line to pick up their registration package.

"I've been here for about fifteen minutes, and you?"

"I just got here, but I had to stop at the Hilton, to see if my books arrived."

"I'm at the Hilton too, but the publisher sent my books here by accident." Jasmine responded with a slight frown.

"Are you staying at the one on LBJ Freeway?" He asked, wanting confirmation.

"That's the one." She replied with enthusiasm. "Next!" a blond haired woman, whom seemed to be in her sixties, wearing a pair of gold wire framed glasses yelled out; competing with the loud talking of other people in the room, momentarily interrupted their conversation.

"Good afternoon I'm Mrs. Devereux; I'm here to pick up my books and author package."

"Good Afternoon! May I see some form of identification please?" Reaching inside her purse, Jasmine retrieved her driving license and handed it to the woman. The gray haired woman, who looks like a feisty grandmother, searches a sheet of paper, filled with names. "Here you go Mrs. Devereux." The woman said, placing a check mark by her name and handed Jasmine her package; then the woman turned around and called out to an assistant, to retrieve Jasmine box of books. Jasmine waited patiently for Darius to get his author package.

"Let me give you a hand and walk with you to your car." Darius offered as he picked up the box.

"I don't have a car. The hotel shuttle had dropped me off."

"Well, you could ride back with me if you like. I rented a SUV."

"Oh that would be perfect. Thank you!" The two maneuvered their way through the crowded room, heading to the parking lot.

On the trip back to the hotel, they talked about family life and why their spouses still were not supporting them in their writing endeavors; even though their book sales were doing very well. They also talked little about this upcoming conference. A few minutes later, they arrived at their destination. Darius exit the vehicle and walked around to the other side and open the door for Jasmine; extending his hand out for hers. Placing her hand in his, she thought to her herself, *what a gentleman, Eric never had done this for me.* He then retrieved the box from the back seat and placed it on one of the hotel's luggage cart. They both agreed to meet for dinner in an hour, at Barrington's; the hotel's restaurant. Waving goodbye to one another, they both went in separate directions; Darius walking toward the consigner desk and Jasmine grabbed onto the cart and walked toward the elevator.

*****

Darius waited for Jasmine in a very comfortable chair in the lobby, reading the latest issue of Forbes magazine and checking out the guests as they passed by in front of him. The elevator door opened and Jasmine stepped out. Dressed casually, wearing black form fitting stretch jeans that complimented her sexy figure, a pair of two and a half inch heels and a beige silk blouse. Her short bob haircut style was impeccable. Even though she was dressed casual, she looked stunning. Darius wanted to hold her close to him with

The Write Lover

no clothing as barriers. He stood up and glided towards her; like the actor's in a Spike Lee movie. They kissed each other on the cheek and headed towards the restaurant. As the restaurant greeter seated them, Jasmine said to Darius, "Excuse me baby, I need to go to the ladies room." A true gentleman, he stood up and watched her walk away before sitting back down. He was mesmerized at how lovely she looked in those jeans, not to mention the sexy walk she had going on. He sat back down thinking to himself, *why couldn't she be my wife.*

During dinner they talked about their books and what they had to offer in their stories that would make their work stand out in the sea of other literary works. While enjoying their glasses of wine and sharing a huge slice of cheese cake, their conversation became steamy. Jasmine spoke.

"I don't understand, how two attractive authors who write romance novels, can have sex lives which are pretty much non-existent; all because our spouses are jealous of our literary talent."

Darius agreed. "It really feels good that we can share our thoughts with one another and support each other's passion to the fullest."

"Yes, it does. My husband never supported my writing. I published my first book behind his back. When he found out about it, we almost ended up getting a divorce. But he came around when he saw the royalty checks floating in. He hates the fact that I travel out of town often to promote my book, but at least he's better than before." Darius listened to Jasmine, nodding his head in agreement.

"Sounds like my wife," he laughed. "Her attitude changed when she saw one of my royalty checks, also. She just read my book and it's been out over a year now."

"That's better than my husband. He has never read any of my work. I tried to read a few chapters to him, but he never sits through a whole reading. He really has no interest." Jasmine glanced at her watch, as she yawned. It was close to nine o'clock and she was a little tired, but not really wanting the night to end.

"Oh excuse me; it's been a long day. I should be going to bed."

"Have one more drink with me, please." Darius pleaded. She couldn't resist his beautiful browns eyes and boyish smile.

They ordered two more glasses of wine and decided to take them back to his room; because the restaurant was becoming crowded and a little bit noisy, they could barely hear each other. Besides, they didn't want to share their time together in a crowded room filled with strangers, since they didn't know when they were going to be at another conference together. Darius paid the check, gathered their glasses and left the restaurant.

Sipping on their drinks the conversation continued to flow while walking to the elevator. Once in the elevator they broke out into laughter when they both reached to press the same button, realizing they were staying on the same floor. They didn't know this earlier since Darius had to take care of some business at the consigner desk and Jasmine had taken her things to her room. The minute they entered Darius' room they placed their drinks on the table, and engaged in a passionate kiss that was long awaited by both parties.

"Hold up Darius. What are we doing?" She asked, pushing back from him.

"Kissing" He said, attempting to return to her lips.

"We can't do this. We are both married." He wanted her so bad, but he also respected her and didn't want to push the issue, jeopardizing their friendship.

"I apologize." He said sincerely.

"There's nothing to apologize for. You're a great kisser." She replied with a smile, as she wiped her lipstick from around his mouth. The wine was getting the best of her, when she suggested, "Since we are writers, what if we got into character and did a little research on a love scene; for one of our future novels? Would that be cheating?"

"Ah...I don't think so," Darius laughed, agreeing to her suggestion. The chemistry between the two was so strong, along with the combination of wine and opportunity, made for a perfect sexual storm. Jasmine had never been with any other man, however she knew in the back of her mind that her husband had been with other women. At that moment, the wine took over and she pulled Darius into her, kissing him gently and passionately.

Passion filled the air as they disrobed each other without losing lip contact. Enjoying the feel of her breasts in his hands he had to put his mouth on them. She held his head firmly as his tongue made circles around her erect nipples. He gently laid her on the bed and she scooted back toward the pillows. Darius couldn't wait to make love to her, but he wanted to taste her sweet nectar first.

"Jasmine, I'm about to take you on an oral experience you will remember every morning when you wake up and every night when you lay your head to rest. She giggled, wondering if he had used that line in one of his books. Her heart was racing because she could not believe this was really happening. She told herself to pull back, but her body told her otherwise. Not once did her husband cross her mind.

With her legs over his shoulders, he held onto her hips as his tongue explored her lubricated tunnel. Jasmine's moans filled the air, acknowledging approval of his work. Her hips gyrated like a professional belly dancer. He could feel her trying to pull away, as her orgasm was building; but she couldn't, his grip held her in position.

"Oh damn, this feels so good." She yelled, as she arched her back and had an orgasm that made her scream out Darius's name. He could feel her body tense up while her legs jerked, indicating a successful climatic experience. He continued to kiss her soft body, not missing an inch, until he reached her mouth. They changed position, as she rolled on top of him. His hands roamed and squeezed her plump buttock. She sat up and took a hold of his hardness slowly easing him inside her; until her thighs rested on his. She began to ride him vigorously. Jasmine's breathing and movements were becoming more rapid with each forward and backward motion. He held firmly onto her hips as she yelled out softly.

"Oh shit! I'm coming…I'm coming."

"Yes baby, come for me." He responded back, as he thrust his hips upward going deeper.

"Oh God!" She screamed, as the intensity of the orgasm consumed her. Jasmine arched so far backward; the top of her head nearly touched the bed. Darius sat up as he placed his hands around her lower back to support her. After about a minute, she rose back up wrapping her arms around his shoulder.

The Write Lover

"Come for me baby." Breathing hard, she pleaded accompanied with a long passionate kiss. Repositioning her so he can enter from the back, Jasmine grabbed a fluffy pillow hugging it tightly, putting her hips in the air so he could get full access for deep penetration. He thought to himself, *her behind feel as good as it looked.* He had to kiss, nibble and lick on it for a minute. He guided his ship into her canal. He held onto her hips as he gave her fast deep thrusts.

Jasmine screamed out in pure pleasure. She balled up the sheets placing her face in the pillow and continued to scream; while saying passionate adjectives. After forty minutes of working on her honey box, Darius could feel the intensity of his orgasm mounting.

"Yeah baby, I'm about to come." Darius blurted, through clinched teeth. Enjoying the view of watching his hard, wet penis appear and disappear inside this sexy beautiful woman's private palace, made him loose his mind. "Baby, I'm coming," he yelled out, as he buried all of his hardness inside her. He released like a firefighter holding a water hose putting out a fire. Jasmine collapsed onto the bed and he lay on top of her exhausted with his semi-hard penis still inside her. They both were breathing heavily, and stayed in that position for a short moment before he pulled out. With his arms around her shoulder, and her head on his chest with her leg between his, she leaned forward toward his mouth and they kissed before falling asleep.

When Jasmine awoke a few hours later, she found herself still in the same position with Darius sound asleep. A smile appeared on her face, as she snuggled closer to him. The ringing of her cell phone startled her as she glanced at the clock that read 2:30 am.

She freed herself from his hold, and made her way across the room, reaching inside her purse to retrieve the cell.

"Hello," she answered softly, not to awake Darius.

"I've been calling your damn phone all night. What the hell Jasmine?" It was her husband, Eric.

"Hey baby, um…yeah…I went to dinner with a few girlfriends and had a couple of drinks. I guess I just dozed off as soon as I made it back to my room. I'm sorry, I didn't hear my phone." She clicked on the lamp and Darius adjusted his eyes, sitting up in the bed. She placed her index finger up to her mouth; indicating to him, please don't say a word. He nodded in agreement.

"What time does your flight leave tomorrow?" Eric demanded.

"Um…I fly out at 7 pm."

"Alright, so how much money did you make on your book sales?" Jasmine rolled her eyes up in the air.

"I haven't made any money, being the book signings is later today." She replied bothered.

"Don't be shopping, spending up all the money you hear me! The car needs a tune up and I promised the boys a trip to Disneyland."

"Yes, Eric." She submissively responded. "I'm leaving as soon as the book signing is over. How am I going to have time to go shopping?"

"I'm just saying." Eric replied, in a more subtle tone.

"Yeah, whatever, I'm going back to bed. I'll see you when I get in." Before Eric could say anything else, she turned off her cell phone. She glanced over at her lover sitting up in the bed. His exposed washboard stomach instantly turned her on. Little did she know his manhood was hard and ready for another round.

"Is everything okay?"

"Yeah" Jasmine answered with a fake smile.

"So why do you have that look on your face baby?" He asked taking a hold of her hand. "I can tell something is bothering you. Is it about what we did?"

"No!" She quickly answered. Though she felt somewhat guilty, Jasmine had never had such an amazing sexual experience in her life. The only man she had ever given herself to was her husband. Eric had never taken her on a sexual journey like Darius just did. She enjoyed everything that Darius had done to her, she could never take that back, it was the best mind blowing sex ever. She just wasn't sure he was real. "Last night was amazing. Thank you baby, I don't regret one second." She said with dreamy eyes.

"Good because, I don't either." Jasmine leaned towards his soft lips and engaged in a tender kiss.

"Let me see how long it's gonna take me to make this thing soft." Jasmine sensually said with a smile, as she began to stroke his pleasure stick.

*****

The event was a success for the two upcoming authors; they had sold all their books. They stopped at Wendy's and had quick bite before heading to the airport. When they at the airport and pulled up in front of the Delta terminal, they gave each other a short passionate kiss. Darius exited the SUV and opened the door for Jasmine. As she stepped out the vehicle, she said, "Call or email me so I know you made it back safely."

Brooklen Borne

"I will baby." He assured her, as he placed her luggage at the curbside check-in counter. They gave each other a hug and a kiss on the cheek, not to show a lot of public display of affection; before Darius returned to the vehicle; driving off to return the rental, and catching his flight back home.

Jasmine sat on the plane reminiscing about her sexual experience with Darius. She had never been so sexually satisfied. She could count on one hand how many times she had experience an orgasm by her husband and her new lover, had her reaching orgasmic euphoria three times last night and twice in the morning; before the book signing. *What has this man done to me?* She thought to herself smiling, as she got comfortable in her assigned seat. She didn't want anyone talking to her, so she turned on her I-Pod, closed her eyes and replayed everything about last night in her mind that she had shared with Darius; as she attempted to doze off.

Her nipples were becoming firm, as she felt her clit pulsating; when the vibration of her cell phone interrupted her sexual relaxed state of mind. She thought it was Darius, but her smile slowly disappeared, when she saw it was a text message from her husband. From the text she could tell he was upset. She hadn't called him before boarding the plane. She began to think of a good lie to come up with because her husband wanted to know her every move. The trip to Dallas was a much needed get-away for her. She would remember the affair in Dallas for the rest of her life.

Jasmine wasn't sure what this meant for her and Darius. He had a wife to go home to and she had a husband and two boys at home as well. *It was just sex, that's all it was. He probably won't call me now that he got the goods*, she thought to herself, as she texted

The Write Lover

her husband back; explaining how she had almost missed her flight due to rush hour traffic and forgot to call him. Jasmine's flight touched down in Sacramento around 4 pm. *Damn! I'm back to my regular life. If it weren't for my two boys, I would just pack up and leave,* she thought to herself, as the plane taxied to the gate.

Darius' Trip Home...

Darius took his window seat in row 15A. As he settled in his assigned seat and buckled up, he thought about the quality time he spent with Jasmine. The flight attendant began to give her safety lecture to the passengers; he didn't hear a word she said, for he was in deep thought. He wondered how life would have been if only he had met Jasmine years ago; he would have loved to have her as his wife instead of Chandra. His thoughts were interrupted as the plane's engine revved and began to roar down the runway for lift off. He felt Jasmine had to be his soul mate because her whole being felt so right. Not to mention, the wonderful sex they passionately shared. He never felt this way before about a woman. Yes, he felt something for Chandra but this was very different.

The one thing he knew for sure was he wanted to experience more of that feeling with her. He wondered why Chandra couldn't keep her body tight like Jasmine's and Jasmine had two kids. Darius didn't understand why her husband wasn't treating her like a Queen. *If she was my woman, she would be the happiest woman walking the earth*, he thought, as he slowly fell into a deep sleep.

Brooklen Borne

A few hours later, the plane was on final approach to JFK when the flight attendant tapped Darius on the shoulder, awakening him, so he could buckle and place his seatback in the upright position. He still had Jasmine heavy on his mind; he couldn't shake the thought of her essence. Somehow, someway, she had to be his woman full time. He didn't know how he was going to do it, but he knew he had to try.

Chapter Two
The Awaited Phone Call

Besides writing books, Jasmine was also employed as an editor of a local magazine. She was busy working on a new advertising project that was going to bring a lucrative contract to the company, so she couldn't work on her latest novel "Love and Relationship" like she wanted to. Her job was emotionally draining and she was considering making a career change, to be a full time author, but she felt she wasn't financial stable; to do so. The money she had made from her debut novel, "Savannah" was put in a separate account, unbeknownst to her husband; who would have used it for his own selfish purpose. Although, Jasmine had always been upfront with Eric, about the money she earned from her book signings, things had changed between them, and she knew, to secure her future, she could no longer be doing that.

Three days had passed and Jasmine hadn't heard from Darius, not even a text. She figured it was for the best, and wasn't sure what she would say to him anyway. She thought to herself sitting in her cubicle, behind her desk; one of many cubicles that made up the office. It was 5:55 pm when she tapped the power button on her keyboard to shut down the computer and gather up her Coach bag for the 1 hr. commute home. Saying good-byes to her co-workers for the day, as she exited the building making her way to her car, her cell phone rang. Not bothering to check her caller ID, she answered it.

"Hello?"

"Hey beautiful!" It was Darius. Her heart skipped a beat as she pressed the remote to unlock the doors to her Nissan Altima and placing her bag on the passenger seat. "Jasmine, are you there?"

"Yes, I'm here. I'm just surprised to hear from you because you never contacted me to say you made it back safely." Inside, she was jumping with joy to hear Darius' sexy voice, with his New York accent; closing the driver's door, getting comfortable behind the wheel.

"I've been so busy with my book tour. I haven't had a chance to touch bases with anyone. Besides, my wife has been traveling along with me on my last two book signings."

"That's good, Mr. Best Selling Author. I read the article in Essence. Nice picture, too."

"Thank you. Soon you'll be quitting that job and doing book tours right alongside me."

"From your lips to Gods ear." She whispered.

"What baby?"

"I said from your lips to God ears." She repeated a little louder.

"Jasmine, the world better get ready for you, because when your second novel drops, I know it's going to be fire. The word on the street, your first novel "Savannah" is still getting rave reviews."

"That's good to hear." She replied smiling, looking at herself in the vanity mirror; on the sun visor.

"Don't sell yourself short baby, you are a very talented author. Anything you write, will be a must read."

"I hope it will be good as yours. I've read the excerpt to your latest novel in the magazine and that's what I call fire." She said still smiling, holding onto the steering wheel.

"Thanks you. Spending time with you in Dallas was so beautiful."

"What happened in Dallas stays in Dallas." She replied, feeling herself getting moist, from the very thought of his touches.

"I haven't stopped thinking about you." Jasmine began to melt, but she quickly regained her composure.

"Really?"

"Yes…it was really nice."

"Yes it was," she agreed, trying to wipe the smile off her face.

"No regrets?" Darius asked in a low easy tone.

"No regrets," she repeated. She hadn't been able to look her husband in the eyes and had been faking headaches every night since she returned home. Jasmine had never cheated on Eric before and she was afraid he might notice a difference if they made love. She felt so guilty deep inside, but another part of her wanted Darius alone in a candle lit room every night. She had sex scenes worked up in her head, but knew they would never materialize because of the slight guilt, she was feeling; she thought to herself.

"Well, I wanted to let you know I'll be coming to Sacramento in two weeks."

"Huh?" She blurted, choking on her saliva.

"Are you alright?" He asked concerned.

"Um…yes, I'm okay. So what's bringing you to Sacramento?"

"I'm coming to see you."

"Stop playing."

"Actually, one of my friends that I was in the military with is getting married. He asked me to be his best man. He and his fiancé put this together quickly since he has to leave for Afghanistan soon. I was hoping I could see you while I'm in town."

"I don't think that's a good idea."

"Why?" Darius asked sounding disappointed. She wanted to say, because I might fuck you, suck you and loose my damn mind if I saw you again. She squeezed her thighs tightly together, trying to control the urge, that had her wanting to masturbate. "Why?" He asked again, when he didn't get a response.

"Um…just because…I mean…," cutting her off, Darius asked,

"Don't you want to see me? I'm dying to be with you again, Jasmine."

"Your wife is not coming with you?" Jasmine asked curiously.

"Nah, she can't take any more time off from work." Jasmine was gently biting on her bottom lip.

"We are both married Darius, did you forget that? We can't keep having these sexcapades."

"And maybe we are both married to the wrong people."

"Yeah, maybe you're right." Jasmine replied in a low voice.

"Does that mean we'll be seeing each other when I fly out to the coast?" She didn't response. "I'll be staying at that new hotel Envy. I hear it's a real nice hotel. Come and share the experience with me."

"I guess we can meet, but only for dinner."

"And some wine?" Darius asked, as he laughed.

The Write Lover

"Be quiet," as she laughed with him. They chatted for a few minutes longer before Darius had to go. She started the car and pulled out the parking lot, thinking about Darius, the way she shouldn't.

*****

Jasmine was exhausted when she arrived home. Before she could bring the car into the garage, she had to move her sons' bicycles out the way. Once in the house she placed her keys on the table; when Eric walked in from the bedroom with nothing on.

"Why are you standing there naked and where are the kids?" She asked slightly annoyed.

"They're at the babysitters, because I want to spend some quality time with you."

"I just got in from work and I need to unwind. Besides we don't have money for a babysitter. We could have made love tonight, when we went to bed."

"I need for you to do your wifely duties!"

"What?" Jasmine asked in disbelief; to the demand that came out his mouth. Eric walked up to Jasmine and took off her jacket and began unbutton her blouse. "Eric! Damn! Did you hear what I said? I'm tired baby." Eric still didn't say a word. He roughly turned her around, lifted her skirt, bent her over pulled her thong to the side, and forced his hardness inside Jasmine's dry vagina. She screamed out in pain as Eric had his way with her. When he finished, he asked her, when was she going to pick up the kids? Jasmine didn't respond, she lay bent over the couch with tears streaming down her face in pain.

Chapter Three
We Could Be Happy Together

    Darius was due to arrive in Sacramento sometime before ten in the morning, local time. He and Jasmine had planned to meet around five in the evening for dinner. She told her husband, she was going with a few co-workers after work, to happy hour. Eric was pissed at first, but then he made plans to hang out with his friends. Jasmine had made arrangements for her sister to pick up the boys and stay at her house for the night, because if she didn't do that, and her husband had to watch them, there would have been a major argument. An argument that would have led to a fight and she would have missed her rendezvous with Darius.

    Jasmine took a half-day off from work and went to the beauty salon to get her hair done. After she left the salon, she made her way to a nearby mall to find a matching bra and panty set from Victoria's Secret. Jasmine thought to herself, *why am I spending money buying* this? *I'm only having dinner with him; he's not going to see this sexy underwear.* She then made her way over to BCBG clothing and found a form fitting red dress and a pair of shoes to match. After getting her outfit for the evening she headed to the Day Spa where she indulged in a full body massage, facial, pedicure and manicure. It was a good thing she made an appointment earlier in the week because the Spa was packed with people trying to get a walk-in appointment at the last minute.

Jasmine was enjoying the day to the fullest; spending more money than she had budgeted for. She was finishing up at the spa, when her cell rang. Looking at the caller ID, it was Darius. A smiled appeared on her face, as she pressed the button to answer.

"Hello," answering, in her most sensual voice.

"I'm looking forward to seeing you." Darius voice bellowed.

"Likewise handsome," She responded glancing at her Movado, black face watch. It's going on five o'clock.

"You know I ditched my boys' bachelor party to be with you. I told him my stomach was acting up, from that airplane junk they served. But there's another guy there, who's going to put together a party for him."

"You didn't have to do that. We're just having dinner, I'm sure you can make his party on time."

"Oh, we're just having dinner?" Darius sounded a little disappointed.

"Yeah," she answered biting her bottom lip, trying to control her feelings.

"Okay, well in that case, you can be my dinner."

"Darius, you are too much!" She giggled.

"I'm already here at Envy. I'll be at the entrance of the lounge waiting for you. I also brought my manuscript from my latest project. I want you to take a look at it and let me know what you think."

"Okay, I'll be there soon." Then she disconnected the call.

The Write Lover

A few minutes later...

Jasmine called her sister, once she left the spa to check on the kids.

"Hey sis, how are my little men doing?"

"They are doing fine and playing with the neighborhood kids."

"I really appreciate you doing this for me."

"It's alright! I enjoy spending time with my nephews."

"Thank you! I love you!"

"I love you too! Enjoy!"

"Ok, bye!"

"Bye!"

Trying to find a parking space in downtown Sacramento was like trying to find a needle in a haystack. Jasmine patience was beginning to wear thin, so she had the hotel valet park the car. The parking attendant greeted Jasmine with a smile, as he opened the door to assist her. Her shapely long legs exited the vehicle followed by her sexy body in her new red dress. She smiled back at the attendant, giving him the keys, feeling like a million dollars as she walked toward the hotel entrance. The valet attendant eyes locked on Jasmine's derriere until she disappeared through the revolving door. The lobby of the hotel was breath taking; the Envy was definitely a five star hotel with its high ceiling, marble floors and glass sculptures. She paused for a moment, admiring the décor before making her way to the lounge. She received admiring stares from both men and woman as she walked across the lobby, like a super model. She smiled back at the few admires, not giving them too much eye contact. Just as she entered the lounge, Darius looked up. His eyes scanned her from head to toe and by the smile on his face; he was very impressed with her appearance. He levitated out the chair and made his way over to her. He was looking pretty dapper himself with a long sleeve, black silk, button-up shirt, black slacks and a brown blazer.

"You look beautiful." Darius said as he greeted her with a kiss on the cheek along with a firm hug.

"I love the hair, it fits you well."

"Well, thank you. You look very handsome yourself." She replied, not wanting to break free from the hug as his firm chest pressed against her breast.

"Baby, you know what you're doing in that dress, don't you?"

"What am I doing?" Laughing she asked.

"Well, seeing how all eyes are on you right now, you must be the finest lady up in here." She looked around noticing the male species, were sneaking glances at her. She began to blush as Darius took her arm in his and stated, "But right now, you're all mine." They made their way to the restaurant on the 25th floor. The view of the Sacramento skyline from the glass wall elevator was absolutely breath taking. A fiction writer couldn't have written the evening any better. Jasmine browsed through the first three chapters of Darius' latest manuscript, as he sipped on a glass of wine, waiting patiently for her thoughts. They both deeply valued one other's opinions.

"I wish my wife looked at my work like you do. Let it be told, I wish my wife did a lot of things you do."

"Stop it." Jasmine laughed, sipping the last of her glass of Merlot. "My husband doesn't look at my work either and damn sure doesn't do what you do." She began to chuckle as she placed

The Write Lover

the manuscript back in the folder. Darius just smiled, knowing she was referring to their sexual experience.

"So you really like it?"

"I do! The first chapter grabs the reader's attention, and keeps you spellbound throughout."

"I appreciate your input baby." He reached across the table, taking a hold of both of Jasmine's hands.

"What would it take for us to be together forever?" He said, as he looked into her eyes. Jasmine slowly pulled her hands away.

"Darius, I have two kids and we're both married. We could never be together."

"I like kids. I don't have any of my own. I would love your kids, just as much as I love you; unconditional love with no reservations." Darius didn't have any children of his own and she always wanted to ask why, but figured maybe it was too personal to ask. She knew he had been married for seven years and he was in his mid thirties so it was strange he never had any kids, especially as fine and smart as he was. Jasmine was sure more than a few women would have loved to pop out a few babies for him.

"Please, we could never be together. I could never give you what you need. My tubes are tied, and I'm sure you would want your own children. What am I saying? I would never leave my husband and you would never leave your wife. We are just friends. It is what it is. We can't make this a love thing. Too many people would get hurt and…" Darius cut her off.

"It's too late. I've already fallen in love with you."

"No you haven't." She replied shaking her head.

Brooklen Borne

"I know what I feel baby." He sincerely spoke, as he pulled out his wallet to pay for dinner.

"No! Let me pay. You paid in Dallas, so dinner's my treat," Jasmine said reaching for her credit card. He placed his American Express Card on the table.

"I got this! Put your card away baby." She didn't argue as she placed her credit card back in her purse.

"Thank you for dinner."

"You're welcome pretty lady and thank you for coming."

"I really enjoyed this evening. Being that it's still early, you can make it to that bachelor party."

"No, I'm going back to my room and chill. Too bad you have to go. Are you sure you can't stay?"

"I'm afraid so." She responded, taking out a tube of lip-gloss from her purse to touch up her lips and placing a piece of gum in her mouth. Darius watched her every move.

"Too bad, because I had a surprise for you in the room."

"Yeah right, I bet you did." She laughed.

"Seriously, I brought you a gift. Look, I'll be busy all day tomorrow with the wedding and my flight doesn't leave out until three in the afternoon on Sunday, so maybe we can meet for breakfast. I could give it to you then. I would love to see you again before I leave. Okay sweetheart!" *Damn, this man is so sexy*, Jasmine thought to herself, looking into his eyes. She was now curious, wondering what in the world he could have bought her? The waiter came and took the credit card but not before offering them a chance to order desert. They both declined. A few minutes later the waiter came back with the receipt. Darius signed and collected his copy.

"What did you buy me? I hate surprises."

"You'll just have to wait until Sunday."

"I can wait over there on that comfortable couch while you go to your room and get my surprise." She started walking toward the couch.

"No! If I give it to you now, then you won't show up on Sunday,"

"I wouldn't do that." Placing her hand on his chest, giggling.

"Yeah! Right!" Darius said jokingly, as he placed his hand on the lower part of her back.

"Well, come on. I'll come with you to your room because I'm dying to see what you bought me." Darius' face lit up as he took a hold of her hand and entered the elevator.

"Umm, you smell good." She said, leaning toward him.

"You smell good as well, with your sexy self." He replied, looking into her eyes. The elevator came to a stop on the fourteenth floor and they exited.

He slid the firm plastic key card in the slot on the door and the click sound, accompanied by a small green light, indicated the door was now unlocked.

"You wait out here. I don't want you to think I'm trying to seduce you or anything."

"You got jokes huh." She responded, placing her hand on his bicep, pushing him aside as she entered the room first. He took a deep breath looking at her behind, and followed her inside. "Wow, this is nice." She stood a few feet from the door, taking in the view, looking around the plush suite. Modern furniture and paintings filled the room. The marble floor looked like you could eat off of it. Fresh flowers were the center piece, on one of the tables. It was more like a condo. Darius' cell phone rang and he glanced at the number.

"I have to answer this, excuse me baby for a minute." He informed, walking toward the kitchen area. Jasmine sat down on the chaise looking out of the massive window at the city lights while overhearing Darius' conversation. Jasmine knew he was talking to his wife because of the questions being asked. A few minutes later, off the phone, he walked back to where Jasmine was relaxing on the chaise.

"Sorry about that."

"It's okay." Jasmine assured him. He made his way over to the leather suitcase that was lying on the bed. He quickly unzipped it, reaching into the side pocket and pulled out a rectangular box, gorgeously wrapped in fancy gold paper, with a red satin bow.

"This is what I got for you honey." He handed her the gift. "Go ahead baby, open it." With a smile, she gently removed the bow from the box, wondering what in the world could be inside. Finally after fighting with the bow, she opened the box to find a gold necklace with a diamond cross charm.

"Oh my God…this is beautiful!"

"You like it?"

"I love it." Smiling, as she took the chain out the box, holding it in front of her face.

"I remember you telling me that you had lost your necklace a few months back…so here's a new one. Don't lose this one. It cost me a pretty penny."

The Write Lover

"I can't accept this Darius. My husband is going to ask me; where I got it from. How much did it cost? I really don't feel like answering any of his dumb questions."

"Yes you can. Tell him, your sister gave it to you. But make sure you fill her in, before you get home. Here, let me put it on you." She stood up and turned around, as he placed the necklace around her neck, securing the clasp. The sparkling cross looked so elegant lying on her chest, just above her cleavage. She felt the touch of his lips, gently on her neckline and both his hands held onto her slim waist. He slowly turned her around and their lips merged as one. Wrapping her arms around his neck, as they passionately kissed, her body pressed firmly against his. Then she came back to her senses, breaking off the kiss, placing her head on his chest, ending the moment.

"We shouldn't be doing this." She whispered.

"I'm sorry, I don't want to make you uncomfortable but after we spent the night together in Dallas, I just can't get enough of you."

"I know honey. I feel the same way." She whispered, taking a deep breath and staring off to the side.

"So what are you thinking about?"

"Um…you don't even want to know, but I can't act on that thought. I have to go. I'm sorry Darius." The disappointment in his eyes broke her heart but she had already asked God for forgiveness, and had been beating herself up inside about what they shared in Dallas.

"You don't have to be sorry, sweetness. I understand!" He smiled, holding her face, looking into her eyes. "Let me walk you out."

Brooklen Borne

"Okay." Jasmine replied, with tear filled eyes, picking up her purse and following behind him. Her mind was telling her that she should give back the necklace, but her heart said to keep it. It was a part of him. Besides, the sparkling diamonds on the cross really looked good on her. Darius held the door open for Jasmine, but she couldn't bring herself to walk out. She wanted him as mush as he wanted her, and the feeling in her heart and southern hemisphere took control. She pushed the door closed, dropping her purse on the floor, attacking him with a deep passionate kiss. He pulled her into him, kissing her back with intensity. She began unbuttoning his shirt, kissing on his chest. Slowly walking backward, he led her to the bed. So many emotions were running through her head. She pushed him back onto the bed so he could get a good look as she slipped off her dress. Standing only in her black thong, bra and high heels, the look on Darius' face and the bulge in his pants told her he was ready to put in some work. He leaned forward, reaching for her.

"Lay back baby and watch me." Keeping her heels on, she stood above him on the bed, swaying her hips back and forth, licking her lips, giving him a show. Her alter ego combined with the intake of wine earlier, had totally consumed her. Standing over him, she freed herself from the restraints of the laced bra and began to massage her breasts with light pinches on her nipples. Lowering onto her knees, she unzipped his pants reaching through the slit of his underwear, to take a hold of his penis. She gently stroked it getting herself hornier by the second. Sliding his penis in her mouth gingerly, checking her gag reflexes, he moaned with approval. Darius couldn't remember the last time he had oral sex performed on him, especially with the type of skill that Jasmine was performing.

He always had to beg Chandra to do it and she could never get it right. She opposed to giving him head, but loved it when he performed on her. Darius' body was in a state of shock as Jasmine began to firmly suck and rapidly stroke his hardness. She spread her arms out to the side, taking him all in without any hand assistants. "Damn!" he blurted out, taking a hold of the side of her face with both hands, pumping harder in her mouth. A few minutes and deep pumps later, she felt him tense up and release. She swallowed, as she continued to suck, making sure she got every drop. Looking up at him, she could see his eyes were still closed and he was licking his lips. Finally he spoke,

"I'm in love with you Jasmine. If you were my wife, I would never leave home and if I had to travel, you would have to come with me baby."

"That sounds nice." She responded, wiping her mouth, and kicking off her heels. She cuddled next to him relaxing her head on his chest, listening to his heartbeat and wishing she could stay with him forever like this in his arms. He kissed her on the lips and told her he wished there was a rewind button.

"The same here baby." She replied with closed eyes, savoring the moment.

"We could really be happy together Jasmine." He said seriously meaning his words and stroking her face softly.

"I know we could. It's a beautiful feeling, how we click so well, huh? We've only known each other for a short time, but it feels like I've known you my whole life." Kissing her, he rolled on top, removing her lace panties, throwing them to the floor. He began kissing on her breasts, knowing this was one of her weak spots, almost bringing her to an orgasm. He slowly worked his way, down her flat stomach, positioning himself between her legs. Sliding his tongue inside her vagina ever so gently, flicking his tongue on her clit with light pats and firm suction.

She began moaning loudly, breathing hard, and her hips were in a rhythmic gyration. Jasmine raised her head to look down at this man in action, giving her an oral fix that brought tears to her eyes. She held onto his head for dear life as she thrust her hips upward, screaming out his name as she came. She grabbed a pillow to hold it over her face, while her body continued to shake uncontrollably.

"You can have this every day baby." Darius said to her in a soft tone.

"Darius, what are you doing to me? Are you trying to turn me out?" Jasmine spoke looking into his eyes. He didn't say a word; he just slid his hardness deep inside her. She immediately held him tightly and moaned. Their moans filled the room, like a symphony orchestra at Carnegie Hall, as they matched each other's rhythm perfectly. Not missing a beat, he raised her legs onto his shoulders and went even deeper into her love canal. She dug her nails into his shoulders, biting her bottom lip; then she remembered, and lightened her grip, because she didn't want to send him home to his wife with scratch marks all over his back. After taking a few more deep strokes, Jasmine rolled over on top of him. Sitting on his lap, he held her hips while she rode him, like a cowgirl at a rodeo, going up and down, round and round. Jasmine grabbed his hands and placed them on her breasts so he couldn't control the penetration by holding onto her hips. After a few strokes she changed positions, now riding him backward. She began to work her voluptuous behind, teasing him. He alternated his hands between her hips and butt cheeks, squeezing with every powerful stroke, they both delivered. Slowly going up and down, raising her kitty to the tip of his penis, then pushing down and back hard against his pelvis. This drove him crazy. He still had not come, and her legs were beginning to cramp.

"I know you are not getting tired on me. Turn that pretty ass around." He instructed, as he came up behind her, taking a hold of her waist and entered deep. Her moans, sounded like a standing ovation at a stage play to his ears. Looking down, watching her butt jiggle, when his thighs made contact, made him appreciate the moment; as he went even deeper. Her moans turned into screaming words of passion with each thrust that was delivered. Perspiring, her hair stuck to the sides of her face; with her eyes closed and mouth wide open, Jasmine gathered the cotton sheets in her grasp, as her body trembled to an out-of-body orgasmic experience.

Feeling his own orgasm nearing, Darius began to pump harder and faster. A few minutes later, he released his warm cum inside her. Both dripping with sweat, and breathing heavily, he collapsed on her back. Her grip of the sheets loosened, as she was recovering from the intense love making. Now able to close her mouth and opened her eyes, a slight smile of total satisfaction, appeared on her flushed face. *This man is amazing; I wish he was my husband.* She thought to herself.

*****

Brooklen Borne

As Darius got comfortable in a seat on the Blue Airport Shuttle Van, to take him home, he smiled as he stared out the window thinking about his lovely experience with Jasmine, in Sacramento. He was on his way home to his spouse and Jasmine was at now at home with hers. His feelings for her were so strong, but he began to wonder, were they both just filling a void in their lives by being together.

"Can you turn on the radio to a jazz station or something?" He asked the driver, hoping the music would help clear his head.

"Yes sir," the driver replied, as he changed the station to WBGO Jazz 88. Darius closed his eyes leaning his head back against the cloth seat, listening to the smooth tunes when his cell phone vibrated alerting him, that he had a call. He pushed the button on his phone, answering on his blue tooth.

"Where are you?" Chandra's voice blurted.

"I'm in the van on my way home."

"Oh, okay. I have a surprise for you when you get home baby. How far away are you?"

"About twenty minutes away. What's the surprise?" He asked curiously.

"It wouldn't be a surprise if I told you, now would it?"

"Alright, I'll see you in a few."

Before long, the driver pulled up in the driveway of Darius' five-bedroom brick home on the outskirts of Queens. Chandra came running out. Darius thought that was strange of her. She never was so anxious for him to get home before. He noticed the loose fitting brown dress, she was wearing, seem like she bought it from a maternity store. She planted a firm kiss on his lips, scanning him up and down.

The Write Lover

"Hey baby. I missed you."

"You did?" He responded, with a curious expression. The driver retrieved Darius luggage from the back of the van. Darius tipped the driver kindly, before making his way into the house.

"Are you hungry baby? I cooked."

"You cooked?" He chuckled to himself knowing, she must really have had a surprise for him if she cooked. She hardly ever cooks, they mostly ordered out or he would do the cooking. Chandra was not the kind of wife that liked to cook or clean, and Darius often wondered why in the world he married her.

When he thought back to how they met five years ago, he knew it was her body that attracted him to her. When they met she wasn't a thin woman, nor was she a big woman but she was thick in all the right places and carried her shape well. However, over the past five years she had gained a good thirty pounds. In Darius eyes, she was now over weight and he did not find her as sexy as he once did. Chandra had attempted several different diets and exercise programs, but she could never stick with them. Darius had even attempted to work out with her, but she would just whine and complain the whole time and they would end up arguing. Darius never brought up the weight issues, even though it bothered him, he didn't want to hurt her feelings.

"So what's the surprise?" He asked as he entered the house setting down his luggage in the foyer. The aroma of Pillsbury rolls scented the air. He was quite hungry. "Um, it smells good in here."

She took him by the hand and led him to the round glass, dining room table; which was set up with lighted candles and dinner plates awaiting him. He scanned the table and saw wine glasses and his favorite foods: baked chicken breast, white rice with vegetables, and a basket of buttered bread rolls.

"This looks great."

"Thank you." She smiled, as Darius pulled the chair out for her, to be seated at the table. Then he excused himself to go wash his hands. He returned and took a hold of Chandra's hand, saying a quick prayer before they indulged in the food.

"So how was the wedding and please tell me you didn't go to that bachelor party." Darius wiped his mouth with the napkin trying to figure the best way to answer the question.

"No, I didn't and you wouldn't believe who I ran into."

"Who did you run into honey?"

"Jasmine Deveraux! You know the author from Baby Girl Publishing. Anyway, instead of going to the bachelor party, I had dinner with her and we went over a few manuscripts."

"Oh, is that right." She replied, looking at him with a clinched jaw.

"Yes, the buzz is one of her books is up for some award."

"It seems like you are always making time for her on your trips."

"Ah, come on Chandra. She's married with two kids. We are writing partners."

"And where did this reviewing of the manuscripts take place?"

"At a restaurant."

"Ummm," she groaned. "I sure would like to meet this Jasmine, who is so involved with my husband. I read her last book, she's a good writer. She's like your competition in your genre, isn't she?"

"In a way, but we are both about to sign with the same publisher, so we keep each other on our toes; since we do write in the same genre. Anyway, so what's the surprise you have for me?" He asked changing the subject. Chandra's face lit up with a bright smile.

"Well...it's been a long time coming and I know your going to be happy... Baby...I..."

"You're pregnant!" He exclaimed, cutting her off, almost elevating out of his chair." Chandra gave him a mean look.

"No, I'm not pregnant. Where would you get that idea from?" Darius sat back down; feeling like all the life had just been sucked out of him.

"I just thought…"

"We've talked about this Darius. Why you can't get it through your head that I'm not ready to have a baby right now?"

"Well, when will you be? We've been married for five years and we are not getting any younger. You know how bad I want a baby."

"I know!" She snapped. "With everything that I am trying to accomplish in my career it's just not a good time right now. As I was saying…um, I wanted to surprise you and tell you I made my first million dollar home sale, yesterday. I got a fat commission bonus. No one in the office has ever sold a million dollar home in their first year of real estate. I bought us a fabulous new bedroom set." She smiled, taking a hold of his hand. "I was hoping we could break in the new mattress tonight." Darius didn't respond he just picked up his plate from the table, and walked into the kitchen to wash the dishes. Chandra followed with her plate.

"You're not going to say anything?" She nagged.

"I'm happy for you." He muttered.

Brooklen Borne

"Look baby...I'm thinking, maybe I'll stop taking my birth control pills next year and we can start trying then. Okay?"

"That's what you said last year."

"I know...I know, but this real estate job is really taking off for me right now. It's not the best time to get pregnant and you're always gone, traveling with your book tours, to say the least. Neither one of us will have time to take care of a baby."

"I would make time for my child. That would be my first priority."

Chandra was growing upset that Darius was pushing the baby issues again. She was very apprehensive about getting pregnant. Before she and Darius met, she had gotten pregnant by her college sweetheart Carl. They got married and bought a house as soon as they found out. They were so happy preparing for their baby. Picking out names and fixing up the nursery for their baby. Chandra carried the baby nine months and was ecstatic about their bundle of joy.

Unfortunately, she delivered a stillborn, eight-pound baby girl and Chandra had been traumatized ever since. Not to mention her and Carl ended up getting their marriage annulled due to them fighting and not being able to get along after that tragic event in their lives. Chandra went into a deep state of depression. Even with intensive counseling, she was still not able to put closure on that part of her life. After a few years, she was ready to move on and the first night she went out with her girlfriends to a spoken word night club she saw Darius. She thought to herself, he is a very handsome man, but dismissed the idea of ever getting with him. She thought a man who looks like that must have a woman or a few girlfriends. Then two days later when Darius walked in the realty office where she worked, she knew that was a sign of them getting together. From that day on they hit it off, and one year later they were married. Darius always expressed to her from the jump how much he wanted children. When she told him about what happened in her past, he was genuinely kind to her and helped her realize it was not her fault; unlike Carl did. Chandra was afraid the same thing would happen with Darius and having a baby was the last thing she wanted to think about. Darius was very sensitive about her past, which is why he was so careful whenever he would bring up the subject, but he was growing frustrated now.

"With this lovely dinner and you being so anxious for me to get to the house and seeing you in that dress…I thought maybe you were pregnant. That looks like a maternity dress." Darius blurted, loading the dishwasher.

"Excuse me?"

"I'm just saying, you have picked up some weight."

"AND!" She yelled.

"I think you need to start working out with me again, that's all." He mentioned, knowing what he was doing. Darius was trying to start an argument so he could lock himself in his office, that way he could work on his stories all night, and she would not bother him nor would she want to have sex from him. Having sex with her was getting to be a full work out, trying to lift her and flip her over. She weighed more than him now and he found himself often not being able to stay hard when they had sex. She gasped for a deep breath.

"I'm going to pretend I didn't hear that." They continued to load the dishwasher and clean up the kitchen without any words being spoken. Darius grabbed his luggage and went up stairs to their master suite, to unpack and take a shower. Lucky the phone rang and Chandra paid him no attention as she chatted on the phone with her girlfriend, bragging about her real estate sale and the bedroom set she had just bought. Darius was quite impressed when he entered their bedroom. The massive wooden bedroom furniture consumed the room. It was something he probably would have picked out himself. He unpacked quickly, pushing his clothes to the bottom of the hamper when he smelled Jasmine's perfume aroma on them. Then he hurried, making his way into the shower. After a long hot shower, he felt like a new man. Drying off, he wrapped his towel around his waist walking out the bathroom to find Chandra waiting for him on the edge of the bed with a revealing long satin nightgown.

"This is new too." Chandra grinned at him, referring to her nightgown. Darius forced a smile on his face.

"Nice. I like the bedroom furniture good choice. Now tell me, what drawer my pajama pants are in?"

"That drawer on the left but you won't need them." She said, seductively, as she stood in front of him, slowly removing his bath towel.

Darius was not in the mood but he didn't deny her. They began to engage in a deep kiss, He closed his eyes and imagined he was kissing Jasmine's soft lips. His penis got rock hard with that thought in mind. He removed Chandra's nightgown, exposing her large naked body. He kissed her on the neck and then turned her around demanding her to get in the doggy position as she lifted her thick ass in the air. He penetrated her and she let out a deep moan. He closed his eyes once again and thought about Jasmine, which made him stay hard as he gave one of his best performances.

The Write Lover

Chandra began screaming loudly on her second orgasm, as Darius came hard.

"Damn honey, that was off the chain. What has gotten into you?" She asked breathing hard, pulling the sheet over her breasts. Darius smirked, getting out the bed, walking toward the bathroom, and under his breath he mumbled…"Jasmine."

Chapter Four
The Truth Comes Out

One year had passed and many things had transpired in the lives of Jasmine and Darius'. Their contract obligations were fulfilled with their separate publishing company, now they both had signed on with Firestorm Publishing. The publisher decided to do a marketing deal for both of their books and a few other new authors who had just signed on with the company. Jasmine was blessed to sign a lucrative three book contract with the publisher, thanks to Darius. He had really tightened up her last manuscript and helped her through the grueling process. They had been touring together on their book signing for the past six months, meeting up in different states every few weeks promoting their work.

Jasmine was finally getting paid good money to do what she loved, writing novels. The more her books were being exposed in the right venue, the more her book sales grew. Now she was starting to see four and five figure checks. Jasmine was still a little apprehensive however, she did decide to resign from her job at the magazine so she could focus a hundred percent on her writing and book tours. That did not sit well with her husband at all.

Jasmine's husband job wouldn't allow him the time he wanted to travel with her, so she would be left alone to go out of town to promote her book. She didn't mind, because it was like a mini vacation for her. Eric was starting to complain more and more about them not spending enough time together. Jasmine toured a lot and was very busy writing her next novel and taking care of their two sons. She and Eric were growing apart and it was beginning to show in their sex life. The main factor really was the love she had for Darius. Jasmine tried her hardest to push the feelings away she had for her lover, but each time they saw one another she needed to be held by him.

When Darius and Jasmine scheduled had then in the same city, at the end of the day the two lovers would find themselves tangled up in the sheets for hours fulfilling each other desires. They would snuggle after making love and brainstorm about their next novel collaboration. Everything seemed perfect for them. Darius was the perfect man in her life except for one thing, she was still married and so was he.

Jasmine's husband knew about Darius. She told him he was a great author and good friend who helped her with her writing. She thought it was crazy to even allow her controlling husband to talk with Darius on the phone from time to time, but she didn't want her husband to think something may be going on with them even though it was. If her husband had any thoughts about them, they were squashed when he found out that Darius was married and his wife accompanied him a few times on their book tour, even though she hadn't done so thus far. Jasmine felt somewhat guilty about doing that, but when she was with Darius it was like she was someone else and wasn't cheating on her husband. She and Darius had a special relationship; they just understood and supported each other to the fullest. Jasmine sat on her bed packing her bags for a

The Write Lover

literary conference in New York when she began to daydream about Darius' slow deep thrust inside her.

She was becoming moist as she closed her eyes. Her heart began to race when the door to the bedroom suddenly opened. She jumped, delivering her from her mental pleasure. It was Eric.

"Are you alright? What are you jumping for?" he asked, looking concerned but more annoyed.

"I'm always jumpy before a literary conference. I worry about the turn out and the speeches I have to give."

"Well, let me help you relax." He got on his knees and lifted Jasmine's nightgown, kissing her legs and thighs moving up towards her stomach. She knew it was more to satisfy him than her, but she went along to fulfill her wifely duties.

"Are the kids still up?" She asked, stopping him with her hands.

"Relax baby, they're sleeping." He assured her, as he pulled down his pajama pants exposing his hard-on. Laying Jasmine back on the bed, he mounted her in the missionary. Jasmine tensed up from the pain of the dryness of her vagina. There was no foreplay, just straight to the action. She was not ready for him to enter her.

"Slow down Eric!" She pleaded, trying to get some pleasure out the deal but Eric ignored her and began gyrating faster and faster as he let out a grunt and came. "I know you didn't already come. You didn't even try to satisfy me. You mount me, fuck me, and then roll off. What's up with that Eric?" Frustrated, she got up from the bed and stormed into the bathroom to take a shower.

Eric didn't respond to her resentment. Fifteen minutes later, when Jasmine re-entered the bedroom from taking a refreshing shower, he was sitting up in the bed eating chips, and watching television.

"What's up with you?" Jasmine asked naked, searching in her drawer looking for a nightgown. "You need to learn to take your time with me. Foreplay would be nice."

"I'm sorry baby, I was just so horny." She stood up, slipping her nightgown over her head. "Our sex life is straight, right?" He inquired.

"Why would you ask me something like that? And why are you eating chips in the damn bed?" She barked mildly upset, as she got in the bed. He closed the bag of chips, placing the bag on the nightstand; before turning on his side. Pulling himself closer to Jasmine, who had her back turned to him; still visibly upset.

"I'm sorry baby." Eric whispered, placing a kiss between her shoulder blades; as he cuddled her. She found it quite odd he was doing that, because they hadn't cuddled in a very long time. A few moments later, she heard him snoring and knew he had fallen asleep. Jasmine gently removed his arm from around her waist and sat up on the edge of the bed. It was time she was honest with herself. She was no longer in love with her husband, and no matter how hard she tried to be happy it was not in her. Holding her head, thoughts of being in bed with Darius had Jasmine moist, wanting to feel his touch and probably would be on her third orgasm; if they were together. Tomorrow couldn't come fast enough, for her to fly out to New York. She continued to think, that if it weren't for her children, she would be long gone from this marriage.

The Next Day in Manhattan...

The Write Lover

Darius was rudely interrupted by his wife, who snatched his earpiece out his ear while he was listening to his iPod.

"What the hell?" He snapped.

"Have you heard one word I said?" Chandra snapped back, placing her hands on her hips, staring him down. "I know we didn't come into Manhattan to sit up in this hotel room. I booked the room a day early before your big book conference for us to get away from the house and put a spark in our relationship. We could have done this shit at home." She nagged.

Darius put away his iPod, as he began daydreaming about what he was planning on doing to Jasmine, when she arrived. He needed to figure out a way to ditch Chandra, with the quickness. He hadn't mentioned to her that Jasmine would be coming to the conference.

"What do you want to do?" he sighed.

"Do you love me Darius?"

"Huh?"

"It seems like your head is somewhere else. We barely even make love anymore."

"Of course I love you. I've just been overwhelmed, with this book tour and putting together some other projects." He lifted himself off the lounge chair walked over to her, giving her a big hug. Chandra hugged him back feeling relieved. She placed her hand in his crotch area, and began massaging his manhood.

"I know what you need." Chandra whispered in his ear. Holding onto his wrist with a firm grip, she lowered herself getting on her knees. She then loosened his belt and unzipped his slacks.

"What are you doing?"

Brooklen Borne

"What you say I never do." She giggled, pulling out his semi-hard penis and slowing licking the tip.

Darius perked up, surprised by his wife's gesture which was completely out of character for her. He couldn't remember the last time she went down on him. He felt awkward at first and tried to enjoy it, but she just wasn't doing it right. She kept scraping her teeth against his hard penis and could not take all of him in her mouth. His manhood began to get soft, so he put his hand on the back of her head, trying to get into it by forcing himself deeper into her mouth. She pushed his hand away and mumbled for him not to do that. Darius rolled his eyes, looking down at Chandra making a fool of herself.

After five minutes, she pulled back looking up at him.

"Don't come in my mouth!"

"You know what? Just forget it." He pushed her back, placing his manhood back into his boxers.

Chandra wiped her mouth with the back of her hand. "I try to do you a favor and that's how you treat me. See if I ever go down on you again." She snapped, standing up.

"You don't do it right any way!" He growled angrily.

"So who does it right…huh?" Chandra yelled. "Has somebody else been sucking your dick while you've been on your little book tours, Mr. Big Time Author. Tell me…how am I not doing it right?"

"Do you really think I wasn't getting head before I met you? What you said wasn't even called for."

"Well, what the hell am I supposed to think, when you say some shit like that to me?" Chandra spoke with an elevated voice, as she walked into the bathroom.

The Write Lover

Darius took a deep breath, looking at his watch. It was almost 8pm. He couldn't help but wonder if Jasmine had arrived yet and what room she was staying in. Since his wife seemed to be at his hip all day, he hadn't had a chance to call her and give her an update. Chandra had been getting on his nerves more and more each day that passed and he was beginning to question if he really wanted to continue with this marriage because fighting seemed to be all they did lately. Chandra came out the bathroom with a toothbrush in her mouth, busy brushing her teeth searching in her handbag. Darius just rolled his eyes, as she retrieved a piece of gum; strolling back into the bathroom. He knew if he got up after going down on her, and rushed to brush his teeth and get some gum she'd be offended. He just shook his head laughing.

She was just trying to push his buttons. He wanted to go off on her, and tell her that Jasmine could show her a thing or two about how to please a man orally, but knew it wasn't the right thing to say; so he kept his thoughts and comments to himself.

"Let's go to the bar and have some drinks." Chandra uttered, coming out the bathroom chewing gum.

"Yeah, let's do that." He answered, retrieving the hotel key card off the dresser, just before they walked out the door.

Jasmine had taken a late flight out of Sacramento, so she could attend her son's baseball game. She had been to New York once before in the summer time, but never in the spring and wasn't sure how the weather would be so she packed like always; something that she would be comfortable in, regardless of the weather. She was making her way to her room to relax, from the long flight and to get ready for the book signing and discussion panel in the morning. She was surprised he hadn't called or emailed her to see when her flight would arrive. She was beginning to wonder if their love affair was coming to an end. They spoke a few days ago and he told her he would be at the conference, he had also mentioned that it was a strong possibility his wife would be with him, but wasn't sure at the time. Jasmine was keeping her fingers crossed, hoping he was able to leave her at home. The bellhop followed behind her with luggage in tow, as they made their way to the elevator. The elevator doors opened, when she went to enter, she was surprise to see Darius. Chandra's eyes locked on Jasmine, from head to toe.

"Hey Jasmine!" Darius said with a surprised expression.

"Hey Darius," She smiled back, before looking over at the woman holding on to his arm tightly with a partial smile. Jasmine had been dying to see what his wife looked like. She had seen a picture of her, but to see her up, close and personal was different.

"Jasmine, this is my wife Chandra. Chandra, this is Jasmine." Jasmine thought to herself, *she's beautiful, not at all like what she saw in the picture.* She wasn't wearing any make-up and her hair was pulled back in a ponytail. *She was on the overweight side but her clothes looked very nice on her.* Jasmine couldn't help but notice her pretty grey eyes, knowing they were real and not contacts.

"It's so nice to finally meet you Jasmine," Chandra spoke, with a hard New York accent; extending out her hand. They shook hands firmly as Chandra stared her up and down again. "Feels like I already know you girl." She said with a smile; displaying a perfect set of teeth.

The Write Lover

Jasmine was disappointed; that Chandra had came, but understood he couldn't make up any more excuses for her not to come, as he had done the past couple of times.

"Likewise" Jasmine responded, as they stepped to the side not to block the elevator, letting the doors close. The bellhop waited patiently as Chandra rambled on.

"Girl, I read your book. I can't wait until the sequel comes out. I'm dying to see what happens with Zaria," Chandra expressed with excitement. The last time the two women spoke on the phone their conversation turned into a thirty minute talk about her book. Ironically, Chandra was a big fan of Jasmine, but haven't read any of Darius' work.

"I'm glad you liked it. I'm busy wrapping up the sequel now." Darius stood silent with a slight smile on his face, secretively eying Jasmine's perfect figure down to her pedicure toes. "Baby, you didn't tell me, how beautiful she is." Chandra laughed, hitting him on the arm. He laughed with her. Jasmine could see Darius was uncomfortable, with the two of them meeting face to face; not to mention, the awkward feeling she, herself was harboring.

"Um...her picture is on the back of her book." Darius replied.

"Well, it's always good to put a face with a name or should I say a voice." Jasmine added, clutching onto her shoulder bag taking a deep breath.

"Yes, it is," Chandra agreed. "We were just going to get some dinner. Why don't you join us?" Chandra invited.

"No thank you. I think I'll just order room service. I'm tired from the flight but thanks for the offer. Are you ready for the panel questions tomorrow?" Jasmine asked Darius, trying to contain herself. She just wanted to grab him, kiss him and tell him how much she had missed him. It was hard for her to see him standing next to his wife. A little jealousy came across Jasmine, even though that was a right, she didn't own.

"Yeah, I think so." A smile lit his face. Chandra interrupted their conversation.

"Are you sure you don't want to come with us? Then you both can talk about that book stuff at dinner. Maybe you'll disclose the inside scoop about the sequel of your next book."

"Chandra, Jasmine wants to get to her room. Let's go. We'll see you tomorrow." Darius said as he and Chandra began to walk away.

"Okay, but promise me we can do lunch tomorrow." Chandra added.

"Sure," Jasmine replied as she and the bellhop entered the elevator. Jasmine waved at Darius with a slick grin thinking what an awkward moment.

When Jasmine got to her room, she tipped the bellhop and shut her door glancing around the plush room. She was dying to take a long hot bath. She slipped out of her clothes walking around the room naked. She went into the bathroom and began running water in the enormous spa tub. She had been nagging Eric to remodel their bathroom and put one in. So she took full advantage of this nice suite and oversized bathtub. She added her oils and liquid bubbles, and sank into her "Calgon" moment; it felt like heaven, sipping on her Merlot and enjoying the complementary fresh in-season fruit tray.

It was coming up on midnight, and Jasmine was not at all sleepy. Darius was weighing on her mind. The thought of Darius in the same hotel as her probably making love to his wife was burning her up inside. She wanted Darius to be hers exclusively, but she understood her place in their relationship. It was what it was. She would often fantasize how it would be if they both weren't married. She knew they were soul mates. They had so much in common. She and Darius enjoyed the same movies, music, and a shared passion for writing. Jasmine loved everything about Darius. He was fine, smart, and sexy and knew her body better than she knew herself. She desired everything about him. It seemed that since he was now a very well-known author, most women were hot for Darius as well. During each book tour, more and more women would show up dying to take a photo with him and slip him their number. It stated clearly on the back of his books that he was married, but that didn't matter. Darius would always empty his pockets full of phone numbers, then call and check in with Chandra at home and end up in bed with Jasmine.

Jasmine had questioned him about if he was seeing anyone else. She knew if he cheated on his wife with her, who was she to think she was anything special. It bothered her, especially since they were having unprotected sex. But, he assured her he would never sleep around with loads of women and would always be honest with her. Strangely enough she believed and trusted him, but was also sure to get her Pap smear and checkups. Darius get a full physical as well. They both shared their results of negative STD's and HIV tests.

After she finished her bath and another glass of Merlot, she sat on the edge of the tub and began to oil her legs and feet. She was still restless, even though she knew she needed to get some sleep; because she had a full day tomorrow. A knock at the door startled Jasmine. She put on her bathrobe rushing to see who it was.

"Who is it?" She yelled, just before looking through the peephole.

"It's me." Darius' smooth voice responded. She gently opened the door half way, happy to see him but trying to play it cool, in case Chandra was with him.

"What are you doing here?"

"Can I come in?" Jasmine opened the door wider, gesturing for him to enter.

"Where's your wife?" She asked glancing outside the room.

"And how did you know what room I was in?"

"She went to sleep after her third Strawberry Daiquiri, and I knew she was going to sleep like a baby. And to answer your second question, the bellhop made out with a fat tip." They both laughed. I didn't want the front desk calling your room, because that would have spoiled my surprise visit.

"Did you get her drunk on purpose so you could come up here and seduce me?" She giggled, grabbing his hand, pulling him into her, not wasting a moment to plant a kiss on his soft lips. Her body relaxed into his as her robe came undone; he could feel she was naked. Jasmine broke their kiss by stepping back to close her robe. "Isn't your wife gonna roll over and notice that you're not by her side?"

"Nope, come here!" Darius responded, pulling her back to him.

"I don't think this is a good idea…besides…I'm pretty sure you were having sex with your wife and I'm not trying to be anybody's sloppy seconds." Jasmine blurted softly, being upset with herself, for letting her emotions slip out.

The Write Lover

"You'll never be my sloppy seconds and we didn't have sex. After coming out the shower, she got in the bed and went straight to sleep. To be honest we haven't had sex in weeks."

"Is that right, why?"

"Because, of you!"

"Me?" She replied with a surprise expression.

"Yes baby, ever since the first time we made love. I couldn't get you out of my head, and I know you were the one baby, I wanted to spend the rest of my life with."

"Awww honey." Jasmine placed her hand on the side of his face.

"I missed you like crazy." He whispered, lifting up her chin for her to look him in the eyes. "I love you Jasmine. I just want to be with you." He kissed her neck softly, running his hands down her back. "Umm, I love your smooth soft body." He breathed to her.

"I love you too." She whispered back, as their lips locked in an intense kiss. They walked slowly backward, falling on to the bed. Darius didn't waste any time caressing her breast with his tongue. Jasmine loins were wet and ready for him. She began unbuttoning his shirt, and jeans. Now fully naked and without hesitation, he buried his face between her legs and began making love to her, orally. A few minutes later, her body began to quiver. With her eyes closed, she was enjoying every micro second of this wonderful experience. She needed a space shuttle to bring her back down from the sexual high, she was feeling. The kind of sexual experience her husband never introduced to her. She climbed on top of Darius, kissing down the middle of his body; until she reached his harden manhood. Gently guiding it into her warm mouth, she began to swirl her tongue around the crown, before slowly moving down the shaft, taking it all the way down her throat.

"Umm!" He let out a deep moan. She tasted his pre-cum, which made her suck him firmer, but she wasn't ready for Darius to release just yet. She wanted him to come inside her. Giving him one last lick from the base to the tip, she whispered to him.

"Make love to me baby." She needed him more than he knew. Her back arched and her mouth opened wide as he guided his manhood into her pleasure palace. She locked her legs around his back, assisting him deeper inside. Jasmine moans were like applause to the performance of the deep, rhythmic thrusts her lover was giving. Their bodies became one and danced to their own music. They gently kissed each other's neck and shoulders. The heat of their passion became more intense as their bodies shined with sweat.

"I missed you so much." She whispered, gripping his butt and pushing him deeper inside her. Her body was his to do what he wanted. The loving he was putting on her was so good; she was having back to back orgasms. He rolled over, positioning her on top. One of her favorite positions was riding the erection, while he lay back and massaging her breasts. He enjoyed watching her skillful movements as she gyrate her hips, accompanied by a chorus of moans and passionate endearments. With her hands on his shoulders and his on her waist, the intensity of their rhythm increased, until they both came at the same time. Jasmine fell upon his chest breathing hard. Both trying to catch their breath, they just enjoyed the comfort of each other's embrace. The moment was magical.

The Write Lover

"Wow!" Jasmine expressed, wiping perspiration from her face and rolling off him onto the bed.

"Damn, that was...great baby." Darius added, as he braced himself on his elbows. "It gets better each time we're together."

"I agree...honey. It would be on every night if we lived together." She smiled with starry eyes, admiring him. "We are each other's stress relief pill. We would have little or no stress, if we were under one roof.

"You're right," he responded, now sitting on the edge of the bed, running his hands over his head.

Every time he was with Jasmine sexually, or just in her presence, he felt like a new man. He thought about breaking off his love affair with her several times, but he knew he couldn't. He needed her in his life. He was in love with her more than he wanted to admit. He had also thought about asking her to leave her husband several times; he wanted her for himself. He was willing to take the responsibility of helping her raise her sons, without the help of their biological father.

With Jasmine's youthful appearance no one would ever guess she was in her mid thirties or for that matter a mother of two. She had delivered two sons and still had a picture perfect body. She's the epitome of beauty from head to toe, but she was not at all stuck on herself and often down played her looks. Guys would approach her all the time during the book tours, asking her to let them buy her drinks and what not. She always politely declined. One other thing Darius admired about Jasmine was, she worked out faithfully, taking care of her body.

"You better get back to your room." She advised Darius, running her hand down his back.

"Yeah!" He answered just above a whisper, as he put on his shirt; letting out a deep breath. Jasmine knew by his tone and the look on his face that something was bothering him.

"You want to take a shower? I'm sure you don't want to go back to your room smelling like sex and bath oil," Jasmine suggested, as she pulled the sheet over her nude body.

"I hate washing your scent away." He replied, standing up, looking at this beautiful, sexy woman wrapped in the sheet, and wishing he could stay all night with her.

"Do you?" Jasmine smiled.

"Yes sweetheart. I do!" I'm in love with you."

"The feeling is mutual baby." Jasmine responded, caressing his back.

"Huh?" Jasmine responded confused.

"I'm gonna ask Chandra for a divorce. I'm not happy with her and I realize that more and more when we are together." Jasmine was speechless.

"Okay, well, umm," she began stuttering.

"I'm not asking you to leave your husband. I just… well, I haven't been happy in my marriage for quite some time. And I know you haven't either baby. We need to be honest with each other. We should be together."

"Darius!" she cut his words short. Ignoring her interruption, Darius continued.

"I want you full time. Look, I'm not going to pressure you into anything. I'll be waiting for you whenever you decide to leave your husband. We are going to be together and grow old together."

"I can't hurt my kids Darius. It's not that easy for me to walk away from my marriage."

"I know…I know, but what about you? What about your happiness?"

"It's not about my happiness. I have to think about my kids." Without a response, he took a hold of her hand, planting a soft kiss upon the back of them.

"I understand honey, handle your business."
Positioning herself, she placed her head on his chest as the tears flowed down her cheeks.

"Don't cry honey."

"What are you saying to me, Darius? Is this over? Are you going to move on and look for another woman to marry?"

"Nah, it's not even like that. You're going to be my wife; you just don't know it yet." They both laughed at that statement as he wiped away her tears with his thumb.

"You're too much." At that moment, Darius' cell phone began vibrating.

"Ah shit." He checked the caller ID, while reaching for it on the nightstand. "Damn, it's Chandra."

"I guess she wasn't sleeping as hard as you thought after all." Jasmine commented, as he gestured for her to be quiet; placing his index finger on his lips.

"Hey baby." He answered. Jasmine could hear Chandra's loud voice through the receiver questioning his whereabouts.

"I had a headache. I just came down to the store in the lobby to get some extra strength Tylenol. I'm on my way back up."

"Okay, see you soon." They both disconnected the call.

"Boy you're in trouble." She teased jokingly, letting out a giggle. He rushed to the bathroom for a quick wash up. A few short minutes later, he emerged from the bathroom; dressed.

"I'll see you tomorrow. Think about what I said."

She walked him to the door and they kissed good-bye, just before he opened the door and disappearing down the hallway.

Jasmine went to sleep confused, thinking about, what Darius had said to her.

Chapter Five
The Two Women

The Next Day...

Jasmine had never been a breakfast person. She just needed a cup of black coffee and she would be ready to start the day. The meet and greet was scheduled for two that afternoon, so Jasmine had time to kill. It was just about ten and she was still in the bed. She was enjoying the moment of sleeping in, and not having to wake up to her boys begging for cereal and fighting with each other. Her husband would always roll over and leave her to deal with the issues. If he didn't have to go to work, he would sleep until noon or until she nagged him to get out of the bed, to cut the grass look after the boys' while she ran errands.

She picked up her cell phone and called home to check on the family, but to her surprise no one picked up the phone. She disconnected and called her husband's cell phone, but he didn't answer that phone either. It went straight to his voicemail. She laid back on the pillow, thinking to herself, she would later try again. She began to wonder what happened to Darius after he left her room last night, leaving her still horny but content. Jasmine was hoping he had played it cool with his wife so she wouldn't expect anything.

She was not looking forward to running into him with his wife, but she knew it would be inevitable. She pulled her tired body out of the bed, grabbed the telephone and called the concierge to find out the location and hours of the hotel's gym. After obtaining the information, she decided to take advantage of the time and get in a work out.

Jasmine had given her sister a small business loan to finance a fitness studio, and it was beginning to take off. She enjoyed filling in for her sister every now and then and thought about even teaching her own classes; but she knew she didn't have extra time to do that, especially with her writing career taking off and raising her sons; but she kept her body tight, just in case she changed her mind about teaching. Her husband would never approve of it any way. He already complained that she wasn't home enough. However, he didn't mind her teaching the belly dancing classes she taught once a month on Thursday. He enjoyed looking at all the other women that would come to learn the exotic movements.

After Jasmine worked up a sweat on the treadmill and hit the punching bag for twenty minutes, she felt revived and headed back to her room to take a rejuvenating shower, before slipping into her favorite tight jeans with a silk fitted blouse. After putting on her heels, she gave herself a look over in the full body mirror. She put on a simple coat of natural make-up to enhance her beauty and some lip gloss. Jasmine was heading down to check out her area and make sure everything was set up the way she liked it. The last literary meet-and-greet conference in Phoenix was all right, but did not have the big turn-out all the authors were hoping for. While she was checking in at the registration desk, Jasmine ran into a few of the other authors she had met during her travels. She made her way to her assigned table and started unpacking.

"Well, if isn't Jasmine Deveraux," she heard a deep voice say. She looked up and saw Terrance.

Terrance was a well known literary agent. He had been trying to get Jasmine to sign with him for months now. He stood about six-four, fair skinned, and very easy on the eyes.

"Hey Terrance, how are you?" Jasmine replied, as she continued to unpack her books for her table display.

"Ms. Deveraux, you know if I was your agent you wouldn't be unpacking your books. You would have someone else doing that for you."

"Is that right?" She knew having an agent came with a price and she preferred to cut out the middle-man and negotiate her own contracts with the publishers. Terrance smoothly pulled a business card out his suit jacket, handing it to her.

"Why don't you take my card and give me a call? We can sit down and discuss me becoming your agent." Terrance paused, while looking at her figure from head to toe before continuing. "Why don't we have dinner tonight and we can discuss a lot of things." She shook her head knowing what he was implying. He just wanted to get between her legs.

"I don't think so." She replied, not taking his card. He smiled taking back his card, placing the card back in his jacket.

"That's your loss sweetheart. So um, I hear the buzz that you and Mr. Hamilton are writing a hot romance novel." How he knew about that, she wondered. It wasn't public information just yet. They just finished the manuscript a couple of weeks ago.

"Oh, yeah, and where did you hear that from?"

"I hear things through the grapevine."

"Is that right?"

"I saw you working out in the gym this morning and I was going to stop and say hi, but you were working that punching bag pretty good. So I just watched for a second enjoying the sight," he laughed. "Your husband is a lucky man, or shall I say Darius."

"What are you implying?" Jasmine raised her voice becoming agitated.

"Well, when I see you guys together at these literary affairs, you two seem pretty close."

"We should be. We are friends and colleagues," Jasmine snapped. Terrance lifted both hands in the air as if he was surrendering.

"Look, I'm not mad at him. There is no way I could just be friends with a fine woman like you without wanting to get a little closer." She rolled her eyes at Terrance, wanting to strike him in the face. *This man is nothing but a straight up snake,* Jasmine thought as she balled up her fist. He kept looking at her body as if she was a well-cooked steak, giving added attention to her cleavage.

"Well, if you don't mind I really need to finish setting up."

"I understand. Have a good day, Ms. Deveraux," He winked at her before turning to walk away.

"Umm, who was that handsome man?" A woman's voice asked. Jasmine turned around to see who it was. It was Chandra, checking out Terrance as he walked away. Jasmine couldn't believe her eyes. Chandra looked ten times better than the night before. Her hair was in loose curls wearing a cute jean skirt and a silk blouse. Jasmine glanced behind her and noticed she was alone.

"He's a literary agent. How are you this morning?" Jasmine asked as she took a deep breath.

"Hmm very nice," Chandra replied, watching Terrance making his way across the room, then turned her attention back to Jasmine. "Well I've been better." The look in her eyes told Jasmine that she wasn't the same happy woman she was yesterday when she had met her. She wasn't sure if she should pry or not, so she quickly changed the subject.

"Where's Darius? Shouldn't he be setting up?" Jasmine asked, as she continued stacking her books on the table, trying not to make eye contact with Chandra.

"He's coming. He's been acting real shitty to me girl. I should have never come here with him. I don't think he really like me coming with him when he does these book tours."

"Why would you think that?"

"Just because he…I don't know…acts different like I'm annoying him or something. When he's in the zone with his writing and book stuff, it's like I'm invisible to him. He pays me no attention and then he wonders why I'm not ready to have a child."

"Huh?"

"Oh, I thought you knew Darius and I don't have any children. He's been nagging me about it for years, but I'm really not feeling the whole mommy thing, ya know. I'm pushing forty and it's too late for me to be trying to pop out babies now. Do you have kids?"

"Two boys, seven and nine," Jasmine spoke proudly. She was also stunned that Chandra was sharing so much of her personal information to her like they were the best of friends.

"People look at me like I'm crazy when I tell them I don't have any kids, nor do I want any. I don't think you need to have kids to be a complete person. Besides, Darius and I haven't been having sex enough to make a baby, even if I wanted to."

"Okay," Jasmine laughed uncomfortably.

"Oh, I'm sorry, girl. I've just been running my mouth about my personal life?"

"It's alright."

"Here comes Darius now." Chandra informed, looking over her shoulder. Every time Jasmine saw him her heart skipped a beat.

"Hello ladies," he greeted, with a movie star smile.

"Finally decided to wake up huh?" Chandra asked sarcastically.

"I had a hard time falling asleep last night." He responded, looking around the room. Now focusing on Jasmine, he asked,

"Are you ready for the crowd?"

"I hope there is a crowed," she sighed.

"Oh, I think it will be a better turn out than Phoenix." Chandra took a hold of Darius' hand, holding it was more for show, than actual feelings. That touched a nerve with Jasmine. It showed a little on her face.

"So why don't we all go get lunch before everything starts." Chandra suggested.

"That's a great idea, my treat!" Jasmine could not believe that Darius had just invited her along to have lunch with him and his wife. *What was Darius thinking, having me and his wife sitting next to each other eating and laughing like one happy family?* She thought to herself; wondering if she go or not.

"Well I…" He cut Jasmine off.

"No excuses. Let's go!" He demanded.

"Yeah, I'm starving." Chandra added, reaching for Jasmine's arm.

"Well alright," she agreed, reluctantly giving in.

After a quick stop at the ladies room to get her mind right, Jasmine joined Darius and Chandra at the Café in the hotel. Chandra questioned Jasmine about her family, making small talk, until their food arrived. Chandra went on and on about her hectic real estate job, how she just sold her first million dollar property, and how she was the real estate agent of the month. It was more than obvious that she loved her job. She talked about the housing market for a good twenty minutes without any pause.

Darius kept giving Jasmine the eye so she discretely took off her shoes and ran her foot between his legs licking her lips, letting him know it would have been on, if his wife wasn't there. Chandra didn't have a clue what was going on inches away from her, she was too busy going on and on about real estate. Then Chandra's cell phone rang, freeing the two from a conversation they didn't really want to participate in.

"It's Walter from the office. I need to fill him in on what the Johnson's are looking for baby." She said to Darius as she excused herself from the table and hastily walked toward the restaurant exit. Jasmine waited until Chandra was far enough away from the table before she said,

"You really think you smooth, having your wife and your lover, sitting together having lunch with you. I must be crazy!"

"I'm sorry baby, but she was asking twenty-one questions about you this morning so I wanted you to have lunch with us so she wouldn't think anything is going on between us."

"What's really on your mind Darius?" Jasmine asked, not following what he said as she placed a fork full of mashed potatoes in her mouth.

"To divorce or not to divorce, is the question?"

"You really need to be sure that's what you want to do?"

"I'm sure!" replied Darius, giving Jasmine direct eye contact. Their eyes locked for a moment. Then she quickly looked away and shook her head.

"I love you so much Darius." She whispered to him. "I really wish we could be together. This is so confusing." She raised her head up towards the ceiling, trying not to let any tears escape from her eyes. She never thought in a million years her feelings would become so strong for him.

"I know baby, and I…" She cut him off quickly, when she saw Chandra approaching.

"So um, when are you leaving, tonight or in the morning?" Jasmine asked Darius, changing the subject as Chandra sat down.

"First thing in the morning, I wish we could fly out tonight though, because the bed is uncomfortable." Darius replied, catching on to why Jasmine changed the subject so quickly.

"I slept in it just fine, and besides how would you know honey, you slept on the loveseat?" Chandra interjected, coming in on the conversation. She looked at Darius as she resumed eating.

"Now that couldn't have been comfortable," Jasmine added, as she took a sip of diet Coke, through a straw.

The Write Lover

"No love seat tonight baby. You'll be sleeping like a baby when I get done with you." Darius rolled his eyes, laughing her off and thinking, not if I can help it you won't.

"Don't act shy everyone knows those erotic scenes you write in your books had to come from experiences, and I'm glad to be the lucky lady you get to do your research on." Jasmine choked on the soda, coughing until she recovered; covering her mouth with a napkin.

"Now, Chandra!"

"Oh please Darius, Jasmine is a grown woman, she knows what's up."

"Well on that note, I'm going back to my room, to change and get ready. Thank you both so much for lunch. You guys, it's been fun."

"Yeah, maybe next time your husband will be able to accompany you and we can double date or something?" Chandra suggested, with a wide smile.

"That sounds like a plan." Jasmine responded, giving both of them a hug, before exiting the restaurant. Jasmine couldn't believe how fake Chandra was acting. An hour ago, she was complaining about how, she and Darius didn't have sex often enough to plan for a baby. Now she's taking credit for Darius' sex scenes. *That bitch doesn't have a clue!* Jasmine thought to herself as she waited for the elevator, which seemed to be taking forever and a day. She was trying to digest, not only her food, but the whole conversation that had taken place.

Jasmine entered the elevator, pressed the illuminated button corresponding to her floor, and exhaled. The doors began to slide shut, when a hand stopped the door from closing all the way. She looked up to see Darius, making his way onto the elevator alone, with no Chandra following behind him. Before she could say a word, he placed his arms around her and gave her a loving embrace. He apologized for the awkward conversation that took place.

"Darius baby, what are we doing?" She whispered.

"I need you." He responded, placing soft kisses on her lips. She broke their kiss as the elevator came to a stop on the 11th floor where her room was located. He stepped back from their embrace, as the door chimed and opened. Not looking at him, she stepped out, and he followed.

"What are you doing on my floor? And where is your wife?" she asked, pulling her plastic key card out of her purse. He gently took the card from her hand and opened the door, not answering her question.

"What do you think you're doing, Darius?"

"I'm coming with you in your room." He replied with a smile, holding the door open for her.

"You are cutting it real close. What if your wife comes looking for you? Besides, we have to get ready, the meet-and-greet starts in an hour."

"She won't come looking for me. We had a disagreement after you left the table and I just stormed off. She's mad at me right now, so she could care less where I'm at."

"You two had a disagreement? I thought she was going to tighten you up tonight?" Jasmine questioned, dropping her purse on the table and taking off her three inch heels.

"What she said at the table was uncalled for. She really can work my nerves sometimes but enough about her." Darius removed his shoes as well. "Come here baby."

"I don't know about this."

"You know you want me just as much as I want you." Holding onto her waist and gently pulling her into him.

"Of course I do, but…," Jasmine turned her head to the side, now looking out the window.

"My wife doesn't know what room you're in or what floor you're on. Try to relax." He kissed her softly on her shoulder, removing her blouse then swiftly unsnapping her bra.

"Baby I ran into Terrance earlier today, that so called literary agent," she spoke, while he lowered the zipper on her jeans. "He was asking a lot of questions about you and me. He even knew that we had written a book together."

"Umm hmm, and?" Darius asked, lowering her jeans to the floor.

"It seemed like he was letting on, that he knew we were having an affair or something. You haven't mentioned us to anyone, have you?"

"No baby, I would never do anything stupid like that. People may say stuff just to start gossip. I see the way he looks at you. He's just jealous that he can't get next to you. As far as him knowing about the book, he probably got that from the publisher. Now, enough talk about that fool." They fell back onto the bed and began kissing and grinding against each other. When his cell phone rang, killing the moment.

"Damn." He reached over pulling his phone out of his pants. "Hello." Jasmine sat up on the edge of the bed looking at her watch. They had less than an hour before the meet-and-greet and book signing started.

He gestured for her not to move, indicating he wasn't going to be on the phone long. "Don't worry about where I am. No Chandra, I'm sick of your shit. You should have stayed home then. It was uncalled for." Jasmine listened silently. She could hear Chandra yelling at the top of her lungs at him. He grew angrier by the second, and just disconnect from the call, dropping the phone on his clothes that were lying on the floor.

"You too need to square things away before we have to be downstairs."

"Come here baby." He continued, ignoring her question. She crawled back toward him, planting a sensual kiss on his lips, trying to get the angry look and wrinkles off his forehead.

"Put on a condom first baby." She whispered reaching onto the bedside table, retrieving a Trojan brand condom out of the box of three; she bought and handed it to him. He placed it on and before she realized it, he took a hold of her waist, pushing her down onto his hard penis. He held her breast, squeezing them gently as he thrust his hips upward into her. He knew that massaging her breasts was her spot, and just like clockwork she jerked and yelled out in ecstasy, and her body became limp as she came extremely hard.

"Shit!" Jasmine whispered, trying to catch her breath as she fell onto his chest. They rolled over, now Darius was on top placing her legs over his shoulder, as he entered. Biting her bottom lip, she dug her nails into his forearms, not caring if she left a mark. Darius was taking all his tension and aggression out on her and she didn't mind. He was pumping her so hard, the wonderful feeling she was receiving, made her climax twice in a matter seconds of each other. The headboard was hitting the wall with a rhythmic beat when he noticed a painful look on her face.

"Are you alright baby?" He asked, stopping in mid stride.

"Oh yes baby, we gotta hurry up."

"Alright…I'm about to cum soon." He spread her legs apart as far as they could go and pulled her into him, releasing in the condom. Jasmine held onto his ass pushing him deeper inside her as he continued to release, wishing she could have felt his warmth inside her. He slowly rested on her chest letting out a deep grunt. They rested for minute to catch their breath.

"Umm, I need you like this more often baby." He whispered in her ear, still breathing rapidly. They stared into each other's eyes smiling, a moment later there was a hard knock at her door. Darius and Jasmine looked at each other with a surprise expression.

"Oh damn," Jasmine whispered, grabbing the robe off the chair going over to the door. Darius got up grabbing his clothes. "Who is it?" She yelled, putting on her robe.

"Hey Jasmine, it's me Chandra." Her eyes almost popped out her head as she tied her robe looking back at Darius. He stood there with his clothes in his hand as she gestured for him to go into the bathroom.

"Hold on, just a moment." Jasmine mouthed the words to Darius, *What do I do?* He motioned for her to open the door as he entered the bathroom closing the door behind him. She took a deep breath before opening the door slowly.

"Hey Jasmine," Chandra greeted, looking frantic and crazy as she pushed past Jasmine, looking around her room, falling onto the sofa. "Darius and I just had a big fight. I thought maybe you'd know where he is?"

"Umm, I'm sorry to hear that. I was just about to get in the shower."

"I apologize girl, for barging in on you. I just…I don't know…I needed someone to talk to. I thought maybe he would have come to your room."

"My room? He doesn't even know what room I'm in and how did you know where my room was?" Jasmine questioned. Chandra eyes were red like she had been crying. Jasmine instantly felt guilty, but at the same time was wondering could she smell the sex that was lingering in the room.

"I looked on the conference sign-in sheet. Does Darius ever talk about me to you?"

"Huh?"

"I mean, I think something's going on with him. I think he may be having an affair?"

"I can't imagine him having an affair."

"I don't know. I just…something seem different. I can't lose him. I know he really want kids and I've been rejecting that whole idea since we've been married. I should never have gotten that abortion."

"Abortion?" Jasmine echoed.

"Darius doesn't know. About two months after we got married, I got pregnant. I didn't tell him. I was not ready to have a baby. We had only been married for a few months and the thought of getting fat and my real estate career was just taking off, so I went behind his back and had an abortion. I told him I had a yeast infection to get out of having sex."

The Write Lover

"Damn Chandra!" Was all Jasmine could say, hoping Darius didn't storm out the bathroom and kill her where she stood. At that moment, Jasmine glanced down and noticed Darius cell phone on he floor by the side of the bed. Chandra broke into a deep cry.

"Maybe I should try to call him again." She pulled out her cell from her purse.

"No! Don't do that." Chandra looked at her like she was crazy. "Just give yourself and him a little more time to cool down."

"Yeah, maybe you're right. I'm sorry for barging in on you like this."

She wiped her tears away and stood up. Jasmine positioned herself in front of the bed to block the view of Darius cell phone.

"I'll tell you what. After the book signing, let's go to the bar and have a drink. Let Darius do his book stuff and give him some space. I'm sure you guys will be fine." Jasmine walked Chandra to the door, playing it off, hoping she couldn't smell his cologne on her. "I have to hurry up myself or I'm going to be late."

"Thank you Jasmine." Chandra said with a half smile as Jasmine as opened the door, for her.

"I'll see you later." Jasmine told her smiling back, closing the door quickly. Darius stormed out the bathroom looking like he was going to murder someone, with tear filled eyes. Jasmine stood there unsure of what to say or do.

"I'm going down for a murder case."

"Shh! She might hear you." Jasmine rushed, picking up Darius' phone and handing it to him.

"Fuck her. This is some fucked up shit. She took it upon herself to abort the pregnancy without informing me about anything. After all these years telling me that she was only on the pill to keep her period regular. She's been lying to me all these years." He spoke with fire.

"Darius baby, I know it hurts but you can't let on that you know. Then she'll know you were in here or that I told you."

"I don't give a fuck. You two aren't best friends."

"Please Darius, just calm down."

"CALM DOWN! That bitch just told you she killed my baby. All these years she knew I wanted a child. I'M MORE THAN UPSET. YOU HAVE NO IDEA, JASMINE! YOU HAVE TWO KIDS! HOW IN THE HELL WOULD YOU KNOW HOW I FEEL?

"Don't fuckin' yell at me!" She responded, slightly raising her voice. He didn't say a word; he just slipped on his shoes. "Are you going to confront her? Let me know right now, so I know how to handle her."

"Nah, I'm gonna play her little game, since she wants to play in the big leagues. Then I should hurt her like she hurt me and tell her you and I have been fuckin' you for over a year."

"What! Have you lost your mind?" Darius had really pissed Jasmine off with that statement. She knew he was hurting and upset but now he had gone too far.

"Fuckin'? That's all this has been, huh?"

"No, I didn't mean it like that I…"

"Darius, you better leave before I slap the shit out of you. Now I'm pissed. Get out!" Jasmine demanded. Darius shook his head and stormed out the room. She locked the door before rushing to take a quick shower.

Jasmine was a nervous wreck as she rushed to get dressed and thinking about the argument she just had. She was running twenty minutes late for her book signing but she finally made it. Jasmine glanced over at Darius' booth and he was nowhere to be found. She was praying he didn't go and confront Chandra. Jasmine could not focus as she greeted her fans. She was distracted every few minutes looking around for him. Chandra wasn't in the area either. Finally, about thirty minutes later Jasmine saw Darius making his way to his booth as the whole crowd started to migrate over to him. He smiled, taking pictures and signing books like he didn't have a care in the world. Jasmine was worried that he had gone back to the room and killed Chandra. She was still unraveled because they had never got into an argument before.

"Look at him over there putting on a happy face like everything is so great." Jasmine heard a voice say as she looked up and saw Chandra standing over her, looking in Darius' direction. Jasmine took a deep breath as she stood up.

"Looks like the majority of the people moved over to his booth."

"Yeah...he loves that shit. I think his career as a writer is more important to him than anything," Chandra mumbled with an attitude.

"You ready for that drink?" Jasmine asked.

"You all done?"

"I need a break. I'm ready for that drink," responded Jasmine as they walked out the room. Sure enough Darius looked up and saw them walking through the door, heading towards the lounge.

"I need a strong drink right about now." Jasmine said, taking a sip of her Long Island ice tea.

"Darius came back to the room, shortly after I left you. He just rushed past me and took a shower, not saying a word. He's a bastard sometimes." She expressed stirring her drink with the plastic, red straw, just before taking a healthy sip.

"Did he?"

"Yeah! You know I think things would really be different if we had kids. I'm going to throw my birth control pills away."

"Maybe you should tell him first."

"No, I'm gonna surprise him." Just then the waiter asked.

"How are you ladies doing?"

"We're fine, thank you." Chandra responded. She continued, "So Darius mentioned something about the two of you writing a book together?"

"Yeah, it was recommended by our publisher. He thought it would be a good since both of our writing styles blend well together." Chandra turned her eye up at Jasmine like she had more questions to ask, but she just sipped on her drink instead. Then she finally asked, "What did you think of Darius when you first saw him?"

"Huh?'

"I mean did you think he was cute? Did he try to come onto you? You look like his type. Did you fuck him?" Jasmine gave off a nervous laugh in shock that she came at her like that.

"You need to put that glass down because to ask me a question like that, I know that drink went straight to your head. To answer your question, no I didn't fuck your husband. Yes, he's a very attractive man but I have my dick at home waiting for me. Besides, we are both married and we keep our relationship strictly professional. I told you that before." Jasmine wanted to get up and run out the lounge, but she played it cool, taking sips of her drink. That lie rolled off her tongue so good she almost believed it herself. Just then her cell phone rang, to the tune of "Say Yes" by Floetry. She rushed to answer, knowing it was Darius.

"Excuse me, it's my husband." She lied to Chandra, taking the call, giving herself some space.

"Why are you calling me?"

"So you and Chandra are home girls now?"

"Shouldn't you be signing books and taking pictures?" She asked smartly.

"Shouldn't you be signing books instead of trying to be best friends with Chandra?"

"I'm not trying to make friends with your precious wife. I'm just trying to keep her off balance, in reference to our love affair; so don't get it twisted. Look, I don't have time for this drama. I have enough of this bullshit to deal with at home, with my husband. I'll talk to you another time. Bye." When Jasmine returned, Chandra had finished her drink and was ordering another.

"Look Chandra, I have to get back to my booth; so I'll talk to you another time."

"Okay girl, if I don't see you before you leave, have a safe flight back to the west coast.

It was nice meeting and talking with you. Maybe we should exchange phone numbers so we can stay in touch."

"I'm sure I'll catch up with you before I leave. I really have to get back in there." Placing a ten dollar bill on the bar before rushing off, she didn't want Chandra's number and definitely didn't want her to have hers. Chandra gave Jasmine a funny look as she watched her quickly walk away.

Feeling very uncomfortable about the day events, Jasmine decided to take an early flight back home. She didn't want to stay another night in New York. Instead of staying to Sunday morning, she figured it was best to fly out that evening. She wrapped up her book signing, made all her appearances and went back to her room to pack. She did not want to run into either Darius or Chandra, because she had enough drama for the day. The bellboy gathered her suitcases and told her a cab was waiting for her down stairs. He followed her as she settled her room bill at the counter before proceeding to head out the massive glass door. Darius was walking into the lobby, laughing and talking with some female. She was a beautiful woman, extremely tall, and slim. She looked young by her baby face. It was obvious she was bi-racial by her light complexion and wavy hair. Jasmine was going to completely ignore Darius, but he stopped her in her tracks.

"Hey Jasmine!" She just looked at him, still feeling annoyed.

"Ms. Deveraux, oh my God…I love your books. I went by your table but you were not there. It's so nice to meet you face to face. My name is also Jasmine, but everyone calls me Jazz." She threw her hair back, extending her arm, taking a hold of Jasmine's hand, shaking it almost wildly. "Do you have a book readily available that I can purchase from you?"

"I'm sorry, everything is packed and in the taxi. Give Darius your information and I'll get an autographed copy to you."

"Thank you, Ms. Deveraux, or should I say Jasmine?" The woman rattled on with a big smile, before Darius interjected,

"Excuse my manners. Jazz is a model with fashion fair."

"Well good for you," Jasmine smartly replied, pulling her hand away from Jazz, and wondering if she was Darius' new freak of the week. Jasmine began to wonder a million things, like if he was

The Write Lover

fucking her too, and she began to feel like a used fool at that moment.

"Darius told me you guys have completed a romance novel together. I can't wait to read it." Jasmine just smiled, dividing her attention between the two. It took every fiber in her being, to stay cool.

"Well, it was nice meeting you Jazz, but my cab is waiting and I really have to go."

"It was nice meeting you as well." Jasmine turned and walked away.

"Let me walk you to the cab. Jazz, I'll talk to you later."

"Okay."

"You don't have to walk me anywhere!" Jasmine spoke with contempt.

"What's your problem?" Darius asked upset, following Jasmine to the taxi.

"Nothing, you better hurry up and get back to your friend…no better yet…" Jasmine stopped in her tracks and angrily snapped. "You should check on your wife who's probably throwing her birth control pills away as we speak."

"What are you talking about?" Darius asked in a low voice.

"Just…I don't know. Everything is messed up. You, me…it's over, Darius."

"What!"

"I can't do this with you anymore. We should have never gotten involved with one another. Let's just stick to a professional writing relationship, nothing more okay?"

"I don't know why you are trying to talk so fast, but I caught on to what you said about some birth control pills. Did Chandra say something to you?" Jasmine could see the sadness in his eyes, then the anger.

"I have to go."

"Wait." He motioned to the cab driver, to give him a second.

"I have to get to the airport."

"So this is how you want it to end? Why Jasmine? You know how I feel about you."

"Do you feel that same way about Jazz? Will you be fucking her tonight?" Jasmine asked in a cold, calm tone.

"She's just a fan, nothing more."

"Yeah, well…I got to go." Jasmine turned away, trying to prevent the tears from escaping her eyes and rolling down her cheeks. He gently turned her back around and they looked deep into one another eyes, and before she knew it, tears began to travel down her cheek. Darius wiped her tears away and attempted to kiss her on the cheek when Jasmine moved her face, not allowing the kiss to take place. Darius didn't say a word; he just watched her get into the taxi and drive away.

Chapter Six
Good News or Bad New First?

    The communication between Darius and Jasmine wasn't like before. Two months had passed and since they last spoke to one another. Darius didn't understand why Jasmine acted the way she did toward him, so he wasn't about to call her; even though she still held the key to his heart. Jasmine felt deep down inside that she shouldn't have left New York the way she did being mad at Darius. The feelings and intimacy she shared with him and the moral obligations for her husband and children had her head all messed up. But one thing she did know for sure, she was in love and it wasn't with her husband.

    Jasmine was having her suspicions about Eric stepping out on her. All of a sudden he was working late a lot. He came home the other night around one in the morning; saying he took another guy shift, who had gotten sick, but he never bothered to call; informing her of his late arrival. She thought it could be her own guilty feelings, which had her tripping. She had gone way too far with Darius, but she didn't regret it because he made her feel like a woman. He loved every part of her mind body and soul. Her heart wouldn't let her deny that he was indeed her soul mate, but she knew if her husband ever found out about it he'd probably kill her. She thought about picking up the phone and calling Darius to apologize, but forced herself to stay angry with him. She thought that would be best for the both of them.

As Jasmine glanced at the touring schedule for their book, *"Being Homeless Is Not an Option."* She knew Darius was supposed to be in Sacramento. She canceled all her touring schedules for their book, and told the publisher to leave all the promotion appearances to him. She had made that decision when she was furious with him on her way home from New York, after their fight. She had dialed the publisher's number so fast acting on her emotions, telling them she didn't want to have any parts of promoting the book with him. The publisher didn't question her; they just cleared her off the rest of the schedule. She knew she would lose a lot of money from the book sales, but at that moment she didn't care.

Jasmine knew that the only way to forget about Darius was to focus on her marriage, and get things back on track in her life. But it was easier said than done, because at the same time she was dying to hear his voice. She was hurting inside and needed his touch. *I'm so messed up in the head, how did I, let myself get to this point. Why couldn't my husband love me and make love to me, like Darius.* Shaking her head, and pacing the floor, trying not to give in, knowing he was in her city, she couldn't contain her feelings any longer and picked up the phone. She put her pride aside and dialed his number.

*****

The Write Lover

Darius was in Sacramento for a meeting, with a senior editor for a major magazine. He was trying to relax in his hotel room after the five and half-hour flight. As he laid on the bed, his mind wandered off and he began to think about Jasmine. Glancing at his cell phone he wanted to dial her number something terrible, but the more he thought about her canceling all the book promotions, sadness filled his heart. The past two months for him, had been a nightmare without her. The only good thing going on was their book, *"Being Homeless Is Not an Option."* It was flying off the shelves and getting a lot of buzz. Darius had asked Chandra for a divorce and had moved out of their home. He wanted so bad to tell Jasmine about the divorce paper he filed, but his pride kept him from calling her. He figured it was best to leave her alone. He knew she would never leave her husband for him. So he decided to start a new life and try to forget about her. His focus was now working on his next novel project, *"Based on a Lie."*

He flipped through the channels trying to find something on television, to kill a few hours before the late meeting when his cell phone began to vibrate.

"Hello." He answered without checking the caller ID.

"Hey sweetheart, how are you?" A sensual female voice replied on the other end.

"Who is this?"

"It's Jasmine." She said, with a hesitated tone in her voice, unsure how he would respond.

"Hello Jasmine." His heart skipped a beat as he replied. He was filled with joy to hear from her.

"I'm doing fine but how did you know I was in town?" He asked puzzled.

Brooklen Borne

"I already had the schedule. Did you forget? How have the tours been going? What else been going on with you?" Jasmine questioned, feeling a nervous energy inside of her.

"You should be here with me, this is your hometown. Everyone was asking why you're not touring, and I told them you had to take care of personal business."

"Good! I knew you could hold it down and yes, I should have been there with you, but everything was getting so complicated with us Darius. I know you're still angry with me and I deserve it, but I want to come and make it up to you."

"If you're coming, be here by four o'clock; because I have to meet someone." Jasmine's heart stopped, wondering who that someone could be.

"Okay, I'll be there. I really need to see you." Without a response, he disconnected. Her heart sank. She didn't know what to think. Darius had never been this cold to her. She began to look back and thought to herself, *who is this someone Darius was talking about? Could it be that model Jazz?*

Jasmine became so overwhelmed that she started to cry as she sat down on the bed. She mumbled out loud, *please God, help me. I hope I didn't lose him to someone else.* A few hours later, Jasmine got herself together and picked out the sexiest dress she had in her wardrobe. *I'm not giving up without a fight*, Jasmine said to herself out loud, as she wiped the remaining tears from her face, and began to pull herself together.

Jasmine arrived at the hotel at three forty-five, fifteen minutes ahead of time. Her heart was pounding, in her chest as she knocked on his room door.

"Who is it?"

The Write Lover

"It's me, Jasmine." He opened the door wearing nothing but a towel wrapped around his waist. She could smell the scent of his cologne, Obsession Night by Calvin Klein; one of her favorites. The sight of him made her nipples hard and her kitty moist. She used every ounce of discipline she had, not to jump on him and sex him where he stood. She walked into the room and saw his clothes laid out; on one of the two beds that occupied the room. Her eyes swept the room for signs of a woman…there was none. He gave her a peck on the cheek, not the loving sensual tongue greeting she was use to getting from him. He turned away and continued to get dressed.

"What's up with that?" She asked referring to the greeting, she received.

"You look great in that dress." He replied, ignoring her question. She walked closer to him as he pulled up his pant before sitting down in the chair, to lace up his brown lizard Belvedere shoes.

"I'm sorry for acting the way I did toward you in New York. We had that big argument, Chandra was asking me a hundred and one questions, and when I saw you with that model, I just lost it." He didn't comment on what she had just stated. He stood up and walked toward the closet to put on his mock neck and jacket. As Darius walked away, unbeknownst to him, she reached out for him but slowly brought her hand back as her eyes became full. After straightening his jacket, he walked over to her, lifted her chin giving her a peck on the lips.

"I want to apologize for yelling at you when Chandra said what she said in the room. I don't like arguing with you either. I asked Chandra for a divorce." Jasmine didn't know what to say, she just looked at him. I didn't let on that I knew about the birth control pills. I just confronted her about other things and it led into it. Let's just say she came clean with everything. She had no clue I was in your room or that you might have told me. However I did tell her I was in love with someone else." Jasmine sat on the bed speechless, fearing someone had already taken her place. "I'm in love with you and I know you are not going to leave your husband for me. I would never ask you to do that. I've already moved out the house and my lawyer is drawing up the papers; so that part of my life will soon be over." Darius glanced at his watch. "What does your schedule look like for the rest of the day?" He asked adjusting his jacket, changing the subject quickly.

"It's open."

"Good! I want you to come downstairs with me. I have someone to introduce you to."

"Okay" She said nervously. He placed his hand at the small of her back as they walked out the room.

When they reached the lobby and walked in the restaurant, a beautiful woman with a mocha complexion stood up with a big smile when she saw Darius. Her hair was pulled back in a ponytail and she wore little makeup. The print silk dress this woman had on brought out her sexy curves. Jasmine's heart sank. Darius introduced Jasmine to the beautiful lady.

"Jasmine, this is Faye. Faye, this is Jasmine."

"I finally meet Ms. Jasmine Deveraux?" Faye was awed with excitement. Jasmine looked over at Darius like he was crazy for introducing her to his new woman.

"Yes, and you are?" She hesitantly replied.

The Write Lover

"I'm Faye Simms from Essence Magazine." Jasmine had a puzzled look on her face. Faye picked up on it and looked at Darius, then back at Jasmine.

"You didn't receive a letter?" Faye asked Jasmine with a look of concern on her face.

"A letter?" Jasmine answered unsure, while giving alternate looks from Faye to Darius.

"Let's sit down and I'll tell you what this meeting is about." Faye informed, getting comfortable in the booth. She began to explain to Jasmine what was going on when the waitress came over to take their order. Jasmine wasn't really hungry so she ordered a house salad and a glass of water.

Faye ordered the same thing while Darius ordered a Philly cheese steak, fries and a coke to wash it down. After the waitress left to put in their order, Faye continued, "You and Darius will be featured in Essence next month. You both won Best Romance Novel and Best Author Collaboration of the Year Award. You should have received a letter in the mail."

Jasmine remembered receiving something the other day from Essence but didn't open it. She had so much on her mind, not to mention an argument with her husband. She had completely forgotten about the letter and left the house without opening it. Jasmine gave Darius a playful punch on the arm and he broke out in laughter.

"Yes, I received it but I didn't get a chance to open it." Jasmine said, with a slight smile from the good news, Faye just blessed her with.

Everyone enjoyed their lunch as the specifics were given to both of them, along with a mini interview for the magazine. When the interview was over, Faye and her photographer took a couple of photos of Darius and Jasmine. After the photographer got the delivered shot, Faye conveyed her congratulations on behalf of the magazine and her goodbyes. Then she sent a bottle of wine to their table and departed the restaurant. Darius and Jasmine stayed in the restaurant for a little while longer, talking about their good fortune as they enjoyed the bottle of wine.

"Let's take a walk downtown, look around and enjoy the moment." Darius suggested as he sipped the last of his wine.

"That sounds good to me. What about the bill?" Jasmine replied when they stood up to leave.

"Essence covered it. We're big time now baby." He replied as they both laughed and exited the restaurant.

The two felt on top of the world as they walked along Capitol Avenue in downtown Sacramento. All their hard work and dedication to their passion of writing was beginning to pay off. He started filling her in on what she missed on the book tour.

"This is a great day." Darius cheered as he stopped in his tracks and gave Jasmine a big hug. As passersby's walked around the embraced couple, not paying them much attention as they continued on their personal journey among the crowed streets.

"So can we put that whole New York fight behind us? I've missed you so much!" Jasmine asked with a smile.

"I've missed you too baby." Darius replied, tilting Jasmine head upward so she could look him in the eyes just before engaging in a deep intimate kiss. He broke their kiss and told her, all is forgotten.

"I've never seen you upset like you were; when you overheard that news about Chandra having an abortion. I know that must have really been hard for you to hear." He looked away from her taking a deep breath. "I apologize for yelling at you. I guess it's not in the cards for me to have any biological children."

"What do you mean?" She questioned.

"When I was younger my high school sweetheart, whom I thought I was going to marry and raise a family with, got pregnant. She got pregnant by another guy she met at a party. I was bustin' my butt doing the right thing keeping all kind of girls off me, letting them know I'm faithful to my girl. To make a long story short, she had me fooled. After the initial shock, I walked out her apartment and never looked back."

"Oh, I'm so sorry."

"I'm not. I really loved her, but the guy she was messing with gave her syphilis and she miscarried. I ran into her some years back and she told me she couldn't have any kids, but wanted to suck my dick for five dollars. Yes, she's a crack head now. One bad decision can mess a person up for life." Jasmine covered her mouth with her hand in shock by what Darius was telling her. She could see the pain in his eyes.

"I really wanted to be a dad, so when I heard what Chandra told you about having an abortion, I just...I just lost it. She deceived me by getting the abortion. I could never forgive her for that. One good thing I can say about all of this...I met you. You're the best thing that could have ever happened to me. We're still writing together and our books are selling like hot cakes."

Jasmine blushed, feeling her heart flutter. She held her tears back, giving Darius a tight hug. His cell phone began to vibrate. They broke their embrace as he looked at the ID. "It's my mom." He began to talk and laugh with his mother after sharing the good news. "Yes, she's here with me." Jasmine looked at him with a strange look on her face. He handed her the cell phone. "It's my mother."

"Hello. Yes ma'am. Thank you. It's my pleasure. I hope to meet you as well. Okay, you take care. Okay, bye-bye." Then she handed the phone back to him.

"I know, alright! Okay, I will. I'll call him as soon as I get off the phone with you. I love you too Mom. Bye-bye. My mother's always nagging me about my brother. Saying we need to stay in contact more with one another. Hold up a second, let me call him real quick, baby."

"Okay, I need to make a phone call too," Jasmine told Darius, pulling out her phone and walking the other way so they could both have some privacy.

Darius shook his head watching Jasmine's tight figure as he called his brother Darnell. After a few rings, his brother picked up.

"Hey Darnell, it's me Darius. How are you?"

"What's up, bruh? Did mama tell your punk ass to call me?"

"You know she did. I'm in Sacramento."

"Great! I was going to call you anyway."

"What's up?"

"Well, there's a new restaurant opening in North Hollywood called Soul City Café, and Stacey, the owner, has been bugging me about you. She just finished reading your book, *Being Homeless Is Not an Option*." That's the collaboration book you did, right?"

"Yeah."

"Man, everyone is talking about that book. I got the signed copy you sent me and I haven't had a chance to read it yet. I've been so busy, but anyway she asked if you could come to the opening and sign her book. She told me, you could even set up a table and sell some books if you like. She's a big fan. But this event is going to be in two days."

"So when were you going to tell me?"

"I was dialing your number, when you called me. Can you make it?"

"For sure! I'll be there and as a matter of fact, I may bring the co-author, Jasmine Deveraux, with me; if her schedule permits."

"That sounds good. Mama told me you and Chandra was calling it quits. What's up with that, bro?"

"Yeah, man. I'll fill you in later."

"Yeah, I guess we got a lot of catching up to do.

"I will call my publisher and have a hundred books over night for the event."

"You have the address?"

"Yeah, I have it I'll be there tomorrow."

"Cool! See you then. Darius disconnected the call, filled with excitement about the news as he approached Jasmine who had just finished her phone call.

"Is everything alright?" He asked her when he noticed a disturbed look on her face.

"It's just Eric. He telling me he has a business trip all of a sudden. His supervisor can't make the trip, so now he has to fly out to a site in the morning."

"Oh. I was about to ask you, if you wanted to take a road trip with me to L.A."

"Tonight?"

"No baby, tomorrow morning. We have a book signing in L.A. at a new restaurant. I'm going to rent a SUV for the road. I think it's only about three hours from here to Los Angeles."

"Yeah, it is. Hmm…sounds like fun. Let me make a phone call and see if my sister can keep my boys.

Jasmine was able to get her sister to watch her kids. Then she called Eric to tell him she was needed in Los Angeles for an unscheduled book signing/reading. To her surprise, he didn't argue with her, like he usually does; probably because, he was leaving out of town himself.

"I'm cleared to go to L.A." Jasmine rejoiced, with a big smile, placing her phone back in her purse. He placed his hands around her waist, holding her firmly. As much as she wanted to bed him down, she didn't return to the hotel with him; because she had to hurry home and pack. She figured, she would have time to rock his world, on their road trip.

Chapter Seven
Road Trip

Darius rented a fully loaded Lincoln Navigator for their trip to Los Angeles. He had called their publisher and had them overnight 100 books to his hotel in LA. He wasn't sure how many people would line up to buy their latest novel, but he figured a hundred would do.

When Jasmine arrived at his hotel early the next day, Darius was already waiting for her in front and greeted her with a kiss, before taking her luggage, and loading it in the back of the SUV. Being comfortable for the three hour trip, she wore a mini blue jean skirt, a white tank top, and a pair of white sandals'. He admired her casual look. In his eyes if she wore a trash bag, she could make it look like an expensive article of clothing that came from Milan, Italy. They snapped in their seat belts and headed for the freeway.

"What's in the bag?" He asked, noticing her struggling with the plastic bag by her feet.

"It's a road trip snack bag. All of your favorite candy, chips, and stuff."

"Thank you baby, but you're the only snack I need." He joked, looking over at her briefly, taking his eyes off the road. She started blushing.

Brooklen Borne

"Answer me this one question? I know I must love you because I don't even know where I'm going? I know you said LA to see your brother but that's all I know. You see, I just hopped in the SUV and go with you anywhere," She joked.

"I just need to check in on my brother. Oh yeah, and he set up a book signing for us at some new restaurant called Soul City."

"I need to buy an outfit for the special occasion."

"I'll take you shopping to get whatever you need to be fly, sweetheart."

"Oh, really! Like Rodeo Drive, Beverly Hills fly?" Jasmine asked with excitement. He laughed.

"Well, I don't think you need a fly outfit from Beverly Hills for a book signing in a restaurant, but for you I'll buy whatever you want baby."

"Awww, you're so sweet." She leaned over, giving Darius a soft kiss on his cheek. He smoothly slid his free hand up her knee and between her legs, resting the blade of his hand against her crotch. He could feel the heat between her legs starting to generate. She closed her eyes and lightly bit down on her bottom lip, thinking how good his hand felt resting there. She opened her eyes and saw him watching her reaction.

"Hey, keep your focus on the road." She laughed, moving his hand away.

"Remove that thong and let me relax you."

"That won't relax me. That would make me want you to pull this vehicle to the side of the road, and get busy."

"I can do that!"

"No crazy. Keep this under control, until later on." She replied, reaching over and gently massaging his semi-hard-on. That was starting to bulge in his jeans. "Anyway, what does your brother do?"

"He's an entertainment lawyer. Yeah, my mother sent him off to the good college to get his law degree, and when it became my turn to go to college there was no money left." Darius joked. Jasmine laughed.

"I could have still gone off to college because I had an academic scholarship, but when I found out my girlfriend was pregnant; I thought it was best for me to join the Marine Corps so I could provide for her and the baby. Besides I was a hard head and the Corps was the best thing for me."

They both talked about everything under the sun, from football to who was going to win on Dancing with the Stars. They laughed and listened to music as they playfully fought over turning to different radio stations. They finally found an old school station they both agreed on. The Isley Brothers song came on, *'In Between the Sheet.'* "Oh no they didn't…that's my jam." Jasmine screamed, as she turned the volume up, snapping her finger to the beat, whining and grinding in her seat. He laughed, enjoying her playful attitude. She had no idea how much she was turning him on. He wanted to pull the Lincoln over and make love to her right on the side of the road, but he played it cool and bobbed his head to the beat as she tried to sing on key. After being on the road for nearly two hours, Darius was becoming a little tired and needed to stop at a rest stop and use the restroom.

Jasmine got out stretching her legs; she leaned on the front of the SUV, with her arms folded, as she waited for him to come out the restroom. It was a bit chilly, but she admired how peaceful it was as she watched a few people walking along the beach. She took a deep breath, closing her eyes, taking in the scent of the ocean when Darius came up behind her, wrapping his warm arms around her body and kissing her softly on the back of the neck.

"It's beautiful out here."

"Almost as beautiful as you," Darius added.

"You're Mr. Mack Daddy. You always know what to say, don't you?" She giggled, as he took a hold of her hand and began to walk towards the beach. Jasmine kicked off her sandals and Darius took off his shoes as they made their way down the beach, putting their feet in the water. Though it was a cool breeze, the water was a nice temperature.

"So why I gotta be a Mack Daddy, huh. You wanna fight?" Darius joked, kicking the water, getting her wet.

"Oh, I'm going to kill you. You wet my hair punk!" She splashed water back on him, getting his shirt wet. She rushed him play fighting, but he laughed blocking her love taps. She splashed more water on him, getting his pants wet, and off running; knowing he was going to get her big time. He chased after her but didn't splash her back. He lifted her over his shoulder, smacking her on the butt as she screamed and laughed, trying to break loose. He walked up to a big rock that had a cut out from years of water erosion, and gently laid her down .

"Oh, my hair…I hope you plan on helping me, wash it tonight."

"I'll do whatever." They embraced in a passionate kiss. She felt his manhood stiffen, as he pressed against her. She wrapped her arms around his neck, grinding back against him. She felt him lowering his zipper, and then moving her thong to the side. He gently entered her. She welcomed his hardness letting out a deep sigh. They found the perfect secluded spot, to revive their desire, as they began to make love. They came at the same time, just as a vehicle pulled up in the parking lot.

He quickly rolled off her, pulling her skirt down when he noticed a big camper truck pulling into a parking space. She sat up laughing, shaking her head at him and adjusting her wet blouse. He adjusted his manhood and zipped up his jeans, helping her up to her feet.

"I can't believe we just did that." She whispered. He just laughed, reaching for her hand.

"I've always wanted to make love on the beach." He said to her in a low voice, as they made their way back to their SUV; watching about ten Mexicans unload out of the camper, rushing to the restroom. Jasmine shook her head trying to get the sand out her hair. Darius pulled his wet shirt off and retrieved another shirt out of his suitcase. After a quick shirt change they were back on I-5 heading south.

"Wake up sleepy head." Darius said, tapping her on the leg as he pulled up to the hotel valet. Jasmine sat up yawning and adjusting her eyes. Darius placed their bags on the gold plated luggage cart, before heading to the front desk; to check in. Once in their suite, Jasmine didn't waste any time rushing into the shower. While she was doing that, Darius ordered room service and then joined her in the shower to help wash the sand out her hair. It was quite sensual and she enjoyed taking a shower with him. Jasmine was glad she decided to cut it short, because it was so easy to manage. It would have been unbearable if she would've kept it long.

They could hear someone knocking on the door. Darius got out the shower, wrapping a towel around his waist; it was room service. He retrieved some money from his pant that were lying on the bed and gave the young man a tip.

"What did you order? I'm hungry." She asked Darius, coming out the bathroom with a towel wrapped around her shapely body and one around her head. Darius stuck a strawberry in her mouth from the fruit tray, looking into her eyes.

"I'm hungry too." He grinned looking her up and down. She knew what he was implying, as he attempted to remove her towel.

"Oh no, you don't." She stopped him. "I have to blow dry my hair first. You're not going to let me get any rest, are you?"

"You can rest later."

She laughed, shaking her head at his comment while getting her hair supplies out her bag and dashing back to the bathroom. He put on a pajama pant and a T-shirt, pulled out his laptop and sat on the couch to check his email as he ate his hamburger and fries. Jasmine ordered Fish and Chips with a diet coke.

After applying body oil on her flawless skin, she slipped on her blue, boy cut panties and matching see through lace tank top. She sat next to Darius, with her food.

"What are you doing?" She asked, looking at his computer screen. He just looked at her with a boyish smile.

"Why are you looking at me like that?

"You look so beautiful."

"You tell me anything."

"No baby, why do you say that?"

"You know you're charming and you always know what to say. So how many girls do you have on your starting line up now?" Darius gave her a confused look.

"What do you mean?"

The Write Lover

"All the traveling you do. I know that women throw themselves at you. And now that you are pretty much a single man, I know you must have a few prospects."

"I don't put myself out there like that, Jasmine!" He replied, reassuring her position.

"What do you mean? You're fair game now and once all these women know you're divorced, they are really going to be coming out the wood works at you. I'll soon be just a memory." She then got up and walked over to the table, taking a sip of her diet soda.

"You know that was really uncalled for. You know how I feel about you. You know I'm in love with you."

"And I know you don't have to be faithful or obligated to me. I'm married."

"I know you're married!"

"Just promise me, you'll be honest with me; that's all I ask. Don't be stringing me along with all your other chicks, okay? We almost never use condoms when we are making love, and I just need to be sure I can trust you." Darius shut off his computer, taking a deep breath, growing frustrated and unsure of what to say to her, without saying something that might make her more insecure. "Oh man!" Jasmine said as she rushed over to her purse, retrieving her phone. She forgot to call her sister and inform her, that she arrived safely to L.A. She had a brief conversation with her sister, and children before hanging up and finishing her food.

Darius indeed had a prospect and her name was Rosanna, the only other woman he was considering taking up a relationship with. On a flight back from a book tour a month back, he met Rosanna and her adorable daughter, Amijah.

Brooklen Borne

They were seated next to each other on the plane and began chatting. Rosanna was a beautiful Puerto Rican woman that favored Jennifer Lopez. Rosanna was 28 years old, newly divorced and a single mother raising her 5-year old daughter on her own. She was a six grade teacher at P.S. 150, in Brooklyn, New York. What attracted Darius to her even more than her looks was, she didn't have a clue who he was, like most other women did. He and Rosanna hit it off and the two exchanged numbers. Because Darius' divorce was not final he hesitated to call her. Then after not hearing from Jasmine for a month, he decided to call Rosanna. They chatted often on the phone and through email.

Rosanna and Darius met for lunch and shared an intimate kiss. However, it was an uncomfortable kiss for Darius. It wasn't like Jasmine's kisses. But he thought he would give her the benefit of the doubt, and hoped that maybe the next time they kissed it would be better. Due to his busy schedule, he didn't have much time to talk to or see Rosanna, as often as they both wanted. As soon as Jasmine hung up her phone Darius grabbed her hand.

"Look, I'm going to be honest with you Jasmine. There is one other woman I had talked to, but I haven't sleep with her." Jasmine heart stopped.

"Not yet!" Jasmine snatched her hand away from his. "Who is she? Do I know her?"

"No!" She rolled her eyes at him, feeling her temperature rise. But she knew their relationship was complicated, after all she was still married. She knew he was too handsome of a man to be alone for long. Any woman in their right mind would want to get up with him, in a heartbeat.

"I liked it better when you were married?"

The Write Lover

"Huh?"

"At least I knew who you were sexing?" Jasmine snarled.

Darius took a deep breath, running his hand down his face. He didn't want to argue with her. He had seen this jealous side of her before, in New York. He wasn't sure how to continue this conversation. As she sat at the table eating her food, he put away his computer, and crawled into the bed, relaxing with his hands behind his head. An awkward quietness filled the room.

Jasmine finished her food, went to the bathroom and brushed her teeth. When she came out Darius was lying in the same position. She crawled in the bed next to him, and laid her head gently on his chest.

"Are you mad at me?" She whispered.

"I could never be mad at you." He whispered back, pulling her closer to him.

"I'm sorry baby. I just get so confused about my feelings for you. I love you so much and to know you are with another woman burns me up inside. But there's nothing I can really say or do about it; because I'm still married."

"I'll always be honest with you baby. I never want to betray your trust…never."

"You promise?"

"I promise!" They engaged in a kiss and made passionate love.

Chapter Eight
Soul City

Darius and Jasmine did not fall asleep until the wee hours in the morning. They were asleep for a few hours when Darius cell phone rang, waking him up. He answered the phone groggily. It was his brother asking did he make it to L.A. yet. He told him yes and would stop by to see him in about three hours, after he and Jasmine got themselves together. Jasmine was still sleep, snuggled close to him, when he gently slid out of bed, making his way to the bathroom. He brushed his teeth and splashed water on his face to wake himself up, when he heard his cell phone ringing again. He rushed out the bathroom to answer it so it wouldn't wake Jasmine; however, when he came out the bathroom she was up holding his phone in her hand and glancing at the number on the caller ID.

"Rosanna is calling." With no expression, she handed him the phone. Darius took the phone from Jasmine pressing the button, rejecting the call. "Why didn't you talk to your other girlfriend?" Jasmine asked sarcastically as she slowly, eased her sculptured naked body out of bed. "Forget I ever said that." She recanted.

"Jasmine…!" He started to speak, but she cut him off. "It wasn't my place, to say that to you. I'm sorry." Apologizing as she made her way to the bathroom, rushing to the toilet to release her full bladder. She took a deep breath, running her hands over her face trying to fight the jealous feelings that was consuming her. *What in the world do I honestly think could come out of this relationship besides amazing sex?* She thought, looking in the mirror. Why was she jeopardizing her marriage and taking time from being with her boys to be with Darius?

At that moment, she realized she was going to have to be honest with herself and end this relationship. She didn't want to ruin the fun they were having, so she contained her thoughts and feelings, and looked forward to the book signing but after tonight, she must tell him, it was over. Jasmine began to question herself, why she even called him after two months of being apart. She should have just let sleeping dogs lie. She brushed her teeth, let out a few tears, said a quick prayer, and came out the bathroom. He was patiently sitting on the edge of the bed, waiting for her return.

"So what are the plans for today?" She asked in a cheerful tone, which surprised him.

"Want to go shopping?"

"Now you know I don't mind that." Jasmine said with a smile. Darius was surprised she didn't ask any more questions about Rosanna. So he didn't bother to bring it up either. They went to have a bite to eat before going to Fox Hill mall, where she found two pairs of shoes and two outfits to match, along with some accessories. Darius loved making her happy. He spent over $1,500 dollars, but he didn't mind, because he thought she deserved to be pampered. After sharing an ice cream sundae, they headed to his brother's house.

*****

The Write Lover

Jasmine was mesmerized by the huge houses in the upscale neighborhood they drove through as they approached his brother's house. She was taken back, when she saw the silver Bentley parked in the driveway.

"Is this your brother's house?"

"Yes baby." They stood at the massive wooden carved front door as Darius rang the doorbell once. A couple of seconds later the door swung open and for a split second, she could have sworn, Darius had a double. His brother Darnell was the spitting image of him, except he had more gray in his goatee than Darius. They greeted each other with a brotherly hug and a big smile.

"Darnell, this is Jasmine. Jasmine honey, this is my brother Darnell."

"Ms. Jasmine Deveraux my bighead brother told me so much about you." Darnell spoke excited, taking her hand and gently kissing the back of it, "Nice to meet you."

"Likewise, I see charm runs in the family." She replied with a smile, as they entered the massive foyer. Jasmine was in awe of the shiny white marble floor and beautiful crystal chandler above. She glanced around as they followed Darnell into the family room. She noticed the photos on the mantel, with Darnell posing with several celebrities, such as Celine Dion, Martin Lawrence, Jennifer Lopez, Brooklen Borne, Samuel L. Jackson, Russell Crowe, Angela Jolene, and Brad Pitt.

"Are these your clients?" Jasmine asked. "Darius tells me you're an entertainment lawyer."

"Yes, they are clients and friends." She also admired the fresh beautiful tulips, in the glass vase in the center of the coffee table, as they got comfortable on the couch in the family room. Darnell offered them a drink, however, they both declined.

"Where are Nicole and the girls?" Nicole is Darnell's wife, and she's a high profile corporate lawyer.

"Oh yeah, she told me to tell you hello. She and the girls are in Washington, D.C, for the National Scripps, Spelling Bee contest out there."

"Wow! That's great! Jasmine, my brother has the cutest little girls, Ciara and Cezanne. How old are they now?" Darius asked.

"Twelve and nine," boasted Darnell proudly. "Yeah, I wanted to go, but I had to stay behind and be the Master of Ceremony for the grand opening tonight. Now, if only I could just get a boy," Darnell laughed.

"At least you are blessed with two gifts from God. I just want one boy, girl, I don't care." Silence filled the room for a second and Darnell wished he hadn't made that comment. He knew how bad his brother wanted a child and from the little information Darnell heard from their mother about Darius divorcing Chandra, he knew that was part of the reason. Darnell had been happily married to his wife Nicole, for nearly fourteen years now.

"So Jasmine, it's nice to finally meet you. My brother has been bragging about you and your writing skills. From what I hear your books are off the chain, winning awards and everything."

"Well, I think our styles mesh well together." Just then, Jasmine's phone began to ring in her purse.

"Excuse me gentlemen, I have to answer this. Is it okay if I step out onto your patio?" She politely asked.

"Sure!" Darnell stood up, opening the sliding glass door for Jasmine as she stepped outside. The patio ran along the whole length of the back of the house. There was a seamless pool with a Jacuzzi next to it. The landscaping around the pool was so impeccably beautiful.

"Damn bro…she's bad." Darnell whispered to him. "I know you're doing more than writing books with her." Darius laughed Darnell off, not responding to the question. Darius had not told anyone about his relationship with Jasmine, not even his brother.

Darius had always called his big brother for advice about women, career choices and business. But as they both got older, Darius now thirty-five and his brother forty, he felt it was time to be his own man and make his own decisions without calling his big brother for advice. That's why he didn't tell Darnell about his affair with Jasmine. "Well, what's up?"

"We are just friends." Darnell knew his brother wasn't being honest with him. So instead of asking him the question again he asked, "Is she the reason you and Chandra are getting a divorce?"

"No. Chandra and I are getting a divorce because we have different agendas." Darius went on to explain about the abortion Chandra hid from him and how their relationship had been falling apart for a long time, especially in the past year.

"Damn! I'm sorry to hear about that."

"No need to be sorry." added Darius, looking out the sliding glass doors at Jasmine walking on the patio, laughing and talking on the phone. Darnell noticed the look in his brother's eyes when he looked at Jasmine.

"So are you moving on with Jasmine?"

"She's married. Didn't you look at her bio on the back of the book?"

"Oh…no, I haven't."

Brooklen Borne

"It's real complicated," Darius mumbled, steering back at the coffee table.

"I'm sure it is."

"As bad as I want to tell her to leave her husband, who beats her down, belittles her career and treats her with no respect; knowing I could love her so much better, I can't ask her to do that. She has two sons and I never want to be a home wrecker."

"I feel you." Darnell replied, taking a deep breath. Darius went on to tell his brother that he had put his house on the market in New York and was in the process of finding a new place.

"Since Chandra is a realtor you should have no problem selling it."

"Nah man, I went with another realtor, because that way I know things will be done right and hidden shit; she might come up with."

Darnell suggested that he move to LA. Darius told him he would consider it with all his traveling it seemed to always bring him back, to the West Coast anyway, and it would be nice to be closer to Jasmine. Jasmine opened the patio sliding glass door, and enter the house.

"Okay, big-time authors, let me tell you two about the restaurant slash night club, opening tonight." Darnell said, as he began to go over the details of the evening events. "I'm going to have a table set up for you two to sign your books during the party. It's not formal but it is dress to impress, and there will be many big time Hollywood folks there, not to mention, they are looking for new material. This could be your break into the movie business."

*****.

The Write Lover

Darius and Jasmine left Darnell's house excited about the party and possibly making some major connections, at the event. Darnell had scheduled for the books to be picked up from their room. The two headed back to their hotel to relax before getting ready for the party.

"You look amazing." Darius complimented, the red fitted dress, which had a "V" cut down the front, stopping just above her navel and matching "V" cut down her back, stopping at the base of her spine.

"Awww, thank you baby. I must say you are looking mighty fine yourself." She replied, admiring how his clothes fitted his frame. He was wearing a white silk shirt, black slacks, along with a black blazer, which he complimented with a black brim hat and black lizard shoes.

Darnell had sent a limo to pick up Jasmine and Darius. On the way to the restaurant/club, the two sipped champagne, and chatting about whom they hoped to meet. Darius was focusing on meeting movie producers to pitch a movie or a television series deal for a script he was currently working on. Jasmine was excited about the blessings, their career may receive tonight. When they arrived at the restaurant/club, it was chaos. There were several limos out front and flashing cameras. It was definitely a red carpet event. Jasmine felt on top of the world, with photographers snapping pictures of her and Darius; as they exited the limo. She smiled uncontrollably as they made their way to the front door. Darnell spotted his brother and Jasmine right away, walking over to them, with a lady by his side.

"Darius, Jasmine. I would like to introduce you to Stacy. Stacy is the owner of Soul City and who was dying to meet you both.

Stacy, this is my brother Darius, and his close friend and co-author, Jasmine."

"I'm your biggest fan." She grabbed Darius hand shaking it firmly.

"Thank you." Darius said with a smile. Stacy was a tall woman or at least her six-inch heels made her appear tall. Jasmine couldn't make out what ethnicity she was. She had that exotic look like Kimora Lee Simmons. It was obvious she was bi-racial by her hair texture and her light skin. She was an attractive woman, but hand on a little too much make-up.

"It's nice to meet you." Stacy said to Jasmine, moving in between the two, taking a hold of Darius' arm.

"I have to get a picture with you tonight. I'm so excited you came. We have a table set up for you to sign your novel. My girlfriends will all be there, to purchase that fabulous book as well. Your book is scheduled to be read next month, by our book club. I've read all your other books since your action series, "Savannah." and "Savannah's Fury." Stacy just rambled on, running her mouth, a mile a minute.

"Thank you…thank you very much." Darius kept repeating.

"Oh, there's my girl Carla. Come on, you have to meet her." Stacy grabbed Darius' arm, pulling him off into the crowd as Jasmine and Darnell were left standing there. Darnell and Jasmine looked at each other.

"I apologize for that."

"Its okay, no matter how much money you have, some people just aren't home trained." Jasmine said laughing, not taking Stacy's rude behavior personal, as they entered the restaurant. Just then a waiter walked up to them with a platter of drinks. Darnell picked up two glasses of champagne, handing one to Jasmine.

"Thank you." Jasmine quickly took a sip, trying to calm her nerves.

"If you don't mind me saying you look amazing in that red dress." Darnell complimented her, while giving her a look over. It wasn't hard to tell why his brother had a thing for her.

"Thank you." Jasmine said half-aloud, over the busy chatter, while scanning the room; feeling a little out of place.

"Come on, let me show you where the two of you, will be set up to sign your books." Jasmine followed Darnell through the crowd of attendees, to a beautifully decorated table, set up in the corner of the club section of the restaurant. The table was draped in red, with a black cloth runner. A vase with red and black flowers donned the center of the table. The color coordination, between the table decoration and the two featured authors were not planned. Their books were already stacked up neatly with a thirty by thirty-six picture poster of them, flanking the table. Jasmine thanked Darnell as he excused himself to greet other guests. Before long, Jasmine was swamped with people walking over to her introducing themselves. Darius and Jasmine scanned the room, looking for each other.

She politely introduced herself and then took her place behind the book signing table, wondering when Darius was going to make his way over. Shortly after Jasmine began to sign a few books, Darius appeared out of nowhere sitting next to her.

"Oh, I thought you got lost." Jasmine mumbled to him.

Brooklen Borne

"Sorry, I was pulled away like that. Stacy wanted me to meet her friends and take a few pictures, but it looks like you handled the crowed well."

"You know how I do." The both chuckled at the comment. Before long their table was swamped, as they signed book after book, met fans, and took pictures. In no time, all one hundred books were sold. Darnell announced that all the books were sold and how the people that didn't get a chance to purchase, can purchase an autographed copy from their website; then Darnell introduced Stacy. She gave him a kiss on the cheek as he handed the microphone to her; to the applause of all in attendance. She thanked Darnell, for assisting her, in putting the wonderful event together. She also thanked Darius and Jasmine for supporting her event with their presence and book signing. Stacy then went on to speak about the vision of the restaurant and what she planned to feature on her menus. It's a mixture of Creole and Philippine food since she was of both ethnicities.

"I would like to thank you all for coming and I want you to know, from the bottom of my heart, I really appreciate you all. So enjoy the food and let's party baby." The crowd erupted in cheers and applause. Jasmine and Darius mingled together as the energy changed into a club scene. Darius was busy talking to a couple of producer, from Showtime; when Jasmine excused herself to use the rest room. She felt a slight buzz coming on after her third glass of champagne. When she entered the restroom, Stacy and two of her girlfriends were laughing and talking, looking over themselves in the mirror. Jasmine gave them a fake smile, as she walked to one of the vacant stalls.

The Write Lover

"Hey Jasmine, I want to thank you for coming with Darius tonight." Stacy yelled to her. "Girl, please tell me how you and Darius came up with such a romantic novel?"

"One second." Jasmine yelled back, as she finished up her business. When she came out of the stall, Stacy was waiting with her two of her friends, like vultures around a dead animal.

"The story just flowed for us. We based the storyline from past life experiences." Jasmine finally responded, washing her hands.

"Are you and Darius together?" One of the women blurted out.

"No, they are not," Stacy answered for Jasmine. "Jasmine is happily married with two kids. Didn't you read their bios on the inside cover, Carla?" Carla didn't respond. "Darius brother told me he is nearly divorced so…I got DIBBS on that fine man." Stacy said, like she was some Queen Bee. They all laughed except Jasmine.

"Tell me Jasmine, since you and Darius are good friends, is he seeing anyone right now? Girl, give me the 411 on that fine man you accompanied here." Jasmine was speechless, unsure what to say to Stacy.

"That's something you need to ask him." Jasmine replied fixing a few strands of hair that hung out of place.

"Well, who cares? That's one fine man and maybe if I try hard enough I might knock that someone out the way. Shit, maybe I can even hook up with him tonight and then we can act out one of those loves scene that you two write about."

"Okay." One of Stacy friends yelled out, co-signing what she said; as they all laughed at the comment, walking out the restroom. Jasmine stood there trying to get her thoughts together.

Brooklen Borne

"Bitches!" She mumbled under her breath. As Jasmine made her way back to the party, she didn't see Darius so she walked over to the bar; for another needed drink. Someone gently tugged at her arm, slightly annoyed she turned to see who it was; it was Darius. Her expression changed to relief.

"Come on sexy; show me what you're working with." He smiled taking her by the hand, leading her to the dance floor. The bass from the loud speakers vibrated on the floor as he pulled her close to him and they began to groove to the beat. She held onto his neck with one hand and snapped her fingers with the other. He placed his hands on her hips, taking in the beauty that was in front of him.

"Damn baby," he whispered in her ear when she began to swirl and twist her hips around, using her belly dancing skills. Jasmine glanced up and saw Stacy and her girlfriends watching her and Darius like a hawk, Jasmine really turned it on. When she glanced up again, Stacy was all up in her face, and whispered in her ear; because of the loud music.

"Do you mind if I cut in and get a dance with this fine brutha?" Darius held on to Jasmine's hand, not hearing what Stacy had asked, but Jasmine pulled away letting Stacy take her place. Darius look at Jasmine, as if to say, what are you doing? Jasmine disappeared off the dance floor. Being she was married, she didn't want to cause a scene. She went back to the bar ordering a Cape Cod.

She gulped down her drink, quickly ordering another. She was hoping the drinks would calm her down from the antics of Stacy's behavior.

"We meet again." She heard a voice interrupting her thoughts. It was Terrance; the annoying literary agent, standing next to her at the bar.

"Terrance, what are you doing here?" Jasmine asked not impressed with his appearance.

"I'm at all the hot spots, besides Stacy invited me. She's a good friend of mine. We went to college together."

"Oh."

"It looks like your boy Darius, has all the ladies tonight. Stacy and her girls are all over him." Jasmine forced a smile on her face when she saw Stacy and her two friends dancing with Darius.

"That Stacy is a wild one." Jasmine said, as she sipped slowly on her second drink.

"You're working that dress." Terrance said looking as Jasmine butt.

"Thank you." She replied, not really paying any attention to him.

"Would you like to dance?"

"No thank you." Terrance felt a little offended, but didn't let it show. About two minutes later, Darius came walking up to them.

"If it isn't Darius Hamilton," Terrance spoke, extending his hand to shake Darius'. They shook.

"Stacy didn't want to let me off the dance floor. I had to walk off." Darius addressed Jasmine, as he retrieved a handkerchief from inside his jacket pocket, wiping the sweat from his forehead.

"The women love you man." Terrance added.

"I don't know about all that." Darius replied, when Stacy came rushing off the dance floor walking up to them. Jasmine stood there looking at Stacy, getting tired of her being disrespectful.

"Why did you leave me?" Stacy laughed, putting her hand on Darius' shoulder.

"It's been a long day and we're both tired so we are about to get up out of here."

"What hotel are you staying at?" Stacy asked with no shame to her game. Darius answered with hesitation.

"Jasmine and I are staying at the Hyatt."

"Well look, here's my card." Stacy pulled a business card from her purse, and handed to Darius.

"The girls and I would love for you to come to our book club meeting and grace us with your presence and a live reading from your book. And of course, you know anytime you are in LA., you are welcome to Soul City as my guest," Stacy said seductively, not extending the invitation to Jasmine.

"Jasmine and I would like that." Darius responded, not leaving his lover out the picture.

"Thanks for coming." Stacy looked over at Jasmine, then over at Terrance.

"Hey T, let's dance." Stacy demanded, pulling Terrance away from the bar toward the dance floor.

"Baby, are you ready to go?" Darius asked Jasmine, looking at his watch. It was almost three in the morning.

"You know I am, because those two can get the Pope to cuss." Darius laughed out loud.

"Not to mention, rude and disrespectful to you." He added.

"Like water on a duck, her antics rolled off my back. But I must say, she was tugging at my last nerve." They chuckled, looking at them on the dance floor.

The Write Lover

After Darius and Jasmine said their good byes to Darnell, they walked out to the awaiting limo.

"Did you have a good time?" Jasmine asked Darius, as the limo driver closed the door, behind them.

"It was nice. I didn't expect so many people, though." Darius responded, removing his jacket. "Look, I got Marvin McDowell's card, baby. He's the producer at Showtime.

He wants to set up a meeting in reference to turning our book," Being Homeless Is Not an Option, into a movie." Darius handed the card to Jasmine.

"Wow, that's great baby." She gave him a hug, jumping with excitement.

"I'm glad my brother invited us."

"Your brother's friend Stacy was on you, like a hungry dog on a ham hock." Darius began laughing uncontrollably.

"You come up with some sayings baby, but you're right. She was a little straight forward." Darius placed his hand onto Jasmine's lap. "But you know they didn't have anything on you sweetheart." Jasmine blushed. "A few guys walked up to me and asked if you were spoken for?"

"Yeah right," Jasmine laughed.

"For real, I told him to look on the inside of the cover and read your bio."

"Is that right?" She responded, glancing out the window.

"The night was good, but better now that I have you to myself again…" He leaned over, gently kissing her softly on the neck. She rested her head back on the seat feeling the buzz from the drinks she had earlier. Darius was still kissing her neck as he gently massaged her inner thigh. Jasmine parted them, giving in to her erotic desire. She leaned back on the leather seat as he slowly slid up her dress and sliding her thong off sticking it in his pocket. He parted her legs wider as his mouth and tongue found their way to a much needed meal. Resting her hand on top of Darius head, she moaned softly so the driver couldn't hear her. The limousine came to a stop, and they quickly gathered themselves.

"You have me hella horny." Jasmine said, biting her bottom lip.

"I'll take of that, as soon as we get to the suite."

"I have no doubt in my mind." The driver opened the door and the two exited the vehicle; hand and hand.

Chapter Nine
Pick Your Face Up Off the Floor

    A session of light taps on the door awoke Jasmine out of a deep sleep. She rolled over looking at the clock, which read four-thirty. She ignored it rolling over, thinking it must be coming from across the hall. They knocked again, before she realized it was their door. She shook Darius to wake up, but he didn't move he was in a deep sleep. Jasmine pulled herself out the bed, looking around the room for something to put on. With only the dim light coming from the brightness of the moon coming through the curtains, she saw Darius shirt. Hastily putting it on, she walked over to the door.

    "Who is it?" Jasmine asked. No one answered. She looked through the peephole, but because she was half-asleep she couldn't see clear. She slowly opened the door. To her surprise, it was Stacy, standing there in a black trench coat and heels, looking like a hooker on HBO's America Undercover "Hunts Point."

    "May I help you?"

    "Oh Jasmine, I'm sorry. I thought this was Darius' room. Could you tell me what room he's in?"

Jasmine rolled her eyes. Stacy looked at Jasmine, realizing the shirt was the same one Darius wore earlier. Her facial expression changed.

"This is his room, but I put him to sleep already." Jasmine smiled, opening the door a little wider, so Stacy could see Darius partially naked; sound asleep. Stacy was speechless for a second.

"Aren't you married?" Stacy blurted with anger in her eyes.

"Don't worry about my status."

"Well, Darius told me to come to his room when I left the restaurant tonight."

"Yeah right," Jasmine laughed. "Look Stacy, I had DIBBS all along, so pick your damn face off the floor and have a good night." She slammed the door in Stacy's face. Jasmine knew Darius did not invite her to his room. She was standing right there when she asked him what hotel he was staying at. Jasmine was slightly upset with herself, because she could not believe she was letting herself get caught up in this madness. Darius sat up quickly when he heard the door slam and turned on the bedside table lamp.

"What the hell?"

"Sorry to slam the door. It was Stacy."

"You're kidding?"

"Nope, she was wearing a black trench coat, probably coming to seduce you. Sorry I ruined it for you, but I told her to give me a few minutes to clean up and gather my things and she could come back." Jasmine joked, being that Darius was half-asleep he wasn't sure what was going on.

"Wait a minute, Stacy was at the door?"

"Yeah, she made it known to me, you told her to come to your room when she left the restaurant."

The Write Lover

"That's crazy baby. You know I didn't say that to her." Darius expounded yawning, not fully awake.

"Yeah, I know."

"I guess she was surprised to see you at the door."

"Yeah, her face hit the floor." Jasmine laughed, turning off the light, getting back in the bed.

"Don't worry next time, I won't be here to get rid of your groupies and you can have the time of your life."

"Baby, why are you playing? You know I don't carry myself like that."

"Umm hmm" Jasmine sighed, as he wrapped his arms around her as they fell back to sleep.

A Few Hours Later...

"Damn!" She said to herself, as she showered. Her period had showed. She was glad she had packed some tampons in her bag.

Jasmine quietly got dressed, and left the room and went to the lobby to see if the concierge could arrange to get a rental so she could drive back to Sacramento. She picked up a complimentary Los Angeles Times and waited in the lobby until they made the arrangements. Ten minutes had passed when her cell rang. It was Darius.

"Hello."

"Baby, where are you?"

"I'm down stairs in the lobby. I'll be up in a minute or two."

"Alright!"

Brooklen Borne

Jasmine was informed that Enterprise rental would have a car out front in a few minutes. When she arrived back at the room, Darius was just stepping out the shower. .

"Where did you go, baby?"

"I'm going to head back to Sacramento. I went downstairs to get a rental."

"Why? I'll drive you home. Did something happen between us that I'm not aware of?"

"I don't want to rush you and I'm sure you want to spend more time with your brother."

"What's really going on, Jasmine?" Darius asked as he finished getting dressed.

"Darius baby, thank you for everything. The shopping spree, the book signing and I had a wonderful time last night."

"You're welcome. So why do you want to leave like this?"

"Darius, I need to be honest with myself. As hard as it hurts, we can't keep seeing each other. This is not right. I feel like a horrible wife and mother. The guilt in my heart is building up. It hurts so much that I love you so deeply, but I can't be with you like I want to. I'm so torn up inside." Tears began to travel down her cheeks. She knew she was extra emotional because her period was on, but she meant everything she said. Darius stood there speechless, before sitting her on the bed next to her.

"Jasmine, I don't know what I'd do without you in my life." He took her hand in his.

"You'll be fine." Jasmine wiped her tears away quickly.

"No, I won't be fine. You're my soul mate. I know that with every fiber of my being. I love you that much." He kissed her on the back of her hand, holding back his tears. He knew he was losing her.

"Early this morning, I realized when Stacy came to your door it will only be a matter of time before people will start talking about seeing you and I together all the time. You know people already are reading into stuff from our novel and before long my husband will probably find out. I just can't hurt my kids like that. As much as I love you, I just…we have to end this."

"I understand you have a family, but…

"I'm sorry, Darius." She said, not letting him complete his sentence.

He took a deep breath, running his hands over his face. "He doesn't deserve you, Jasmine."

"Darius!"

"I'll always be here for you, you know that. Whatever and whenever you need me, no matter what time, I'll be there for you."

"You're such a good man, but I'm sure you'll go on and find a special woman."

"I already found a special woman…you."

"Darius please, don't make this harder than it already is." Jasmine stood up, walking toward the door.

"Can I at least put my shoes on and see you out?" Jasmine nodded yes. Darius hurried, getting his shoes on and hugging her firmly. He walked her out front to her awaiting rental.

"Call me and let me know you made it home safely."

"Okay." They embraced in a tight hug. He didn't want to let her go. Finally, they pulled away from one another. Darius reached in his pocket and pulled out six hundred dollars, handing it to Jasmine.

Brooklen Borne

"What's that for?" She asked, looking at the money.

"Just take it."

"Darius, I…" He cut her off.

"Just take it. You may need gas or something."

"Baby, I don't need six hundred dollars' worth of gas?" Before Jasmine could say anything else, he gently pulled her to him kissing her. It was a kiss they never experienced before with each other, because it was a good-bye kiss.

Jasmine broke away from Darius, worrying how many eyes and cameras may be on them. Not waiting for him to open the door for her, she quickly walked around to the driver's side and got in. Her heart was heavy, as she pulled off, tears flowed down her cheeks. Darius just watched her drive away. He knew there was nothing that he could do. He had just lost his soul mate.

Chapter Ten
It's A Plethora of Things

When Darius landed back in New York he was physically and emotionally drained from the thought and reality of losing Jasmine. He knew he had to hold it together and keep it moving forward because his book was one step closer to making it on the silver screen. But it was bothering him that Jasmine was probably making up with her husband; giving that undeserving man the loving she once gave him. Even though he was tired, he wanted to stop by the house to see how many time the house was shown for the day. When he pulled up in front of the house, he could see the close blinds that a light was on in the dining room and master bedroom. *"I'm going to have to inform them, the electric bill is still in my name."* He said to himself as he exited his car.

Darius entered the house and to his surprise, Chandra was there. She walked up to him, giving him a hug and a kiss on the cheek. Wondering about her presence, he asked "What are you doing here?"

"My place is being painted and I thought it would be a good idea to spend the night here. I'm not going to mess up anything that would hinder the showing of the home"

"Cool, because I really want us to get from under this house as soon as possible."

"Darius, this whole thing with us has me going crazy. I'm losing weight, not sleeping well and stressing like crazy."

"I see you are losing weight, you're looking good. See this divorce is working for you."

"That's not funny."

"It's not meant to be funny Chandra. I really mean it, you look good. Some couples are just not meant to be married to one another. Also like you, I'm stressing and have to get over this hurdle. I'm just going to focus on my work."

"Since we are here together let's just chill and enjoy each other's company." Chandra suggested as she walked over to the refrigerator, opening it to retrieve a bottle of champagne; pouring them both a glass. They touched glasses and drank the contents with one gulp. Filling the glasses again, they sipped and talked and talked. The bottle was just about gone, and the champagne was taking affect on their judgment.

Chandra leaned in and kissed him on the lips. One thing led to another and they ended up in the bedroom. The bedroom was lit with the warm glow scented candles. Instrumental jazz music filled the air with a sensual ambiance.

"Baby, I have everything in the bathroom for your shower."

"This is real nice Chandra."

"It's time to do what I should have been doing all along."

"And what's that?"

"Taking care of my man sexually, like a wife suppose to have been doing."

"A little too late, don't you think?" Darius said in a low voice, as he undressed to take a shower. The champagne and jet lag, had Darius tired and he was ready for the bed. Chandra sat at the foot of the bed, taking in the sight of his firm physique. Fully naked, Darius turned to go into the bathroom.

"Wait!" Stopping him in his tracks, she walked over to him and gently began stroking his manhood.

"What are you doing?" She didn't answer; she just got on her knees, taking him in her mouth. She looked up at him, to see his reaction. She was a hundred percent better than the last time she attempted this act on him. He couldn't believe the erotic overtone she was sending him. Chandra began to moan with excitement from feeling Darius' full erection in the back of her throat. He leaned against the wall with his eyes closed, enjoying the performance. A few minutes later, she released his penis from being captive in her mouth, stood up, turned around and bent over at the waist holding onto her ankles; exposing her moist, inviting pleasure palace.

"Before you take that shower, fuck me hard just one last time baby. I need you." She said seductively. Darius knew he shouldn't even go there with her, but with a hard penis and consumption of a bottle of champagne, he granted her wish. Holding her waist and slamming his manhood deep, she screamed for dear mercy. After fifteen minutes he removed his erection from the confines of her honey walls and instructed her to stand.

"Whew baby, my legs are wobbly. Damn! You have some good dick." He walked her over to the bed lying down. He began kissing and sucking her nipples, while his warm hands explored. She became consumed by his passion reached for his penis, guiding him inside her eagerly moist canal. She took a hold of his buttocks and pulled him deeper inside.

"Oh yeah baby." Chandra screamed out in ecstasy. The mattress was squeaking as they both went at each other. Darius raised Chandra legs over his shoulders and began working her good, putting his back into it. Chandra was screaming her lungs out with every stroke Darius delivered, not caring who heard her.

"I know this is feeling good to you," Darius said as he thrust himself deep.

"Yes! Yes! You're fuckin' me so damn good. Shit, I'm coming…I'm coming." Chandra's voice changed to the point, she sounded like she was speaking in a foreign language.

Her orgasm was so overwhelming it took her a full two minutes to recover to the point where she was able to speak again. Slightly out of breath, she managed to say, "Oh God baby that was an outer body experience. I never came so hard. I want you to come now." Without saying a word he turned her around. She hugged the pillow, leaving her butt in the air for deep penetration. Standing up, he guided his hard penis inside her. Holding her hips, he started pumping her feverishly. With his eyes closed, in his mind he was making love to Jasmine! Chandra screamed and moaned into the pillow to muffle the pain and the pleasure that was being delivered. She had not felt this way in a long time and with each orgasm, she was falling deeply in love with him again. Darius was so into the sex and thinking about Jasmine he almost slipped up and called out her name. Then it hit him like a ton of bricks, who he was having sex with and pulled out and came just as he cleared her vagina, squirting cum all over booty and lower back. *Man, that was a close call,* he thought to himself. *What the hell was I thinking? I don't want to have a baby with this woman, especially after aborting one of my seeds, without my knowledge.*

He laid down next to Chandra as his breathing was coming back to normal. She snuggled up to him feeling like she was on cloud nine.

"Baby, you are unbelievable. It's been a long time since you put it on me like that."

"I pulled out just before I came."

"Why would you do that? I want to have your baby." Chandra replied, sincerely.

"Is that right?" I don't think it's fair to bring a baby into this kind of situation. We are about to be divorced Chandra. Why now and not before when we first got married?" He almost let the cat out the bag, giving away that he knew about the abortion; of his baby.

"Because, this is what you always wanted, honey. We would make a beautiful child together.

"Why are you so pressed to get pregnant now? You know we already filed papers, to dissolve this union."

"Maybe I don't want a divorce now. The way you put it on me no one can come behind you, and please me the way you do baby." Chandra replied as she snuggled close to him. Darius, not responding, interlocked his fingers behind his head as she fell asleep with her head on his chest. He stared up at the ceiling for a minute, wondering why he had sex with this woman. After about an hour he got up and went into the bathroom to take a shower.

The next morning Chandra gently shook Darius, waking him up. "Baby, wake up…baby."

Brooklen Borne

"Yeah, what's up? Is everything alright?" Darius asked in a groggy state.

"Everything's fine. I just want you to reconsider this divorce thing. I realize now that I should have been more supportive of your work."

"It's more than work Chandra. It's my passion to write."

"I understand baby, but would you please reconsider?" Darius sat up in the bed gathering his thoughts.

"Chandra, it's not just one thing. It's a plethora of things that is wrong with us."

"What else, honey? I'll change. I'll do whatever I have to do to make this union work." She pleaded with him desperately. Not caring anymore he let the cat out the bag.

"Look, I'm gonna lay it on the table for you. I already looked into moving out west where my brother is. With the abortion and everything I can't do this anymore and...," Chandra cut him off, in mid-sentence.

"You knew about the abortion?"

"Yeah, I knew! I can't believe you did that to me, Chandra. You knew how I felt about a family. I would've given up my passion of writing to have a child with you."

"How did you find out?" She had suspicion Jasmine must have told him, because she remembered telling her; about it. Keeping loyal to his source, Darius threw her sent off

"A woman purchased one of my books at a book signing and she told me that she couldn't remember my name or the title of my book to save her life, until one day at work someone with the name of Hamilton came in the clinic to abort. Then she remembered my last name was Hamilton. Then she asked me my wife name. At that moment I didn't understand why she would ask me that, but when I said your name she described you to a tee, then she apologized realizing what she had done; disclosing personal information and that's how I found out. It's a small world huh? It was early in our marriage too, Chandra. But I guess that's part of life learned lessons."

"I'm still your wife. I know you must still love me?" He just looked at her with no expression and said.

"The papers with my signature have already been filed. We're just waiting on our court date. We agreed to be civil to one another. Last night should not have happened. I'm not in love with you anymore." Chandra felt like a hundred bricks dropped onto her chest. Fighting back tears she took a deep breath.

"Then who are you in love with?"

"Myself!"

"Yourself?"

"Chandra, I really don't have time for this. Last night was a mistake and I'm sorry if you thought having sex again meant I wanted to get back with you. I'm really sorry."

"Don't be sorry, just tell me, who's the bitch, you're fuckin'?"

"What?"

"Which whore has been slobbin' on your dick?' Probably one of those book tour groupies, huh?" Darius pulled himself out of the bed, not responding to her accusations and headed straight to the bathroom. He wanted to just come clean with Chandra and tell her who had his love, but he didn't want to put Jasmine out, like that; knowing she was still married. Chandra knew he was in love with someone else. He had to be, because his feelings were so cold towards her. After brushing his teeth and washing his face, he knew Chandra would be waiting on the other side of the door ready to fuss and fight some more. It was too early in the morning and he just wanted to climb back in bed and go back to sleep.

She sat on the end of the bed with tears flowing down her face, and her arms crossed over her chest, waiting for him.

"Is it Jasmine?' She whispered the question to him. He didn't respond. "Answer me, damn it! Was it Jasmine?"

"I'm not going to answer that ridiculous question!" He felt his heart flutter and he grew nervous. He knew he should have just told her up front, but he couldn't.

"FUCK YOU! GET OUT! I WANT YOU OUT THE HOUSE NOW! (Continuing in an elevated voice)You think you're hot shit now since you sold a few books. I was with your ass when you were broke, remember that shit. You know what Darius? I want this all. The house, the cars, hell even the royalties from your stupid book sales. I'm going to take you to the cleaners. I never signed the papers. You better be glad I aborted that baby. I'm glad! You don't deserve a baby from me. You're selfish and always wrapped up into your damn books. The only thing you were ever good for was a good fuck and licking my pussy. I hate you!" Chandra yelled, as she cried. Her emotions completely took over. Fuming with anger, Darius grabbed his clothes off the floor praying to God that he wouldn't murder her, where she stood. He mustered up everything he had inside him, from slamming Chandra against the wall.

"And you wonder why I don't want to have a child with you. I'm selfish, that's bullshit and you know it. Don't sign them divorce papers, do what you have to." He said to Chandra,

The Write Lover

opening the front door walking out; slamming it so hard behind him, the house shook. Chandra dropped to her knees crying even louder.

Chapter Eleven
Baby...I'm Sorry

A month had passed since Darius and Jasmine took their trip together to Los Angeles. Jasmine came to the realization that she loved Darius very much, but she just didn't have the courage to leave her husband for him. She felt like she'd be letting her family down, who thought she and Eric had the perfect marriage.

Darius emailed Jasmine often, giving her reports about how the sales of their book were doing. He had been busy promoting their book in the mid-west. He kept things between them professional, and respected Jasmine's decision to end their relationship; so he would text the updates instead of calling her. He missed her deeply and had even gone into a slight depression, because he was not able to spend time or love her as he once did. He just prayed that she was happy and that her husband realized what a good woman he have and begin to treat her right.

*****

Darius had moved to LA, not too far from his brother's place. He was relieved to get away from the cold weather on the east coast. He enjoyed the sunny warm weather and got use to it quickly. Most of all, he enjoyed being close to his brother and being able to see his nieces more often; not to mention starting a new life. Now that he was officially divorced, he could finally breathe. Chandra never challenged their divorce, in spite of her threats. She had come to the realization that dragging out the divorce would not keep Darius from leaving her. He finally had a few weeks to himself, without any traveling or interruptions, and was spending time focusing on, putting the final touches to his first movie script he was sending to Showtime.

Darius had accompanied his brother to a few well known nightclub events, but he was not much into the club scene. He hadn't sparked up any relationships with anyone, because he felt he needed time to get over his divorce, and his love for Jasmine. He never tried to contact Rosanna either. He figured it was no use since he was moving out west anyway, and he wasn't going to get involved in another long distance relationship. Stacy wasn't Darius type, but that didn't stop her from making many attempts to invite him over to her house, just to have sex. He even declined attending her book club meeting at the restaurant as the featured author; saying he was booked up for the next few months doing appearances. .

It was around noon, when Darius had made a ham and cheese sandwich, poured a glass of Pepsi and eased back in his reclining chair. He pushed play on his Blue Ray DVD player and got comfortable to watch *Tears in the Sun* starring Bruce Willis. At that moment, his house phone rang.

"Damn! Who the hell is this?" He mumbled with a mouth full of food, reaching for the cordless from the dock on the end table next to him.

The Write Lover

"Hello."

"Hello Darius." He recognized the voice right away. It was Chandra.

"Chandra?"

"Oh, so you haven't forgotten my voice." She giggled.

"How did you get this number?" Darius asked, not laughing back. He had just moved into his new high-rise condo and just turned on his house phone two days before. Only a handful of people had this number.

"Your mother gave it to me."

"What the hell do you want?"

"Man, why you have to be so cold to me? How are you doing?"

"I'm good. What's up?"

"I saw you in the Sister 2 Sister magazine all hugged up with Jasmine at some event in LA. So, is she the reason we divorced?"

"Look, Chandra, what do you want? I know you didn't call me to ask me that."

"Nah, actually I called to tell you something else, but it would be nice if you could be honest with me and just tell me the truth about Jasmine. I know you were fucking her, but answer me this…does her husband know? Maybe I should give him a call and let him know."

"Why are you calling my house, playing games trying to start shit? We are divorced and have no reason to be talking to each other. Everything is done, and over with between us, so just stay out my life!"

"That would be easy, but I'm pregnant and I thought you'd want to know."

"Well congratulations."

"Darius ! The baby Im carrying, is yours."

"Excuse me?"

"You heard me."

"Don't you have a life? Why must you attempt to disrupt mine?"

"Yes, I have a life growing inside me. We did have sex, a little over a month ago, remember?"

"I pulled out before I came."

"Well, I guess not fast enough, because I'm looking at this doctor slip that confirms I'm indeed six weeks pregnant."

"Damn!"

"I thought you'd be happy."

"Happy about what?"

"I know how much you wanted me to have your child. Maybe we should rethink our divorce and get back together. I never wanted to be a single mother and I know you don't want to be a part time dad."

"I can't believe this?" Darius mumbled, while holding his head in his hand.

"Believe it. Shit, I'm already having morning sickness and everything." He took a deep breath.

"I was hoping you'd fly back to New York and come with me to my next doctor's appointment in two weeks."

"You're really pregnant?"

"Yes I am. You have a fax machine? I'll fax you the damn papers."

"Do that!" Darius blurted out his fax number. "Fax me the papers and I'll dial you back after I get them."

"You're serious?" She replied, sucking her teeth.

The Write Lover

"I'm dead serious." He said hanging up, confused and upset.

He jumped out the recliner, rushed over to the fax waiting for the papers to come through. He wasn't sure if he should feel mad, sad, or glad. He paced back and forth until the fax machine beeped and the papers came through. He pulled them out, carefully scanning each sheet. His eyes focused on the line that read:
Chandra Hamilton, the result of your pregnancy test shows that you are six weeks and two days pregnant. Darius stood speechless unsure what to feel at that very moment. He dialed his brothers' cell frantically. After a few rings, his brother answered.

"What's up, D-money?"

"Are you busy? I need to talk to you."

"Just about to head out the office, but I have a few minutes. What's up?"

"She's pregnant!" Darius blurted out nervously.

"Who… Jasmine?"

"I wish it was Jasmine. Chandra's pregnant, she just called me and even faxed me the damn papers that read, she's pregnant."

"No little brother, tell me it isn't so." Darnell said with disappointment in his voice.

"That's what the papers read."

"Oh shit. You were still messing around with her?" Darius went on to explain to his brother what happened the last time he saw Chandra. He was sure he pulled out of her before he came. Darnell told him to calm down and that he would be right over.

*****

Brooklen Borne

Jasmine buried herself into working on her novel, "*In the Naked City,*" and focused on her family life.

Her husband had been working late, so she had the task of taking her boys to Taekwondo practice. It had been a while since she had taken them. That was usually Eric's job but she didn't mind. She was doing her best to ease Darius out her mind, but she was still missing him deeply. She prayed, asking God to forgive her and promised herself to be a better wife, even though she knew, why she had stepped out of bounds. She and her husband had a relationship that could have been better, but it wasn't unfixable. Besides Eric being a bit controlling, she had two healthy, handsome sons, a home, a nice car and didn't want for anything. Yes, Darius had rocked her world in the bedroom. He did things to her body that her husband had never done, but marriage was not based on sex and sex was not going to ruin her marriage.

"Come on Kyle and Kai…y'all gonna be late!" Jasmine yelled from the bottom of the stairs, grabbing her purse and keys off the table in the foyer.

"We're comin' ma," Kyle her oldest, yelled back. She slipped on her sandals when her phone began vibrating in her purse. She fumbled around answering it quickly before it went to voice mail.

"Hello!"

"May I speak to Jasmine?" The female voice on the other end asked.

"Yes, this is she. May I ask who is calling?"

"Chandra." Jasmine was speechless not sure what to say.

"Chandra?"

The Write Lover

"Yes Chandra, Darius' ex-wife. I know you two were messing around. I had a feeling you were lying to me when we talked at the event in Manhattan. I also know you're the reason he left me. Does your husband know about your little affair or did you just go back to your happy little married life after fuckin' mine all up?"

"Excuse me!"

"You heard me."

"I'm sorry you feel that way Chandra. Darius and I are not…"

"Cut the bullshit!" Chandra screamed, cutting her off.

"You shouldn't have called my damn number, if you weren't going to hear me out." Jasmine snapped back, giving off a nervous laugh. At that moment the boys came running down the stairs.

"Let's go ma." They darted pass, running toward the door leading to the garage.

"Get in the car. I'll be right there." She instructed them.

"Look, I gotta go. Don't ever call my number again!" Jasmine hung up before Chandra could get another word in. She wondered how in the world Chandra got her cell number, because she never gave it to her.

"We're late, ma. We gonna have to do extra pushups." Kai whined. Jasmine hissed at him, as she turned the ignition to start up the Range Rover. The call from Chandra threw her for a loop. Jasmine hadn't talked to Darius in over a month. She wondered if Darius had told her about their affair. Jasmine drove in a daze of confusion. She drove as fast as she could without breaking the law. So many things were going through her mind, after that unexpected call from Chandra.

She found a parking space right in front of the building. The boys jumped out, rushing inside and she followed not far behind.

Brooklen Borne

The boys kicked off their sneakers, placing them against the wall in the lobby, before joining the class. Jasmine looked up and saw some lady approaching her children. She noticed her huge belly first. This woman had to be in her third trimester, but she carried her pregnancy well.

She was a beautiful looking woman, which put you in the mind of Keyshia Cole. She wore a cute crop hairstyle and had high cheekbones.

"Hey boys, where's your da-?" The pregnant woman stopped herself in mid-sentence when she noticed Jasmine standing there. "Oh, hi!" She greeted Jasmine. The boys ran pass the woman, not acknowledging her.

"Hi," Jasmine responded as the two women locked eyes. Jasmine looked her up and down; wondering why was this woman about to ask her kids about her husband.

"I'm Lynn." The woman extended her hand. Jasmine slightly hesitated before completing the greeting, shaking the woman's hand. "You must be Eric's wife. I've heard so much about you."

"Really, I haven't heard one word about you."

"Well, my son Xavier is in the same class with your boys."

"Oh! It's nice to meet you."

"It's so nice to meet you too. I'm a fan of your work. I read your book '"Based on a Lie"' and can't wait to read the sequel."

"Thanks." Both women sat down in the lobby.

"Eric is so good with Kyle and Kai," Lynn said as she moved her hand over her belly. "You are so lucky to have a husband so involved with them. My husband is in Iraq and its hard doing this all by myself."

The Write Lover

"I'm sure it is. How long has he been gone? How far along are you? And will your husband be back in time, for the baby's birth?" Jasmine asked, throwing several questions at once, to see how she was going to answer.

"Um, I'm just about six months. I'm also carrying twins."

"Wow, twins. You're going to have your hands full. Thank God I dodged that twin bullet. Twins run in my husbands' family. He's a twin."

"Oh yeah, I think he told me that. Lucky you because carrying twins are no joke." Lynn replied, rubbing her over-sized belly.

"I'm sure. Well, if you'll excuse me I have to make a phone call."

"Sure." The two ladies exchanged fake smiles as Jasmine headed out the door, walking toward her car. She dialed Darius' number as fast as her fingers would allow. She wanted to know why in the world Chandra was calling her. But the call went straight to his voice mail. She hung up not leaving a message and walked back inside to watch her boys practice.

*****

As she and the boys drove home after practice, she stopped at McDonald's to get them something to eat. Lynn was weighing heavy on her mind; it was something about her that wasn't right: Jasmine thought to herself. Just as they pulled away from the McDonald's drive-thru window, she began to question her boys about Lynn.

"So do you guys have a friend name Xavier?"

"Yeah!" Kai said, shoving French fries his mouth. Kai was her youngest, he was almost eight years old and was the spitting image of his father.

"He's my best friend. He has a cool backyard with a pool, mom. It has a water slide and everything."

"Really! You guys spent time at his house?"

"Yeah, lots of times. Dad takes us over there all the time." Kyle her eldest son who favored Jasmine, more than his dad, informed. Kyle had just turned ten and he was already almost as tall as she.

"Like how many times?"

"Usually every time you go out of town. We spend a lot of night over there."

"Spent nights?" Jasmine raised her voice as she pulled up to a stoplight. Eric never told her anything about letting her boys spend the night anywhere when she was gone.

"Yeah!" Kai added.

"Your dad drops you guys off?"

"He comes in sometimes. He and Lynn like to watch the CSI shows together and talk. Daddy fell asleep on the couch a few times and spent the night, too." Jasmine bit down on her bottom lip hard, trying to hold her anger in. She had more than a few questions for Eric, when he came home. Jasmine kept thinking about the way Lynn had looked at her. It took everything in her not to call Eric and ask him 50 questions.

When they arrived home, she settled the boys down and began to help them with their homework. Jasmine poured herself a glass of Merlot, then fixed Eric a steak, and baked potato before taking a shower. She wanted to act cool and not jump to any conclusions

The Write Lover

about Lynn, without talking to him first; but she had more than a few questions for him. Her boys were in bed at their usual nine o'clock time frame. She sat in the living room in a daze, staring at her wedding photos, wondering when her marriage had gone wrong. Her wedding day was the happiest day of her life, besides the birth of her children. She had dedicated her life to Eric's endeavors since high school; she was always by his side. Jasmine prayed that maybe she was just over reacting, but her woman intuition was telling her something different. Eric walked in the house at eleven o'clock.

"Hey baby!" Jasmine heard him say as he turned the light on, walking in the living room. "Why are you sitting in the dark?" Before she could answer, "Ummm, I smell steak."

"Yeah, I made your favorite. How was work?" Jasmine got up from the couch, playing it cool as she planted a kiss on his cheek, making her way to the kitchen to prepare his plate.

"I'm starving," Eric said, as he unbuttoned his work shirt. Eric worked as a technician for the cable company. He had been there for over ten years and was making a decent amount of money. Eric didn't waste any time diving into his meal, eating fast, like always. She just sat across from him, holding back her anger.

"This is good baby."

"Thank you," Jasmine replied, as she stared at him.

"Why are you looking at me like that?" Eric asked, taking a sip of Pepsi from his glass; washing down his food.

"You tell me?"

"Um…what did I do now? I can hear the tone in your voice."

"I fixed your favorite, to remind you, how good a woman, I am."

"Fixing my favorite meal means I'm gonna get some tonight." Eric said with a smile.

"Why don't you ask Lynn?" She blurted out. She couldn't hold it in any longer.

"Excuse me?"

"Lynn, you know, Xavier's mom. The woman you have been spending time with and the boys have been spending the night at her house. How come I didn't know about her?"

"It's no big deal, the boys like hanging out over there. She has a pool and gave the boys an open invitation to come over."

"And you? Why are you spending the night at a woman's house, whose husband is away, fighting a war?"

"What do you mean?" Eric replied looking away. He could never look her in the eyes when he was being dishonest with her.

"Let's just cut through the bullshit. Are you fuckin' her?"

"What?" He yelled.

"You heard me. Are you fuckin' her?"

"You're crazy."

"Answer the damn question!"

"I'm not going to dignify that question with an answer." Jasmine stood up and wanted to slap him in his mouth. She knew he was covering up something.

"Look, Eric, I know things haven't been great with us. I know I've been gone a lot, but I really need for you to be honest with me."

"Have you been honest with me, Jasmine?" He yelled, as he slammed the fork on the table. Jasmine jumped at his sudden outburst.

The Write Lover

"You okay, Mama?" Kai asked, rubbing his eyes as he crept down the stairs.

"Yes baby, Mama's fine. Go back to bed."

"Go back to bed, Kai!" Eric yelled. Kai turned around, making his way back upstairs. Eric and Jasmine's eyes locked.

"Something did not feel right today with that woman, Eric. Just tell me, alright! Have you slept with her?"

"I never cheated on you in all our twelve years of marriage until you started your silly book shit. You're always gone…I have needs, Jasmine."

"What do you mean my silly book shit and you have needs? You mount me; fuck me for two minutes, anytime your little dick gets hard. Then on top of that, you have the nerve to belittle my…."

"Look, Jasmine!" Eric yelled, cutting her off.

"So until I started leaving, huh? How long have you been fuckin' her?"

"It doesn't matter."

"The hell it doesn't!" Savannah screamed. "Do you love her?" He didn't respond. "Oh, My God!" Jasmine yelled out as she covered her mouth, finally putting one and one together. "So she is carrying your twins." Eric still didn't answer. He stood up from the dining room table, carrying his half-eaten plate toward the kitchen. Jasmine followed closely behind him. "You bastard! I had my tubes tied for you. You said you didn't want any more children and you didn't want to use any condoms. Your punk ass was too scared to get snipped, so you told me to get my tubes tied when Kai was born."

"We both decided to have your tubes tied because of your weak heart. Not to mention you almost died. So don't come at me with that bullshit, Jasmine." Tears fell from her eyes, traveling down her cheeks. "Look Jasmine, I'm really sorry. I never meant for this to happen. She's not even sure if the babies she's carrying are mine or her husband's." Jasmine just stood there, with her head bowed. She couldn't say anything. She couldn't even look at him.

"When were you planning on telling me about her, after she had the babies?"

"I'm sorry, honey." Eric whispered.

"Don't honey me!"

"All the times you were gone. Don't act like you've been a saint." Jasmine gave him a funny look, wondering if Chandra had contacted him.

"Excuse me?" She responded with hands on her hips.

"Darius this, and Darius that was all you ever talked about. I was starting to wonder if you were fuckin' him, but I told myself nah, she's not that stupid, she know better. But then I thought about it and remembered all the times you came home after your trips and didn't want to have sex. Probably because you were giving it to him, but that's okay because Lynn was taking care of my needs when you were gone, so now we're even."

"Even? Do you have any proof that I was fuckin' Darius, like the proof I have on your dumb ass? Well, do you?" Jasmine responded, getting up in his face with her index finger less than an inch from his nose.

"You better back the fuck up and calm your ass down!"

"And if I don't?" Jasmine responded with her index finger still in his face. Without warning, Eric slapped her across the face with everything he had. The noise of the slap was so loud, the boys jumped from their beds, and the pain was so intense she almost blacked out as she fell to the floor. He stood over her, grabbed her by the collar of her nightgown, and slapped her two more times; before shoving her back to the kitchen floor. Her face had instantly swelled up, as her eyes rolled back in her head. Eric had laid hands on her once before and she warned him that if he ever did it again, she would kill him. Jasmine thought she was dreaming for a split second, because she couldn't believe he had slapped her three times like that. She tried to pull herself up, by holding onto the counter top, but couldn't. She faintly heard Eric yelling and cursing at her. Jasmine was semi-conscious and her face was throbbing. Blood trickled from her nostrils onto her chest and nightgown. Looking at the blood on her thumb that she wiped from one of her nostrils, she began to cry.

"I TOLD YOUR ASS TO CALM DOWN. NOW GET UP!" Eric continued to yell, standing over her. Jasmine heard Kai and Kyle running down the stairs.

"Mommy!" they cried.

"GET YA'LL ASSES BACK UPSTAIRS!" Eric yelled. The boys were defiant; and didn't move. They stood next to their mother with their hands on her shoulder, crying, trying to help her up.

"I'm okay, go back to bed." She felt so bad that her sons had to see her that way. Not moving, they stayed by her side, sniffling and crying. Mommy is alright, go back upstairs. I'll be there in a minute." Still crying and sniffling, they obeyed her command, but walking away slowly; looking back at her. Jasmine managed to grab onto the counter, slowly pulling her self up. "You better get the fuck out the house before I call the police! Better yet…fuck the police. I told you if you put your hands on me again I was gonna kill you. I really don't want to catch a case for the sake of my babies. So you better get the fuck out this house before one of us leave in a body bag." Regaining her faculties a little better, she opened the drawer where she kept the butcher knife.

"Baby, I'm sorry."

"GET OUT!" she yelled, picking up the butcher knife and slowly advancing toward him. He didn't say another word; he grabbed his keys from the counter and scurried out the door. Jasmine held onto the wall for support, making her way, to lock the door behind him. She then went into the bathroom to look at her face. When she turned on the light and saw her bruised, swollen face, she began crying, sliding down the wall onto the floor. "I can't believe he hit me like that," she mumbled to herself. Kyle and Kai came back down stairs and ran over to their mother holding on to her, crying as well.

The Next Morning…

With the sun peeking through her blinds, Jasmine woke up with a migraine headache. Her telephone was ringing and she didn't remember when she had fallen asleep. *"I must have cried myself to sleep,"* she thought to herself. She wanted last night to be a bad dream, but knew it wasn't by the aching pain on the side of her face. She rolled over, grabbing the phone off her nightstand, glancing at the clock that read 7:45 am.

"Hello," she moaned.

The Write Lover

"Girl, you sound horrible. I thought you would be up. You're usually up at the crack of dawn." It was her sister, Felecia. Her loud voice bellowed in her ear.

"I had a bad night. Eric and I got in a fight."

"You mean a fight, like arguing? You two always get into it from time to time."

"Umm...no; like a Mike Tyson and Holyfield fight."

"Girl, I know you're joking."

"I wish I was." She went on to tell her sister everything that happened the night before. Felecia was so shocked. She told Jasmine that she was on her way to see about her and the boys. Jasmine hung up the phone, and slowly pulled herself out the bed. Making her way to the bathroom and she stood at the sink, looking into the mirror. *"My life is officially a mess."* She thought to herself; as tears departed her eyes, traveling down her cheeks.

"Mommy, can I get some cereal?" Kyle yelled from outside the door.

"Go ahead baby." She said trying to sound like her normal self.

"Are you okay, Mommy?"

"I'm fine baby. Fix your brother a bowl too."

"Okay."

After taking a quick shower Jasmine put on a sundress, fixed her hair, and put on some make-up and sun glasses to camouflage her swollen eye and face. She was somewhat still in shock. She and Eric had never taken an argument to the level that it escalated to last night. Jasmine wanted to call Darius so bad because she needed him more than ever. She retrieved her cell phone out her purse and without a second thought began to dial his number.

"Hello." He answered on the third ring.

"Darius it's me…Jasmine." She spoke in a low tone.

"Jasmine, it's good to hear your voice. How are you?" He said with excitement.

"Umm…I…umm" She fought back tears with a trembling voice trying not to cry.

"What's the matter? Are you crying?" He asked concerned. "What's going on Jasmine?

"Darius…I need you." Jasmine cried. "Eric and I…we got into a big fight."

What happen? Did he find out about us?" Darius questioned, wondering if Chandra had called Eric and spilled the beans.

"Kind of…well…no I mean…I found out about him." Jasmine stuttered as she went on to tell Darius everything that happened. He listened in shock at what she was telling him, trying to take it all in. He was still in a state of shock himself, trying to digest the fact that Chandra was carrying his child.

"You know I moved to LA, so I can get a flight out and be there right in no time. Where's Eric now?"

"I don't know and I don't care. I just want him to come get his shit and get out my life. I never thought in a million years this would happen. You know I could probably forgive him for having an affair. I'm no angel…What goes around comes around, right? But I will never forgive him for hitting me. Never! I should have known better. He cheated on me in high school. It was just a matter of time before he did it again."

"Let me pack some things and I'll be on my way there to see about you."

"You will?" She responded feeling excited and relieved.

The Write Lover

"I told you, I'd always be here for you. I never stopped loving you."

"Darius, I love you so much." The doorbell rang. "Baby, that's my sister."

"Okay, I'll call you when I get in town. There's a lot we need to discuss."

"Okay." She rushed to open the door when she heard Felecia banging hard, as if she was the police. When Jasmine opened the door her sister, asked was she a movie star because, she was wearing sunglasses indoors. Jasmine removed them for her sister to see. Felicia mouth dropped wide open. Her bruised face confirmed how bad she really looked.

"OH HELL NO!" Felecia yelled out.

"Shut the hell up." Jasmine whispered.

"Has Eric lost his damn mind? Did you call the police? Better yet where is he at? I'm gonna fuck him up myself."

"Shut up, the boys may hear you." Felecia poked her head in the kitchen and saw her nephews sitting at the table, eating.

"Oh! Hello Kyle and Kai." She waved to them, sitting her purse down on the couch.

"Hi Aunt Lecia." The boys said in unison. Felecia retrieved a bottle of water from the refrigerator before joining her sister on the patio. Jasmine went on to tell her sister what had gone down with her and Eric. She also got her caught up on her relationship with Darius. Jasmine is five years younger than Felecia, but you'd never know by looking at them. Felecia was a few shades lighter than Jasmine, but they favored each other, they both had high cheekbones, full lips and almond shaped eyes. Felecia was still single and searching for Mr. Right, as she called it. She never stayed in a relationship longer than six months because she was just too picky, and if they did the slightest thing she didn't like, they were gone. She always told Jasmine that she didn't have time for other peoples' bullshit because she "can do bad all by herself."

"Well, this Darius sounds like Prince Charming."

"He's nice, real nice."

"Let me take the boys for the weekend, so you can take some time, to sort things out."

"That would be great, but everything is a big mess and I don't know what the hell I'm going to do."

"First you have to get Eric out of your life, so you can work on your piece of mind. You have your kids to think about." Jasmine looked at sister, nodding her head in agreement. "Are you going to be strong enough to cancel his ass?"

"Do you see this face, all fucked up and shit? I have to be strong."

"That's good, because if you don't, I will handle it for you."

"I got this sis." Jasmine responded, holding her head, as it throbbed.

"I probably would have killed him Jasmine. Shit, my head hurts, looking at yours." They both chuckled. "Here baby, you need something stronger than Motrin." Felecia reached in her purse and gave Jasmine three of her Vicodin. She was in a car accident a few months back, and the doctor prescribed pain medication for her back.

"Can I take this?" Jasmine asked, looking at the pills.

"Yeah, you'll be fine. It will help you sleep and ease the pain."

Felecia packed a suitcase for the kids, for the weekend and told them that mommy and daddy had to work some things out. She had a strong feeling that her oldest son wasn't buying the sugar coated story. She thanked her sister for taking the boys because she definitely needed the time, to self-evaluate. Jasmine glanced at the clock, as her sister drove away; it was going on noon and she hadn't eaten anything all day. She went to the kitchen, made a sandwich. After she ate, she took a Vicodin and laid down. She was comfortably snug in her bed, when her house phone rang. It startled her.

"Hello! Hello!" There was no response to her greeting. "Hello!" She said again.

"Jasmine, don't hang up. I'm sorry for putting my hands on you."

"Fuck you Eric!"

"Baby...I'm really sorry."

"You're gonna be sorry. All I need to know is when are you coming to get your shit!"

Baby, can't we sit down and talk about this?"

"Talk, you say?" Jasmine sat up in the bed, getting pissed by the second. "Yes, we can sit down and talk about how we are going to explain to our children, that their parents are getting a divorce. I can't even stand to look at you. My face is badly bruised and my head is still killing me."

"I know you're upset, but divorce? That's a little extreme, don't you think?"

"You hit me multiple times in the face, damn near knocking me out; that was extreme. There is no way on this God green earth we're getting back together. But what hurt me more than the blow you delivered to my face was that you got some other married woman pregnant. Then on top of that, undermining my passion for writing, I can't find enough forgiveness in my heart to look at you the same way again. You hurt me mentally and physically, Eric. You hurt me like no other person has."

"I know I fucked up baby. I'm so sorry and I…" Cutting his sentence short, Jasmine responded.

"You can come around 5 pm and get your shit. When I get home, don't be there!" Before, he could say anything else; she hung up and laid back down, with thoughts of what her sister had told her earlier and knowing what she needed to do. The Vicodin, began to take effect as she dosed off into a deep sleep.

A Few Hours Later…

Jasmine checked her cell, when she awoke. Darius had text her and told her what room he was in. She text him back informing him she would be leaving the house soon.

After brushing her teeth, she slipped on her favorite pair of jeans, a tank top, and a pair of sandals. She re-applied some make-up to camouflage her bruise with make-up and sunglasses. Her headache was finally gone. She thought to herself, *"Felecia wasn't lying about those pills."*

Once at the hotel, Jasmine valet-parked and made her way to Darius's room. The sun was beginning to set, but she kept her sunglasses on anyway. She took a deep breath and knocked on his door. He opened the door, with a big smile. She could smell his cologne, Kenneth Cole's Black, from where she stood. He tenderly pulled her into him, embracing her in a big hug.

"Hey baby, I missed you," Darius said.

The Write Lover

"I missed you too honey."

"I was just about to order room service. Are you hungry?"

"I could eat a little something."

"Wait! Don't tell me, you want a Caesar Salad, right?"

"Yep, you know what I like," Jasmine responded as she sat down on the love seat, watching him move around the room looking sexy in his simple pair of jeans and button- up white shirt. Darius picked up the phone and made the order, while looking back at Jasmine as he ordered a bottle of Merlot with a grin on his face. She just shook her head at him, with a slight giggle. She knew what he had on his mind.

"So what's up with the sunglasses, Ray Charles?" He asked jokingly as he sat next to her. Jasmine removed them, revealing her bruised face. "He did this baby?" Jasmine took a deep breath and exhaled slowly, not sure what to say. "Baby, did he do this?" He repeated, getting upset. He gingerly placed his hand on her face, taking a closer look. "What happened, Jasmine?" She was so sick of crying, but somehow more tears managed to escape her eyes. Finally the lump in her throat passed, and she broke down and told Darius what had happened last night. He just sat there listening as a disturbed look came upon his face when she told him how Eric had hit her so hard she almost lost consciousness.

"I'm gonna hurt him, like he hurt you." He said, enraged. "Did you call the police?"

"Please, Darius. I don't want anymore drama. It's not like I was being faithful either."

"So does that give him the right to hit you, like he did? I better not see him."

"Enough is enough, honey. I have a handle on this."

Brooklen Borne

"I just...he shouldn't have hit you."

"Just hold me," she whispered. He pulled her into his arms and she rested her head on his chest, as they sat back. She began to cry, letting out all her pain and it felt good to release. He just held her close, massaging her shoulders, wondering how in the world he was going to break the news to her, that Chandra was pregnant. After everything she had gone through with her husband, he figured it would be best not to tell her yet.

They ate and took a nice warm shower together. He gently washed her back, hair, and the side of her face. The Pink Merlot she drank earlier was in full effect. She began to feel much better than when she first arrived. The warm water that cascaded over her body, along with the soothing touch of Darius, made her feel safe. Even though they had not communicated with each other in over a month, they fell right back into each other's arms like they had not been apart at all. Jasmine was becoming horny and wanted Darius deep inside her. Staring at his manhood, made her want to get down on her knees and sucked him until he released in her mouth. She needed to be sexually satisfied and feel loved.

Her thoughts were broken by his voice, telling her he was stepping out the shower to give her some private time. Fifteen minutes later, Jasmine emerged from the shower, dried off and oiled her body, with vanilla essence oil, she had picked up from the flea market two weeks ago. She donned one of his collared, button-up shirts and snuggled next to him in the bed. She just smiled. Darius wrapped his arms around her and continued to watch television. The scent of Sean John's Unforgivable on him made her hornier than when she was in the shower. Now that her pain had subsided, her sexual urge for him took over. She remained cool; as she listened to him tell her about his new place in LA and all the new literary projects he was working on.

She loved listening to his mellow New York accent; because it would put her in a calm place. Her body took over her mind and she began massaging his penis, while kissing him on his ear and neck. He returned the advances, kissing her ever so tenderly on her soft, silky body. She put her hands underneath her thighs as she opened her legs and raised them towards him with the anticipation of what was about to happen. When his tongue made contact with her sugar walls, she arched her back and let out moans of passion, with every pass of his skillful tongue. She removed her hands from her thighs, grabbing the pillow trying not to come so quickly, but she knew that was a war she would lose. Her hips were gyrating with the rhythm of his tongue; she could feel herself about to explode. He knew by the pace of her gyrations, she was on the verge of an orgasm. She took a hold of his head as she tried to push him away, but he had her waist locked in his grip. Jasmine raised her body from the waist up, her back arched, eyes closed and yelled out his name, as waves of pleasure engulfed her.

She fell back upon the bed breathing hard with her eyes closed and mouth open. Entering his hard penis into her private entrance, she began to talk in tongues.

"I've missed you so much baby." Jasmine, manage to audibly moaned. Receiving a few hard steady strokes later, she had another orgasm. "Oh, baby." She gasped, while trying to catch her breath. He turned her glistening body over, bringing her to the edge of the bed and positioned her doggie style. He held onto her waist and was stroking Jasmine like he had something to prove. She gripped the pillow tighter as she buried her face to muffle her screams from each sensual thrust, she was receiving. Sweat glistened off their bodies as he went in and out of her sugar walls. He held on to her hips as he pumped harder and faster, her muffled screams and his loud moans, played acoustics around the room as the aroma of sex filled the air.

"I'm about to come baby." He informed, as he went deep for the last time. "Oh yes!" Darius yelled out as he came holding his position deep inside her until all his soldiers were safely away from their transport tube.

"Oh God!" She screamed out, and her body quivered, as if a cold chill had passed over her wet body.

Jasmine's nerves were so intensified she didn't want Darius to pull out. They stayed in that position with him still encased inside. A few minutes later, they moved further up on the bed with pillow in tow. Darius reached for the sheet and pulled it over them as he wrapped his arms around her like a warm blanket on a cold winter's night. Still exhausted, but totally satisfied they fell off to sleep.

Darius didn't sleep for long. He slid out of bed making his way to the bathroom, cleaning up and putting on his underwear. He sat in the chair next to the bed, watching her sleep. Even though the side of her face was bruised, she never looked more beautiful to him. He took a deep breath wondering where their relationship would lead to now. They had been through so many ups and downs with each other and with their marriages he hoped they finally had the opportunity to be together. Even though he was afraid to tell her about Chandra's pregnancy, but he knew if he didn't and she found out later, she may never want to seem him again.

The Write Lover

He never even called Chandra back after he got the fax; he didn't know what to say to her. Darius wanted a child more than anything in the world, but he never imagined things turning out this way. He was getting in the mind frame to take care of his responsibility; as far as the baby with Chandra, but getting back with her was not an option. Jasmine rolled over slowly waking up. Darius smiled at her.

"Are you watching me sleep?" She giggled sitting up slowly pulling the sheet over her breasts. "Come get back in the bed. I need you next to me."

"Baby, there's something I need to tell you," Darius informed in a serious tone. She immediately felt a pain in the pit of her stomach, unsure what he was going to tell her.

"Uh oh, what? Please don't tell me…you have a girlfriend or something? Damn it, Darius, you should have told me before we…" He interjected, interrupting her sentence.

"No, I don't have a girlfriend. It's not that at all." Jasmine took a deep breath.

"Okay then what?"

"You know I love you?"

"Yeah"

"I see us in a beautiful life long relationship together, as my wife. I know you have a lot, to work out with Eric and all, but I hope you leave him and we can start an exclusive relationship now. I want to meet your boys and everything. I want to tell the public that you are my woman. I'm not rushing anything Jasmine. I just want you to know that."

"I feel the same way about you Darius, but why do I feel there's a 'but' coming." He took a deep breath running his hands over his face.

"Jasmine, Chandra's pregnant."

"By who?" Darius didn't respond. "Oh no! By you?" Darius nodded his head in agreement with her assumption. She stared at Darius unsure how to respond. She was momentarily numb, before she was able to say,

"How far along is she?"

"Um, like six weeks." He read the look on Jasmine's face and went on to explain to her what happen after their trip to LA how he returned home and had sex with Chandra. Leaning her head back against the headboard, trying to process everything, Darius had just said.

"This is crazy! This has to be some kind of nightmare. Both of the men in my life have other woman pregnant. This shit is just too much." She scooted down in the bed, resting her head on the pillow. Darius crawled in the bed next to her.

"Baby, I wish I could go back and change things, but I can't. I do know that I want you in my life and I do know that I'll take care of my responsibility with Chandra, but nothing more." Jasmine didn't respond. She turned her back to Darius and silently wept. He wrapped his arm around her and held her close to him, not saying a word.

Chapter Twelve
Meeting the Kids

Four And A Half Months Later...

So much had transpired in Jasmine's life. The last few months had been a big adjustment. Her divorce was in the process of being final. She now shared custody of the boys with Eric. She had them Monday through Friday while Eric kept them on the weekends, or whenever Jasmine went out of town on her book tour. It was agreed on for the boys to spend the summer with their father since touring was a must during the summer months on the east coast, and the summer season was only a few months away.

It was confirmed that Eric was in fact the father of Lynn's twin girls that were now two months old. Lynn had left her husband to live with Eric in a condo; with the babies. Jasmine absorbed herself in writing another novel and caring for her two boys, but the best thing of all, Darius was now officially her man. No more undercover lover. She had not introduced him to her sons and wasn't sure on how to go about it just yet; even though, he was dying to meet them.

Things were going well in Darius's and Jasmine's life. He was working on several projects, including his own publishing company. Showtime, had offered him a nice contract to turn one of his scripts into a miniseries and Jasmine was assisting him on that project. Jasmine had accepted the fact that Chandra was carrying Darius's child and was going to love that baby as if it were her own. She loved Darius unconditionally and she wasn't going to let anything interfere in their relationship. Darius was flying back and forth to New York, to accompany Chandra on a few of her doctor appointments. At first, Jasmine feared he may slip up, and get back with Chandra for the sake of the baby, but after what he went through with her, she trusted that wouldn't happen. Darius was truthful with her from the beginning and he had never given her a reason not to trust him.

Chandra was entering her third trimester and Darius was very excited she was having a boy. Jasmine was happy as well, because she knew having a child, was something he really wanted. Chandra was still upset that he and Jasmine were exclusively dating, so there was no chance of her and Darius rekindling their defunct relationship. She thought for sure by carrying his child he'd give in and they would be back together. She wasn't going to push the issue about the relationship between him and Jasmine, because she hoped, that once he saw his son's face, he would not want to leave his baby and would come running back to New York to be a family; with her and the baby. She was sure of it. As far as Chandra was concerned, Jasmine was only temporary.

Weekends for Jasmine and Darius were dedicated to each other. Every Friday when the boys left for their father's, she would fly down to Los Angeles to stay with him. She loved being able to sleep in his' arms all night and not having to worry about being caught or washing his scent away. She relished the way he took care of her, especially in the lovemaking department.

It was around five in the evening when Jasmine phone rang, while she was packing for her weekend to be with Darius.

"Hello!"

"Hey baby." Darius soothing voice greeted.

"Hey you! I just finished packing and waiting on Eric to get the boys. He should have been here by now. I might have to take a later flight."

"Well…I decided to come and get you this weekend. I'm already on the road.

"Baby, that's like a four hour drive to Sacramento."

"I'm already in Sacramento. I wanted to surprise you. We can drive down the coast and stay in Santa Barbara. I found a nice bed and breakfast, you're going to love. I know how you enjoyed our last road trips." They both laughed.

"Oh you're so sweet!" Jasmine thought it was strange he wanted to pick her up, because she wasn't fully ready to introduce her sons to him yet. She wanted to give them some more time to heal from the divorce. In spite of that a smile appeared upon her face, when she thought how he was always full of surprises.

"I brought something for the boys. Are they still there?"

"Yes, they're still here."

"Good, so I finally get to meet them."

"Well…I" He interjected, not letting her finish her sentence.

"I want to meet them Jasmine. Have you even told them about me?" There was a long pause of silence. "You haven't, have you?"

"Baby, it's just they been having a hard time adjusting to the divorce and I really don't want to put anymore on them right now."

"Look Jasmine, I plan on being a part of your life full time and you know we've already had this conversation a million times. Do you want me to sit at a Starbucks or a McDonalds and wait for you then?"

"No baby...no...I'm sorry, you're right. Sooner is better than later.

"Okay, I'll be there in a few. I have your address in my GPS." They disconnected and Jasmine dialed Eric.

"Hello." He answered on the first ring.

"You're an hour late." She griped.

"I know...my bad; there was a last minute emergency. I'm on my way now."

"Eric, you could have called me and let me know; that you were running late. I do have somewhere to be." Eric and Jasmine could not hold a conversation for more than a few minutes before they began arguing; however, they tried to hold it together in front of the kids. They had so much anger built up between them; it was like a southern California fire.

"I said, I'm on my way. Where are you rushing off to now?"

"That's none of your business!"

"What you got another man now? That's why you're trying to rush this divorce. Jasmine, I got those papers from your lawyer in the mail. You're not keeping the house! We are going to sell it, I need the money."

"Whatever. I don't have time to talk to you about this. I'll see you when you get here." She slammed the receiver back down on the base before heading down the stairs to see Kyle playing in the back-yard on his skateboard, and Kai in the family room playing on his Play Station.

"Kyle, come inside! Kai turn that off. I need to talk to you and your brother." Kai obeyed without a fuss as Kyle came in through the sliding door.

"What!" Kyle said as entered the house, and closed the sliding the door; like he was paying the mortgage.

"The next time you say "what" when I call you, I'm gonna tear your behind up. Do you understand me?" She informed him, with a stern look.

"Okay mom." Kyle responded, with a better attitude.

"I want to talk to you guys." Jasmine sat on the end of the couch as Kyle sat on the floor and Kai turned his attention to her.

"Your dad is running late, but he's on the way."

"I don't want to go with dad." Kyle responded.

"Why?" She asked curiously.

"I don't like leaving you mom." Kyle admitted. "I hate dad for breaking up our family."

"Hate, is a strong word honey. Don't say that about your father. Besides, you and I had a talk about this."

"I know, but mom, I hate…umm, I mean I don't like those ugly twin babies. Kai and I have to share a room over there and you know how loud Kai snores."

"I do not!" Kai yelled out, in his defense.

"Look! Cut it out you two. I know things have been hard for you guys. I never wanted it to be this way, but I need you to be strong alright? We are still a family. I have a friend coming by, that I want you to meet."

"A friend?" Kyle asked as Kai looked on.

Brooklen Borne

"Yes, I have a male friend; his name is Darius."

"The hell you do." Kyle boldly blurted out as he stood up.

"Boy, watch your mouth. Have you lost your mind?" Jasmine responded angrily.

"So you and dad are never getting back together?" Kai asked.

"That's right baby."

"You're stupid, Kai. Mom would never take dad back. Look what he did to her. I hate him."

"That's enough, Kyle. Don't you ever let me hear you say, you hate your father again? He made mistakes and yes it hurts, but we are not perfect. No one is perfect." Kyle rolled his eyes. Jasmine stood up going over to Kyle and embracing him in a big hug, when the doorbell rang. She was praying it was Eric and she could rush the boys along before Darius arrival.

"Go get your things boys. That's probably your dad. We will finish this talk later." They both sprinted up the stairs and Jasmine took a deep breath, walking toward the door.

When she opened the door, to her surprise it was Darius. He stood there with a grin on his face, looking good with a casual white collared shirt and beige slacks. Without saying a word, he reached for her and they embraced with a hug and gentle kiss.

"Wow that was fast. Come in."

"This is for the boys. It's three of the latest PS2 games." He said as he stepped inside, looking around at the modern furniture and black framed artwork. He felt somewhat uncomfortable entering the home she once shared with her husband. He really could not wait until her divorce was final because he planned on asking her to move to LA with him. He was just waiting for the right time.

The Write Lover

"Yes, they just went up stairs to get their things. Thank you so much, I know they will enjoy this. I thought you were Eric."

"Oh no…" He said, just as they stepped out the foyer and into the open kitchen the boys came down stairs with their backpacks. They looked at their mom, then at Darius.

"Hi. I'm Kai." He greeted Darius with a smile.

"Who are you?" Kyle asked rudely. Darius looked over at Jasmine unsure how to respond.

"Boys, this is Darius. My friend, I was just telling you about." She introduced, slightly nervous.

"What's up fellas? It's nice to finally meet you." Darius said as he extended his hand out to shake the boy's hand. Kyle stepped back and Kai moved forward to accept the greeting with a smile.

"You're my mom's new boyfriend?" Kyle asked, not liking the situation.

"Kyle!" Jasmine snapped. Kyle turned around and walked back upstairs to his room.

"Can I get back on Play Station mom?" Kai asked.

"Yes baby, go ahead and take this. Darius brought three new games for you and Kyle."

"Thanks Mr. Darius." Kai said taking the gift and quickly walking up the stairs.

"Baby, I'm sorry about Kyle." Jasmine took a hold of Darius's hand, pulling him towards the kitchen.

"It's cool. I'd probably be the same way too if I was him, and my mom had a new man." Darius laughed it off, taking a seat on the barstool. Can I get you something to drink?"

"No baby, I'm fine."

Brooklen Borne

"I can't believe you are really here?" Jasmine said overjoyed. "So tell me what happened at the meeting with Warner Brothers?" A big grin crept upon Darius' face.

"The meeting went well. Not only do they want to buy the movie rights to my book "Savannah" they are interested in a deal with our collaboration "Being Homeless Is Not an Option" I'm making sure the integrity of our stories, stay intact."

"Oh baby!" She screamed out hugging Darius for dear life. Stepping back and looking him in his eyes. "Our hard work, sacrifice and patience is finally going to the screen, with the backing of a major movie company. It's a dream come true."

"Yes it is. So I was thinking this weekend we could celebrate. No laptops, no cell phones, nothing baby." Darius suggested, looking serious.

"No laptops baby. You know we always write together on the weekends."

"Not this weekend. I just want to absorb myself into you. No writing, no working."

"Umm...absorb yourself into me. I like the sound of that." Jasmine smiled. The doorbell rang. "Oh shit!" She knew it was Eric.

"It's okay honey." Darius said. "I'll stay right here. You go see your boys off."

"Okay Kyle, Kai, your dad is here." She called for them as she made her way to the door. As soon as she opened the door Eric asked. "Whose BMW is that in the driveway?"

"Hello, is the proper greeting Eric." She rolled her eyes.

"I know you don't have another man up in my house."

The Write Lover

"Your house?" She questioned. "This is not your house anymore." She said with a slight elevated voice. Eric pushed past her, forcing his way inside.

"Where the hell are you going?" Jasmine closed the door, following him. When Darius heard the commotion he jumped off the barstool. He was still furious knowing that Eric had put his hands on her awhile back. Eric stopped dead in his tracks when he saw Darius standing there. They had met only once before a year ago at one of their book tours. Their eyes locked. Jasmine stood nervously, watching what might unfold. Eric looked over at her with a look of disgust before asking,

"How long you two been messing around?"

"Eric...please don't!"

"I knew it was you! Were you fuckin' my wife before we were separated?" Eric's rage had him making a fist. Jasmine looked to see Darius doing the same with both hands.

"It's cool Jasmine." Darius assured in a calm voice, looking over at her but keeping a close eye on Eric. She didn't know what to say when Kai came running into the kitchen, giving his daddy a big hug.

"Hey dad, I'm ready." Eric calmed down a little, as he hugged Kai back.

"Hey little man, you have all your stuff?"

"Yep, did you meet mom's boyfriend, Darius?" Kai added.

"Yes son, I sure have." Kyle came downstairs rolling his eyes, stomping with an attitude.

"You ready big man?" Eric asked Kyle.

"Yes dad." He moaned as he walked out the door.

"Go to the car Kai. I'll be right there." Kai obeyed, but not before giving Jasmine a kiss on the lips and hug while waving good-bye to Darius.

"What the hell are you doing bringing another man in our house?"

"You really have some nerves. Not that it's any of your business, but Darius just came to pick me up."

"So this is my replacement?" Eric asked, looking Darius up and down.

"Bye, Eric!" Jasmine interjected. "You really think you just gonna walk in my house and play step daddy and…" Darius cut him off.

"Eric, before you start throwing stones in a glass house, let me remind you of a few things. One! Kyle and Kai will always know that you are their father and I will never try to replace you. Two! You have a set of kids outside your marriage. Did you wait until you were separated, before you got that other woman pregnant?

Three! Hitting Jasmine the way you hit her, almost knocking her out, reinforces her decision to divorce you. Four! Don't you know what you did to her and your sons will have a major impact on their lives forever? And Five! Your sons will never get the sight of their mother on the floor with a bloody nose out of their mind. Yes, this scene may be messed up but it will get better. I love Jasmine and support Jasmine in her endeavors, if she's with me or not. Can you truly say that from the heart Eric and mean it?" Eric didn't say a word. He knew Darius was on point with what he had said. Eric turned and opened the door and was about to walk out when Darius said. "One more thing, if you ever put your hands on her again, it will be your last." Eric just smirked and continued out the door, closing it behind him. Jasmine let out a sigh of relief as she turned the deadbolt locking the door. She turned around and walked up to Darius, wrapping her arms around his shoulders, as he wrapped his around her waist; standing there in a loving embrace. His phone began to vibrate. Retrieving it from his jacket pocket, to check the number; it was Chandra.

"Baby, we're getting tagged teamed." He said to Jasmine with a wrinkled brow.

"Go head take your call. I'll get my bags." She replied, turning away going up the stairs.

"What's up Chandra?"

"Hey, I'm in the hospital."

"What! Why?" He asked concerned. He knew Chandra was going in her seven months and wondered why she was in the hospital.

"My blood pressure is really high and the doctors said I need to be on bed rest for the next few weeks until the baby comes."

"A few weeks, you mean two months?"

"It's the same, eight weeks, two months. The doctor think Jr. may come early." She replied.

"Can I speak to the doctor?'

"FOR WHAT?" she snapped. "I'm telling you what the hell the doctor told me."

"It just seems weird. The last appointment the doctor said you where doing fine."

"Darius you missed the last appointment."

"I went to the last appointment."

"Well, the one before that then."

"I don't understand you're not due for two whole months."

"Well, unexpected things happen when you're pregnant. So are you going to catch a flight to New York or what? I'm sure you don't want to miss the birth, do you? Or are you busy with Jasmine." Just then Darius glanced up to see Jasmine walking down the stairs.

"Let me speak to the doctor."

"You know what?" He heard Chandra take a deep breath, then a dial tone.

"Damn it!" He mumbled.

"Is everything alright?" He gestured for Jasmine to give him a moment as he searched his cell phone for the doctor's number. He left a message with the answering service to have the doctor call him. Then he explained to Jasmine what was going on. Jasmine found it quite weird that Chandra could be going into labor so soon being that she was only seven months. There were no indications early in her pregnancy that the baby was going to be a preemie. Jasmine poured them both a glass of cranberry juice as they waited for the doctor to call Darius back. She could tell he was very worried. She ran her hand up and down his back. "I'm sure it will be alright." Darius scurried quickly for his phone, when it rang. It was the doctor, returning his call.

"Yes doctor, this is Darius Hamilton. I was calling to find out what was going on with Chandra Hamilton; she said she was in the hospital."

"Oh hello Mr. Hamilton; yes she was in the hospital but I released her a few hours ago. She was complaining of cramps, but I checked her and she's fine. Her blood pressure was a little high though and I told her to go home and get some rest. I ran a few blood tests and everything checked out well. It's just a case of

The Write Lover

Braxton Hicks contraction. Her body is preparing itself, nothing to be concerned about. However, Chandra is saying she is only seven months, but with the size of the last ultrasound we ran today, the baby is measuring way bigger than thirty-two weeks. Either she miscalculated her last period, or you guys are having a pretty big boy." The doctor finished. Darius took a deep breath.

"Well, I was close to nine pounds when I was born."

"Well yeah, that could be it then, but she will be fine. She just needs to rest and stay off her feet, for the duration of the day."

"Doctor, does she need to be on bed rest?"

"No!"

"Okay doctor, thank you. Bye now."

"Bye"

"Is everything alright?" Jasmine asked concerned.

"Chandra is playing games, trying to make me go crazy; saying she's still in the hospital!" He relayed to Jasmine the information the doctor told him.

"Honey you where almost nine pounds, when you were born?"

"Yes, eight pounds nine ounces."

"God bless your mama." They both laughed.

"Are you gonna call Chandra back."

"Hell no! The doctor said she's fine. She's just trying to play games and if I call her back right now I might curse her ass out. He then gathered Jasmine's bags and they headed out the door.

Chapter Thirteen
The Truth

A Month Later...

 Darius and Jasmine had returned to his house from a red carpet event of *American Gangster*, an anticipated box office hit starring Denzel Washington. This was the first time the two had officially gone out in public for a big event as a couple.

 Jasmine had on a beautiful blue sequence dress that hugged her curve and cut low in the back, down to the base of her spine, exposing her back. Darius was in awe when she stepped out the room for the first time with it on. He was quite dapper himself wearing a basic black Armani suit, white shirt, and black tie. They looked so perfect together. Darius had been ignoring the vibration of his cell phone ringing all night, because he knew it was only Chandra, being a nuisance.

 He assured Jasmine that no matter what, he wanted to be with her, and having a baby with Chandra would not change his feelings for her. She accepted it and they continued their relationship as Jasmine's divorce proceeded on with Eric. Their lives were a little complicated, she going through a divorce and Darius' ex-wife being pregnant by him. It was not at all what she had pictured happening in their lives, but they accepted it and continued to move forward. Jasmine was in many ways happy for Darius. He longed for a baby and even if it weren't the way they planned it to be, he would have a biological child.

It was around 2am, when the two love birds could barely keep their hands off each other; as they walked through the door. Standing in the foyer undressing each other, engaged in a passionate kiss, Darius cell phone began to vibrate again. Jasmine pulled back when she felt it. "Who's calling you at two in the morning?" She asked, pulling up the strap on her dress. Darius pulled his phone from his jacket pocket.

"It's Chandra. She's been calling all night. I'll call her in the morning." He was fed up with Chandra calling him everyday making up some excuse about how she was not feeling well. He didn't trust her so he would always call the doctor to find out the real story. Chandra was just using the baby to try to get him back to New York whenever she wanted. He had flown back and forth for the past month to see about her and the baby. Even taking Jasmine a few times, but she always stayed back at the hotel. He knew Chandra would fly off the handle if he brought Jasmine to her house or to the doctor appointments.

"It must be important…answer it!" Jasmine said annoyed. Darius kissed her on the lips and picked her up off her feet and into his arms, carrying her upstairs; ignoring her request. He'd been waiting all night to put it on her. He laid her across his bed, while lowering the straps on her dress; kissing her shoulder blades ever so softly, while gently massaging her breast. "Ummm," Jasmine moaned to his touch, on her erect nipples. The house phone rang interrupting their pleasure. They both ignored the phone as Darius traveled down her body with more kisses and began to pull her thong off, when Chandra's voice came on the answering machine.

"Darius, this is Chandra. I'm not happy about you ignoring my calls all night. I know you have seen my number on your caller ID. Look, I really need to talk to you okay? It's about the baby. The doctors are saying I need to have more blood work done because my fluid is low or something, like that. I was hoping you could come with me to the doctor's office this Tuesday, if you're not too busy…with Jasmine. My girlfriend called and told me she saw you two on television tonight, hand in hand at a Hollywood event. You're hanging out in public now, huh?" Chandra gave off a saucy laugh. Then there was a clicking sound and Chandra said, "Someone else is trying to call me, just give me a call as soon as possible about Tuesday. I need your support Darius." Jasmine sat up in the bed with exposed breast, looking at Darius.

"Call her honey." She suggested. He took a deep breath, growing frustrated, but he knew Jasmine was right. Before he could pick up the receiver, he heard Chandra voice come back on the machine.

"Hey Toni, I just called his home number this time and made up some bullshit story about my blood work to get his ass to New York. He's living big time now in Los Angeles and that bitch Jasmine, is enjoying the red carpet status and shit. That should have been me," Chandra griped. Jasmine covered her mouth. Chandra must have pressed the button one too many times. Now, her conversation was on three-way. Darius put his arms around Jasmine as they both listened intensely to the conversation.

"You're crazy girl, but her dress was hot though." Toni told Chandra.

"Fuck her. She was smiling all up in my face when she came here to New York. All the while she was fuckin' my husband and she had her own damn husband. I'm going to do whatever it takes to get him back. He can't be happy with her skinny ass."

"Obviously he is, and besides, you were giving Charles the pussy every time Darius left town girl. So let's keep it real."

"I needed some dick, so what. Darius wasn't hitting this pussy like he should have been."

"Hmm, how are you gonna pull off this pregnancy thing? Darius thinks you're seven months and here you are really eight months, about to pop that baby out. Don't you think he's gonna wonder why you had the baby so early and the baby is not a preemie."

"Nah, he won't. He hasn't caught on so far. It was seven months ago we had sex, so I told him I was six months. He won't know. He wants a baby so bad he won't care."

"So what the hell are you going to tell Charles?"

"Fuck Charles broke ass. He hasn't sold a piece of property in over a year. I just used him to get some dick."

"Charles should at least know that it's his baby."

"Who cares if I'm really pregnant by Charles, he and I are over. This is gonna be Darius' baby. He always wanted a family, so when this baby comes he'll be all mine again; especially with all that money that comes with him. He'll see this little boy and Jasmine will be history. I'm going to get my husband back!"

"Chandra girl, I don't know, you're playing with fire and you know what fire can do?"

"I'll do whatever it takes to get him back. I should have never signed those divorce papers so fast."

"Like I said you're playing a dangerous game."

"It is what it is. I'll talk to you later."

"Alright"

"Toni!" Chandra yelled into the receiver.

"Yeah, what's up?"

"You're the only person I told this to, so keep it to yourself."

"I'm not one to run my mouth."

"Alright girl, bye"

"Bye." Then the answering machine beeped and went silent. Jasmine and Darius sat there in bed in shock, not knowing what to say to each other. Darius jumped up from the bed. He grabbed the phone off the receiver so fast to dial Chandra back, it fumbled in his hand.

"Baby, what are you going to say?" Jasmine whispered. Darius looked back at her, not responding. "Honey, are you okay? I can't believe Chandra would do something so dirty." Darius did not speak a word, holding the phone to his ear; waiting for Chandra to answer.

"Hello"

"Chandra, its Darius. You've been blowing up my phone all night. What's up?"

"How dare you, not call me back when I call. I'm carrying your child. What if it was an emergency?"

"You know what Chandra; I was thinking we should get a paternity test."

"What? Where did this come from all of a sudden? Are you drunk? Did Jasmine put that shit in your head?"

"No! As a matter of fact hold up. I want you to listen to something." Darius put the phone on speaker and replayed the entire message his answering machine had picked up.

"Darius, I...I-," Chandra stuttered before he cut her off.

"Stay the fuck out of my life Chandra. How could you be so evilly selfish?"

"Darius, I um...I know this is your baby."

"How could you fix your mouth to say that after hearing you talk shit to your girl about this? Knowing that's not my baby."

"It's a possibility. I stop taking pills and..."

"So you telling me you are going to stick to that story, knowing I have you on tape." Chandra didn't answer.

"Yeah, just like I thought. Bye Chandra." He said before disconnecting the call. Jasmine gave him a tight hug, feeling relieved. They open a bottle of Merlot and celebrated the great news; before resuming their love making.

Darius awoke the next morning to the smell and sound of sizzling bacon. He glanced over at the clock, which illuminated 6am. That was the time his body was programmed to wake up. After a quick trip to the bathroom, he made his way to the kitchen where he found Jasmine over the stove. He loved seeing her take control of his kitchen. He noticed she was wearing her work out clothes. She kept clothes at his place, and Darius had even set up, her own computer and desk to work on her writing when she was there.

He made her happy and she looked forward to spending time with him when her boys went with their father on alternate weekends and certain holidays. After all the adultery that was committed within their relationship, they both agreed it would be smart to get tested for STD's and HIV to have a peace of mind. They both realized as adults they had both been careless with their sexual activities by not using condoms. So a few weeks back, they both went and had complete physicals done and the news came back as a clean bill of health, along with the STD and HIV tests saying they both were negative.

Darius and Jasmine made it clear to each other, that without protection they would be committed to each other and have no other sexual partners.

"Good morning, what are you doing?" Darius asked, walking up behind her, greeting her with a soft kiss on her neck.

"Making you breakfast."

"You didn't have to do that baby. You know I'm not really a breakfast person."

"Yeah I know, but I wanted to cook you some grits, eggs, bacon and toast. Enjoy this breakfast while I'll go for run."

"So you want me to sit here, feed my face and get fat while you work out." Darius joked, grabbing a piece of hot bacon and shoving it in his mouth. At that moment the dryer beeped, indicating the load was done.

"The clothes are dry." She said disappearing down the hallway to the laundry room. Darius stood there for a moment, and then followed her to the laundry room where she placing the clean clothes into a basket.

"Baby, you don't have to wash my clothes." She took a deep breath looking up at him, as she placed the basket on the counter near the washer.

"What am I good for then? You don't want me to cook for you or wash your clothes."

"What are you good for? Baby, you're good for more than cooking and washing clothes. I mean I love the nice gesture, but I don't require you to do these things. I can do these things myself."

"I'm use to taking care of a household." She replied.

"I understand that, but maybe you need to get use to being treated like the Queen you are and let me wash your clothes and cook for you." Jasmine froze, looking into his eyes, not knowing how to respond. She never imagined anyone washing or cooking for her. She was always the one multi-tasking, cleaning, cooking, washing and working.

"This is going to take some getting use to." She grinned.

"Probably, but things will be different in a positive way with me, baby."

"What did I do to deserve you?" Jasmine sighed. He pulled her close to him and they engaged in a soft kiss. Jasmine pulled back gently.

"Are you okay, after everything with Chandra last night?"

"I'm fine. Now I don't have to deal with her anymore."

"I know how bad you wanted a child honey."

"Yes, well maybe it's not in the cards for me, because I plan on spending the rest of my life with you and I know you already tied your tubes."

"Well then, maybe I'm not the right woman for you."

"Please Jasmine. I wouldn't want any other woman in the world but you."

"Umm" She smiled. "I would untie my tubes for you." His eyes became wide, indicating he wasn't expecting her to say that.

"Look Jasmine, I would not want you to do that. I'll be happy with you, and the boys. I'll love your sons like my own, they are a part of you honey."

"I know, but still I…" He cut her off.

"This is what I wanted for so long." He just wanted to enjoy this special moment of him and her in the house as a couple, as a family.

"Okay, I can respect that." She kissed him on the cheek as she turned to leave the laundry room. "I'll be back. I'm going for a run."

"Alright baby, be careful." He told her, before she slipped on her running shoes and dashed out the door. The five-mile running track at the local park was within walking distance from Darius' home.

The aroma of the bacon had taken over the kitchen making Darius hungry, so he took a plate from the cabinet and fixed him a serving. He then turned on the laptop computer that was on the counter, logged in and began researching what possibilities and chances Jasmine would have to get pregnant if she did in fact have her tubes untied. He was curiously shocked and honored that she had even suggested that to him.

When Jasmine returned from jogging, Darius had drawn her, a hot bubble bath. He also placed a couple of lit candles around the tub. She was surprised and told Darius she would not get in unless he joined her. She took a quick shower, before getting in the tub. It was very romantic and there was no other place in the world Jasmine wanted to be. Darius washed her back and massaged her shoulders.

"Baby, I was thinking we should take a trip to Vegas."

"Vegas? I haven't been there in a while."

"Yeah, I was thinking we could go there for your birthday next month."

"Oh yeah, that's the big three-five." Darius laughed. Jasmine didn't look a day over thirty, and her body sure didn't look like she bared any children. "Thirty-five is not old."

"Easy for you to say, you're a man. Age doesn't matter." She said, turning toward him.

"It matters for a woman. Our clock runs a little faster than men. Our eggs have a shelf life, your sperm doesn't."

"Yeah, since you put it that way. I guess you are right." Darius agreed, massaging Jasmines firm breast.

"I've never made love in a bathtub." She whispered in his ear as she nibbled gently on his earlobe.

"Don't speak to soon." He whispered back, sliding his erect penis into her gently. She moaned, resting her head on his shoulder Jasmine began moving her hips, matching his rhythm, enjoying the sound of the splashing water and the deep penetration he was giving her at the same time. She rocked her hips in swirls sucking and kissing on his shoulder, as she rode him. They exchanged sweet whispers telling each other how much they loved one another. He wanted her this way for the rest of his life. Just as Jasmine reached her climax, she wondered if Darius truly knew how deep her love was for him. She would do any and everything possible to keep him happy, even if it means untying her tubes. She loved him unconditionally and wanted him to know that in every way possible.

Chapter Fourteen
Moving Forward

Jasmine felt like she was on an emotional rollercoaster, ending a marriage and at the same time starting a new relationship with Darius. Darius himself realized it was a lot on her plate for her to handle. He, himself was also adjusting to the event that had taken place in his life; one finding out Chandra had lied to him about being the father of her baby. But through it all he and Jasmine bond became more solid. They both realized even with all the chaos going on, they had never been happier in their lives, because they were together as one.

The two had enjoyed a passionate weekend together in Las Vegas, for her birthday. He had pulled out all the stops, and booked a fancy suite at the Wynn hotel. She felt like a queen being served. Having her bathwater drawn with rose pedals, riding in a limo, and wonderful dinners. He made love to her throughout the weekend in ways she never experienced with Eric. Sometimes she had to pinch herself to make sure she was not dreaming and that Darius was actually real.

As the sunlight peeked slightly through the curtains, Jasmine rolled over and looked at the clock. When she saw 8:30 am, she panicked, jumping out the bed, not believing she had overslept.

"Baby shit, I'm going to be late for my flight," Jasmine yelled out, tapping Darius who was sound asleep next to her.

"What happened?" He asked, gathering himself.

"Baby, it's already 8:30 am and my flight leaves at ten 'o'clock. Shit!" Jasmine still naked, ran to the bathroom getting into the shower. Today was the day; she was finalizing all the specifics of her divorce from Eric.

This was a very emotional day for her, but at the same time, a day that would bring closure to that chapter of her life; so she could move on with Darius.

*****

"I'm on the phone right now booking you a flight for noon." He informed her, admiring her through the massive glass shower door, with a slight grin on his face. She smiled at him feeling rushed, but she knew what that look meant.

"No, if I hurry I can probably make it."

"No baby, you're not going to make it. What's your attorney's number? I'll call for you and have the meeting pushed back."

"It's in my blackberry on the nightstand. Her name is Bernice Barnes. Eric is going to be hot, pushing the meeting back." Jasmine added. She hurried, drying off and rushing around the bathroom brushing her teeth. When she came out the bathroom, Darius was sitting on the edge of the bed with his laptop; typing.

"Okay baby, so your flight leaves at noon and your meeting has been pushed back to 4:00 pm."

"Thank you honey, you are the best." She smiled, clutching the towel around her chest.

"Are you sure you don't want me to fly to Sacramento with you?"

"I'm sure. I can do this by myself. I never pictured myself being divorced, but you never know what life has in store."

"I hear you. I was thinking…" He paused.

"Thinking about what?" She jumped in, searching through one of many shopping bags spread about the room. He had taken her on a shopping spree and she hit up Victoria's Secret as if they were going out of business. She had Darius pick out all the sexy underwear he wanted to see her in.

"I was thinking about us."

"What about us, honey?" He walked over and took her hand into his.

"I was thinking about you moving to LA with me. You can rent out your house."

"I can't now, baby. With my boys and the custody with Eric…I have to."

"They can come to LA, too. I have enough room for all of you. Think about it."

"Baby, I..."

"Just think about it."

"Eric will have a fit."

"Eric is no longer your husband after today."

"I'm just saying honey. I want us to be a family and be happy together."

"Family? What you already got me knocked up?" She laughed, trying to lighten the mood.

"And how would I do that, Jasmine?" He asked with a smirk on his face.

"I can have my tubes untied according to my doctor. I'm in my mid-thirties and my eggs are still good."

"You would do that for me? I mean I know you mentioned it before. You're serious?" She shook her head yes. "No, I couldn't let you do that. Didn't you tell me you went into cardiac arrest after you gave birth to Kai and the doctors had to revive you? Oh no baby, I would not want you to risk your life like that."

"My hearts fine and besides that was over eight years ago. The way you been rocking my world I'm surprised you haven't already put me in cardiac arrest." She joked. They both laughed.

"You are crazy." Darius shook his head pulling her into his bare chest, kissing her on her neck. "What you just said means a lot to me, that you'd even consider going through an operation to give me a child. We can discuss that later though. Umm, you smell good." He whispered, burying his head into her neck.

"And you smell like sex."

"So come and take another shower with me."

"Baby, I need to get packed."

"Alright, I'll let you slide this time. But I'm starting to get use to taking showers with you. I feel funny when you're not in here with me."

Since Jasmine had a few hours to kill, she turned on her laptop and started working on her latest novel.

"Check this out, baby." Jasmine waved for Darius to come over to the computer, just as he stepped out the bathroom with just a towel around his waist. Darius scanned the screen, reading her work.

"You just wrote all that?"

"Yes, remember I was telling you about writing this story."

The Write Lover

"Oh yeah. Wow, those few pages already got me hooked. You have skills baby girl."

"Thank you."

"Why don't we write it as a screenplay?"

"Oh, that's even a better idea," Jasmine said with excitement.

Chapter Fifteen
Its' Been Awhile

With much thought and research, Jasmine decided to have her tubes untied. Even though she knew there may be a possible risk to her health, she wanted to give Darius a biological child. It was a simple out-patient procedure and the doctor told her in his experience from treating other patients in the same situation as hers, the success rate for conception was over eighty percent. Wanting the gift of life to be a surprise for Darius, she blamed an unusual painful menstrual cycle, for not letting him go inside her. She used her oral skills to keep her man satisfied, during the healing period.

*****

Three weeks had past since the surgery and the doctor informed Jasmine she could resume having vaginal sex. It has been a total of five weeks since they had sex, and Jasmine was very horny anticipating his arrival. She had officially moved in with Darius. She was happy that Kai and Kyle adjusted well, to living with their dad until June, when the school year was over. It was hard for Jasmine not having her sons with her, but she knew it was best for them to stay in Sacramento because all their friends were there, and she didn't want to uproot them in the middle of the school year. Kyle and Kai loved spending weekends with her and Darius in LA, because they would always have a great time. Jasmine was relieved that everything was starting to get back to normal in her life.

"I'm home baby." Darius said when he walked through the door; from a three day literary business trip. Soft instrumental jazz was playing throughout the house.

"Hey honey." Jasmine responded coming around the corner in a red Victoria Secret teddy. He dropped his suitcase to the floor, at the sight of his beautiful and sexy lady. She seductively walked up to him, kissing him passionately. One month without sex was way to long and he needed her as bad as she needed him. Breaking the kiss to look her in the eyes, he said.

"I missed you." He whispered to her as he picked her up walking into the bedroom.

"I missed you more." She replied, before resuming her kiss. Jasmine had scented candles flickering throughout the bedroom. He gently put her down on the bed, undressing as fast as he could. Gently sucking on her nipples, she had a mild orgasm.

"Ah, shit, that feels so good." Come on and break me in." Jasmine said, reaching for his hardness and guiding it inside her. He felt her cradling his hardness, like a baby being cradled in its mother's womb. They moaned in unison as their level of passion rose. She was so wet that every time Darius would move his manhood in and out of her, there was a sucking sound.

"Ohhh…baby, my pussy is talking to you." She said in a whisper. Then she cried out loud, "Damn!" Her eyes rolled up in her head, and she began to speak in an unidentifiable language as the pleasures of having wonderful sex, consumed her luscious body. His joystick was moving in and out of her candy store like pistons on a sports car. Jasmine's hips began to gyrate faster and faster, and then she screamed out as her body tensed up. She shook uncontrollably, as a wave of an intense orgasm consumed her; just before going limp in a relax state. Darius was so glad she came, because he was on the verge of releasing himself. However, he wanted to work his woman from the back.

Turning her over in his favorite doggie position, he held on to her small waist as he re-entered her deep. She screamed out, balling up the sheets in her grasp. Her eyes were closed, and her mouth wide open, with a frown between her brows. It wasn't a frown from pain, but one of pure joy. He was putting in some great work, just the way she liked it. She was throwing it back at him, twirling her booty round and round like a tornado.

He began to grunt, as he repositioned his hands on her behind spreading her cheeks, looking down at his manhood covered with her cum and his pre-cum. The sight was bringing him closer and closer to an orgasm. She began to feel the head of his penis getting bigger, indicating her man was about to give her a cream filling.

"Oh yeah baby, I'm about to come." He said, just as he grunted and released his warm cum inside his woman. She screamed out, squirting and coming for a third time. Hot, sweaty and both breathing hard, they collapsed on the bed with him on her back. Trying to regain their normal breathing patterns, with his semi-hard manhood still inside her exclusive area, he reached around holding his woman close to him; with his hand cupping her right breast.

"We were at it for awhile, sexy lady."

Brooklen Borne

"I can't see the clock well enough, because you fucked me dizzy. All I want to do is go to sleep." Jasmine replied, falling into a deep slumber. Darius kissed her softly between her shoulder blades. The aroma of sex filled the air as the two exhausted lovers slept the night away, feeling ever so content.

Chapter Sixteen
Sister Talk

Jasmine and her sister Felecia sat on the floor in the great room, sorting through hundreds of pictures. They were putting together a collage for their mother's 65th birthday surprise party. Felecia was glad to hang out with her baby sister for a few days. She was still trying to adjust to Jasmine living in LA, and not being able to just stop by and see her whenever she wanted; like when she lived in Sacramento. It was going on midnight and they had been looking at photos for three straight hours.

"Oh My God!" Jasmine laughed, holding up the picture of Felecia when she was about eight years old wearing a lime green bellbottom outfit.

"I remember your ass tried to give me that ugly outfit, so mama could by you two outfits; instead of one." Felecia snatched the picture out of her hand taking a closer look at it, and laughing out of control, remembering that used to be her favorite.

"I loved that piece." Jasmine pulled herself up off the floor, laughing so hard she had to run to the bathroom.

"I know," Felecia yelled out, getting up off the floor and going to the kitchen to pour herself another glass of Merlot. She figured she'd just spend the night, since they were on their third bottle of wine.

"Damn. No more wine for me tonight. I can't keep my ass out the bathroom"

"You sure it's the wine?" Felecia asked, sipping on her refill. "You are looking thick in the hips."

"Shut up girl. I've been working out with my man, so I'm gaining a lot of muscle."

"Are you sure about that?"

"Yeah, Darius and I use condoms. We were very careful about that. I know my body. We did get it on one night, without protection, but I'd know if I was pregnant. I just had my period…wait a minute. What day is it?" Jasmine walked over to the calendar that hung on the wall in her kitchen."

"Ummm…it's June 3rd." Her sister informed her.

"Shit." Jasmine frantically flipped the calendar back scanning through May. "It's June already… shit…. my period didn't come for May. Oh, you got to be kidding me. The doctor said it could take a year for me to get pregnant after the surgery. Maybe I'm tripping, maybe it's just late."

"Or maybe you're just pregnant. Oh, I'm gonna be an auntie again." Felecia began clapping. Jasmine ran her hands through her hair, not caring if she messed up her fresh cut or not.

"I can't be pregnant. Not now!"

"Why? It's obvious that you and Darius are happy together. The boys like him, you guys have everything going on for yourselves."

"Yeah, but we are not married."

"And…like Darius wouldn't marry you tomorrow if you told him you were pregnant."

"I don't want that to be the reason he for us getting married."

The Write Lover

"Girl, please. You want me to run to the 24 hour CVS and get you a pregnancy test so you can stop stressing. It's probably a false alarm. You've been working out like a damn gladiator and sometimes when you work out a lot, your body will act a little funny."

"You have a point, but I'm still worried. If I'm pregnant, I've been drinking wine and I don't want anything to go wrong with the health of the baby. Darius would never forgive me."

"Damn "J", it's going to be alright. I'll go get a pregnancy test tomorrow and we will go from there."

After Jasmine and Felecia finished looking at the pictures, they retired to bed. The sister's slept together, like they did when they were little girls. As soon as Felecia head hit the pillow she was out. Jasmine tossed and turned, wondering if she could really be pregnant and if she was, how would she break the news to Darius? Finally, she fell asleep exhausted, as well.

The next morning, Jasmine was awakened by her cell phone ringing. She grabbed it off the nightstand, answering it irritated, knowing it was probably Eric bugging her as usual about the boys.

"Hello"

"Hey baby." Darius soothing voice came across.

"Hey sweetheart," She replied glancing at the clock, that read 7:45 am; happy to hear from him.

"Sorry to wake you up so early, but I can't sleep when you're not here."

"Aww Sweetie. I can't sleep either, unless you're wrapped in my arm. I wish you were here with me in Phoenix."

"Baby I um... just got a call from my mom. My favorite aunt is in the hospital in Florida and it's not looking to good, so I'm going to catch a red eye flight out tonight, to go see her."

"Oh, I'm sorry to hear that. You want me to fly out there and meet you?"

"No baby, I'll be fine. I don't want you to rush your visit with your sister. I'll be home in your loving arms in two days. Tell Felicia I said hi."

"I will honey." Felecia came into the bedroom, to Jasmine surprise. She thought her sister was still asleep.

"I got the test girl. Wake up." Jasmine sat up quickly, placing her index finger on her lips, for her sister to shut up.

"Dang, I'm sorry." Felecia responded, in a whisper; sitting on the bed, placing the pregnancy test on her lap.

"What test is your sister talking about?" Darius questioned.

"Oh um, she um…just said she wants to go test drive a Benz today. I'm going to go with her."

"Oh alright baby, well…I'll call you when I get to Florida, to let you know I made it safely."

"Okay baby. I love you."

"I love you too." Darius replied, just before hanging up.

"Sorry, but you covered up pretty good."

"Umm hmm." Jasmine yawned.

"I asked the clerk in the store what product I should buy and the clerk recommended this one. She said this is the brand she use to find out that she was pregnant. So this brand is your best bet."

"Thanks sis." She took a hold of the box, looking over the instruction; as she eased out the bed.

"You're welcome."

The Write Lover

"Seeing how I have to pee right now, I'm ready to do this." Following the directions on the box, it brought back memories of her doing this nine years ago. She stood at the sink counter with her arms crossed, waiting for the results. One line meant pregnant, two lines meant not pregnant. Jasmine came out the bathroom after reading the results. Her sister looked at her and noticed Jasmine's mixed reaction.

"Are you alright?" her sister asked.

"Yeah, I'm good."

"Well?"

"I'm pregnant," Jasmine sighed as a smiled crept on her face.

"Is this what you really want to do?" Her sister asked, looking very concerned.

"Yes, I love him so much. He's the real deal Felecia."

"I know he is but what about your health? After Kai, didn't the doctor say you shouldn't get pregnant again because you almost died during that delivery?"

"Yes, I had several tests done on my heart and I did a lot of research. I'm going to be just fine. I just didn't think it would happen this fast. Wow!"

"Call Darius and tell him." Felecia said excited.

"Not over the phone. I'll tell him when he come back home. He's on his way to Florida to see about his sick aunt."

"He's going to be so happy. Oh, I hope it's a girl and she looks just like me." Jasmine laughed, crawling back under the covers. She was so happy and looking forward to share the news with the love of her life.

Chapter Seventeen
Sad News

After seeing her sister off, early the next day Jasmine went back to bed. She couldn't get it out of her head that she was really pregnant. It took everything she had in her, not to tell Darius.

Her sleep was disrupted by the ringing of the phone. She reached for the phone on the nightstand, while trying to adjust her eyes as she looked at the caller ID; it was not Darius and the number was unrecognizable.

"Hello!"

"This is Trooper Foreman of the Florida State Police. May I speak to Ms. Jasmine Deveraux?"

"This is she."

"Ma'am, I'm calling to inform you that Mr. Darius Hamilton has been in a car accident. Your name and phone number was located in his jacket pocket with instructions to call you in case of an emergency."

"Oh My God!" Jasmine spoke loudly and hysterically, as she sat up in the bed.

"He's been in a car accident and has been transported to St. Luke's Hospital. The only information we have at this moment, ma'am, is that he's unconscious." The trooper replied. Jasmine began to cry. The trooper continued. "Ma'am, I have some information for you to write down."

"Yes just a minute, let me get a pen and paper." Jasmine replied sniffling, as she laid the phone down and fumbled in the nightstand draw looking for a pen and something to write on. After a few seconds, she picked the phone back up. "Okay, I'm ready to copy."

"Mr. Hamilton is at St. Luke's Hospital, the address is 4200 Belfort Road. That's four, two, zero, zero, B-E-L-F-O-R-T Road in Duval County in Jacksonville, Florida. The phone number there is 904-299-3700. Did you get that ma'am?"

"Yes I did, thank you sir."

"Okay ma'am, take care. Bye."

"Bye." Jasmine hung up the phone and called Darnell to inform him what had happened.

Seven Hours Earlier...

Darius had left LA on a flight to Jacksonville, Florida to see his aunt in the hospital where his family was going to meet up at. The doctors had only given her a few more days to live. She had been fighting breast cancer for over a year and she was losing the battle. She couldn't fight anymore. When Darius' plane touched down at Jacksonville International Airport around 5 a.m., he wanted to call Jasmine but didn't want to wake her; even though, she told him to do so. He decided he would give her a call later in the morning. After getting his luggage and making his way to the Hertz booth,

The Write Lover

he picked up his rental and proceeded to highway 95 South, heading to his parents' home. He was bopping his head to Paul Hardcastle's Jazz Masters on WSJF 105.5 when a car came out of nowhere and hit Darius from behind. His' car went into a spin doing a three-sixty, hitting a guardrail on the left side of the road before flipping four times down the highway. His car finally came to a rest on its wheels a quarter mile down the road from point of impact. The other driver's car hit the guardrail on the right side and flipped over into the embankment. The state troopers were on the scene in a matter of minutes. Someone had seen the accident take place and pulled over to call 911; before trying to assist the injured drivers.

Darius had suffered some head trauma and was unconscious. He also had a broken left arm, broken right leg, three broken ribs, a pierced lung, and some internal bleeding. The other driver, a fifty-year-old white male from Ft. Lauderdale, was also taken to the local hospital to check his injuries and given a Breathalyzer test. His blood alcohol count was a 1.0, well over the .08 legal limit. He only suffered a few scrapes and minor bruises. After being released from the hospital, the individual that caused the accident was later charged with drunk driving and reckless driving, and they determined he was traveling at a speed of 110 mph.

*****

Jasmine caught the first flight she could get out of Los Angeles, to Florida. She called Darius's mom and gave her the details of his accident and what hospital he was at. His mother Barbara, and Jasmine had hit it off from the very first time they met a few months back. Barbara welcomed Jasmine into their family and was happy that Chandra was out the picture. Barbara told Jasmine she had never seen her son happier in his life.

When Jasmine reached the hospital, she was met by Barbara and Norman, his father. When Barbara saw Jasmine, she quickly walked over to Jasmine while Norman stayed by Darius' side, but still acknowledging Jasmine's presence.

"I'm so glad you could make it baby." Barbara said as she embraced Jasmine.

"I charted a plane and got here as quickly as I could." Jasmine responded as her eyes filled with tears ready to roll down her cheeks at any given second. She couldn't hold the tears back, any longer when she saw all those tubes hooked up to Darius. She stepped out the room and began to cry. Norman left Darius' bedside to join Barbara in consoling Jasmine. After a minute or two, she regained her composure then Norman and Barbara filled her in on the latest news the doctor had reported to them. The doctor had said Darius was in stable condition and his brain waves were excellent. He also mentioned that Darius had to be in great physical shape to withstand such a horrific accident; however, they only gave him a sixty percent chance of a full recovery. Jasmine began to cry again.

"Okay baby, now you have to keep it together. We all have to stay strong for him; he really needs us now," Barbara said, taking some tissue out her purse and wiping the tears from Jasmine checks.

After a few hours, Jasmine told Barbara and Norman to go home and get some rest; she'd stay by his side just in case he woke up. They exchanged hugs and kisses and departed for some much needed rest. Shortly after Darius' parents left the room, a nurse aide entered the room with a pillow and blue flimsy blanket for Jasmine. She thanked the attendant and took the items, and tried to make herself comfortable in the uncomfortable chair that adorned most every hospital room in America.

   She sat at Darius bedside for three days straight, only leaving for an hour to shower and change clothes, and then she would return. She was afraid that he'd wake up and she wouldn't be there. Most of the staff at the hospital was fans of Darius and Jasmine's and loved reading their books; so they let Jasmine take a shower where the doctor's took theirs. Her heart was broken to see the man she loved fighting for his life. All the tubes and machines beeping around him drove her crazy. She was determined to stay by his side until he woke up.

   His brother Darnell came and sat with her and Darius for a few hours; before leaving to go see his aunt. With Darius in ICU and their aunt in a hospital only a few miles away in hospice care, this was a lot for the family to handle.

   She was holding the best information in her heart to tell Darius when he woke up; that she was pregnant. She was praying that Darius would wake up soon so she could share the joyous news. She knew Darius was devastated when he found out Chandra had an abortion, killing a child he always wanted. Jasmine wanted to ring Chandra's neck with her bare hands for hurting him that way. Darius was not the same person for many weeks after that ordeal, he withdrew in every way. He canceled interviews and stopped writing books, which was his passion. He had sunk into a deep depression, even withdrawing from sex. Jasmine had suggested he see a therapist, but after Darius never made an appointment to see one, she just backed off and never brought it up again. She had made up her mind about not wanting any more children, but she loved Darius so much and the love they shared was so deep she would give him the world. She'd never forget the day she told him she was serious about wanting the surgery. His eyes grew big, along with a huge smile. He couldn't believe she would consider doing that, but dismissed the idea and told her he did not want her to risk her health in having the surgery. He never forgot the feeling that came over him when she told him that her heart had stopped when she was giving birth to her son, Kai.

Behind Darius' back, she spoke with the top specialist about her heart condition and ran several tests the past few months on her heart, and the doctors assured her it would be safe for her to get pregnant. She was overjoyed and never thought she'd want another child so badly. She could not wait to see the beautiful child they created together in love.

She sat on the end of Darius' bed, rubbing his feet with lotion, when a different nurse's aide than the one earlier walked in the room with a basin of warm water and a couple of towels.

"Mrs. Hamilton, I need to give your husband a bath."

"Oh, I'm not his wife." Jasmine laughed. "But I liked the sound of being called his last name. I'm his unofficial fiancé."

"I'm so sorry. You've been here every day taking care of him… I thought you were his wife."

"One day sweetie." Jasmine said with a smile, standing up. "But I can bathe him."

"I know that's right." The nurse laughed. "But I think I should do it, because if my supervisor find out that I let you bathe Mr. Hamilton they will fire me."

"Don't worry, if anyone say anything to you, come and get me. I'll get them straight. Also, I use to be a nurse's aide right out of high school." They both laughed.

"Great! Okay. Just let me know if you need anything else." The aide said, walking out the room closing the door. Jasmine turned around and pulled the curtain around Darius' bed for extra privacy. "Okay baby, I'm going to clean you up now." She whispered, like a mother over her child. Pulling the sheet back, she removed his nightgown and began sponging Darius' body, working around all the tubes and IV's. The only question in the back of her mind was how long he would be in a coma.

"I can't be bathing you like this baby, its turning me on." Jasmine giggled, trying to lift her spirits as she proceeded to wash Darius's body with a warm sponge. After washing each part of his body, she dried him off and then she applied lotion to his whole body. She retrieved some clean water and shaved his face. She even changed his linens and gown, tapping into the days when she did this for a living. When the aide came back into the room, she was impressed.

"Wow! You did great"

"Do you think he can hear me when I talk to him?" Jasmine asked, as she sat in the chair next to the bed, taking a hold of his hand.

"I've heard all kinds of miracle stories about people being in coma's, remembering what people had said to them, when they awakened. Keep talking; I think it's great that you are here for him. After all you've done, he better ask you to be his wife." Jasmine laughed.

Brooklen Borne

Holding his hand firmly, Jasmine said, "I hope so because we are expecting a baby and he has no idea. I can't wait to tell him."

"Wow! Congratulations, tell him now." The aide said, grabbing the soiled towels and leaving the room. Jasmine took a deep breath as she looked at him.

"Honey, you have to wake up." She began to cry, but she wiped her tears away quickly. "Please baby. So many people have come to see you, your brothers and so many other relatives. I didn't know you had such a big family, and they all knew who I was too. I guess you've been running your mouth about me, huh?" She giggled. "Your brother Darnell will be back tomorrow. But I told all of them not to worry, that I would be right here with you. Baby, wake up." She leaned closer to him and whispered in his ear. "Did you hear what I said earlier baby? I'm pregnant! You have to wake up and get better so you can help me. I can't do this by myself. I won't dare let you leave me like this." She broke down, crying deeply and burying her head into his chest. When she heard the monitor going off, she jumped back thinking she had pressed on one of the tubes too hard. When she looked up and saw Darius's eyes fluttering open and closed.

"Oh My God! She gasped. "Nurse! She yelled out. "Somebody, please... She spoke panicky as she pressed the button next to his bed; for a nurse to come. He's waking up." At that moment a nurse and a couple of doctor's charged in the room telling Jasmine to leave the room while they tended to Darius. Jasmine paced back and forth in the hallway, worried out of her mind hoping he was alright; while praying silently. When Jasmine turned around, she almost walked into Chandra, who was standing right in front her.

The Write Lover

"How come no one told me Darius was in an accident? I had to hear it on the news." Chandra spoke in an elevated voice.

"You really need to lower your voice." Jasmine told her as she stepped back, surprised to see her. She was the last person Jasmine expected to see. "What are you doing here any way?"

"Excuse me, I was his wife. You're just his girlfriend or shall I say mistress. I have the right to be here."

"That's right Chandra, you took the words right out of my mouth; you was his wife. You're probably the last person Darius cares to see."

Chandra lifted her hand and pointed her finger in Jasmine's face. "Bitch, you aren't nothing but a home wrecker, stealing my husband. I'm going to bust your ass, right here in this hospital."

"Is that right? Just jump then; don't talk about it, be about it." Then Jasmine thought. *Shit! I'm pregnant. I can't risk losing my child, messing with this bitch.*

"Ladies! I'm going to have to ask you both to leave if you cannot keep it down. This is the ICU….please control yourselves." The doctor said, coming out of Darius's room.

"I apologize. Is he alright?" Jasmine asked.

"He's not in a coma anymore and we have removed the breathing tube; he is breathing on his own. The nurse is stabilizing him right now. He's trying to talk, but he's having some difficulty. Which one of you is Jasmine?" the doctor asked.

"I am." Jasmine spoke up, looking at Chandra; as if to say, *I wish you would say something.*

"Mr. Hamilton asked for you."

"Can I see him?" Chandra added demandingly.

Brooklen Borne

"Not at the moment ma'am." The doctor informed. Jasmine didn't waste another second. She hurried into the room to find Darius sitting up in the bed, coughing and the nurse holding an oxygen mask, over his mouth. When he looked up and saw Jasmine entering the room, his eyes lit up and he pushed the mask away.

"Ja…jas…mine." Darius could not stop coughing.

"Baby, shh. Just take the oxygen. I'm right here."

"Mr. Hamilton, please breathe into the mask." The nurse demanded. After a few minutes, the nurse removed the mask and Darius smiled at Jasmine as he reached for her hand. "Where am I? What happened?"

"Baby, you were in a car accident. You've been in the hospital for a week now in a coma." She explained.

"Wow, the last thing I remember was traveling on 95 towards my parents' house, when there was this loud noise. I don't remember anything else after that. I had a dream we were home in bed, and you told me you were pregnant." Darius coughed some more. "I'm trippin'." He grimaced in pain when he tried to lift his arm. Jasmine's mouth dropped open.

"What did you say about your dream?" She asked, as the nurse walked around to the other side of the bed, pushing buttons on his IV. Responding, a little louder than a whisper, he said. "It was just a dream."

"Darius…baby…maybe you were dreaming, but some of that dream is true." Darius sat up in bed as he tried to reposition himself, not really paying attention to what Jasmine had said. Then it hit him.

"What you just said?"

She took a hold of Darius's hand, placing it on her stomach. "I'm pregnant, baby." Tears traveled down the side of her face, and Darius looked at her confused as he gently held onto her hand.

"I thought your tubes were tied?" Darius began to cough.

"I had them untied. That's why I couldn't give you any. I wanted to surprise you with the gift of life; a biological gift from me to you." Darius eyes began to water, with the understanding on the level of love Jasmine had for him.

"I'm happy honey, so happy. Your carrying my child…I'm the happiest man in the world." He said in a weak voice. At that moment, Chandra barged in the room.

"I'm so glad you're okay."

"What in the hell are you doing here?" Darius asked, still not sounding like his self.

"I'm your ex-wife; I have the right to be here." Chandra replied with an attitude.

"I'm fine. Thanks for coming, now please leave." Chandra sucked her teeth, looking at Jasmine. She rolled her eyes approaching the other side of Darius bed, ignoring his request.

"Look Darius, I just want to apologize for everything. I have asked God several times to forgive me for what I did to you. I'm so sorry and when I heard about your accident, my heart stopped. I mean I just wanted to tell you face to face I'm very sorry. I need you to forgive me. I'm trying to change my life and be a better person. I have a son now and I realized that I need to be a better person. I also realize, the dumb decisions I've made in our relationship and I just wanted to say sorry from the bottom of my heart."

"That's good to hear Chandra." Darius responded, sounding clearer.

"Do you forgive me?" She asked, as tears fell from her eyes. Jasmine bit down on her bottom lips, wishing Chandra would just leave. Jasmine could not stand the sight of her.

"Yes Chandra, I forgive you." Darius responded, looking over at Jasmine, knowing she was uncomfortable.

"Good. Now I'm sure there's something that you need to apologize to me about." Chandra said, propping her hand on her hip, swinging her head around and staring at Jasmine.

"Excuse me?" Jasmine replied.

"Darius and I would still be married if it weren't for you."

"Chandra, you need to leave. This is not the time or the place." Darius intervened.

"I got this honey." Jasmine said as she stood up. "He just came out of a coma, not even a good hour. You heard the doctor, say stop the madness and you barge your way in here and continue to bring drama. With that being said, in a New York minute, if you don't get out this room, I'm going to put everything on the line and commence, going straight street on you." Darius reached out for Jasmine's hand.

"Baby you're pregnant, you need to clam down." Chandra's eyes grew wide at that statement.

"Pregnant!"

"Yeah bitch, and this time it's really his. Now please leave." Chandra gave them both an evil look, before storming out the room.

*****

The Write Lover

Eight weeks had passed and he finally had his cast removed off his arm. His broken ribs and bruised body was healing well. Darius was making a remarkable recovery. Unfortunately, his aunt passed away and he wasn't able to attend the funeral. Her home coming was two days prior to him being released from the hospital.

Darius was the happiest man on earth and thanked God every day that he was alive and well, and that Jasmine was going to be the mother of his child. A day did not go by when he didn't rub and kiss Jasmine's stomach. He would even talk to her stomach late at night, when there were lying down and Jasmine said she could feel the baby flutter. Though she was barely showing, her belly was beginning to harden and she could no longer wear her favorite jeans. But she had a lot of stylish maternity wear, to still look fabulous in..

"Baby, guess what I just got in the mail?" Darius said out loud, walking back in the house and peeling an envelope open. Jasmine swung her chair around turning her attention from her computer. She was busy working on her novel, *In the Naked City*.

"What hun?"

"An invitation to the gala, it was a charity event called "Being Homeless Is Not an Option. It's named after our collaboration novel. "

"Oh that's nice. That's the charity we donate to, right?"

"Yes, it's next month. It's going to be nice. A lot of celebrities will be attending. I even heard Maxwell supposed to perform and I know how much you love Maxwell."

"Oh, I hope you don't think I'm going."

"Yes I do and why not?"

Brooklen Borne

"Baby, I don't have anything to wear, let alone standing in heels for hours, right now with my feet swelling up already by the end of the day. I'm pregnant, with child."

"You have some of the most stylish name brand maternity clothes on the market; so don't try to play a brutha." Darius said with a laugh.

"I'll think about it."

"Oh no, you're coming." He demanded, knowing he had a big surprise for her, already set up.

"So now you are telling me and not asking me huh?" She laughed, pulling herself out her chair walking to the kitchen. Darius followed behind her, eyeballing her butt, which seemed to be growing like her stomach and he loved it.

"What's up with the attitude?"

"I don't have an attitude." She yawned. "Oh, I just got an email from my sister, and I'm gonna fly to Sacramento next weekend. A good friend of the family is getting married."

"Okay, so you can jump and fly to Sacramento to go to a wedding, but you can't come to the gala."

"I didn't say I wasn't going. I said I'll think about it." Jasmine slammed the cabinet closed as she grabbed the box of Wheat thins.

"You don't want me to come with you?"

"No, I'm sure you don't want to go to a wedding."

"What's that supposed to mean?" He asked, not liking the way she said wedding. Jasmine was hoping that Darius would have proposed to her by now since she was pregnant, and it was important to her to be married before the baby came. But Darius never even mentioned marriage, and she didn't want to nag him or bring it up, especially with everything he had gone through.

The Write Lover

"Nothing, I'm going to the gala." She replied, leaving out the kitchen and shoving a hand full of Wheat Thins in her mouth. Darius stood there crossing his hands over his chest taking a deep breath. He knew why Jasmine stressed the word wedding. He knew she wanted to get married before the baby came.

Chapter Eighteen
A Sprinkle of Class

Darius and Jasmine were on their way to the big gala in downtown Los Angeles given by Ervin "Magic" Johnson. This event was announced on the radio and television stations, local and nationwide. Who's who was going to be in attendance, from multimillionaire businessmen/women to "A" list movie and television personalities to your favorite singers and rappers. The gala was a charity event called, "Being Homeless Is Not an Option." The gala, was to raise money for the homeless shelters in the greater Los Angeles area, so individuals and families can have decent clothes to wear on job interviews and home placements. This event was going to be a big deal for Darius and Jasmine because it was their charity, which the two started a year ago. They had already donated half a million dollars of their own money.

The limo pulled up in front of the Mandarin Hotel on Sunset Boulevard in West Hollywood. They walked toward the lobby, looking like the beautiful couple they are. Jasmine had on a teal green, floor length, strapless dress, giving just enough exposure to reveal a little cleavage. Even though she was pregnant, she wore one and half inch heels and still had her sexy swagger. Jasmine looked glamorous. Darius of course wore a black tux, black shirt and black bow tie with black alligator shoes. It seemed their presence commanded all eyes on them when they walked into the grand ballroom, and were escorted to their table. There was whispering throughout the crowd, how wonderful the two looked. When they arrived at their table, Jasmine was happily surprise to see her sister and other friends there. She began to cry as she hugged each of them. Shortly thereafter the food was being brought out to the tables. Everyone was having a great time and talking about future projects and endeavors, when Magic Johnson walked out to the center of the stage. Everyone applauded Magic's appearance. He spoke into the microphone and with his famous known smile.

"I would like to thank everyone for coming out tonight to support this great charity. Is everyone having a good time?" The audience applauded and a few screamed out, "Yeah." Magic continued, "As you may know, this charity was developed by two well known authors, Mr. Darius Hamilton and Ms. Jasmine Deveraux." Magic was interrupted, when the audience broke out in applause again.

Jasmine leaned over to Darius and asked, "Do we have to go on stage?" Jasmine didn't really like being in the spotlight.

"I hope not." He replied, with a slight grin.

"I know that grin. He's going to call us up." Jasmine whispered in Darius' ear. No sooner than she got the words out of her mouth good, Magic Johnson called for them to come onto the stage.

"Baby, that's our que." He said, as he took a hold of her hand.

"I knew it big head," She replied, jokingly. Once on stage, Darius shook Magic's hand and gave him a hug before taking the microphone. Magic walked around Darius to give Jasmine a hug and positioned her closer to Darius as he began to speak.

"I would also like to thank everyone in attendance for this special event. This has been a long time coming and I would like to thank the Magic Man for putting this all together. Not only was everyone asked to assist in supporting this charity event, but I need you all to witness something special. Could Mr. Brian McKnight and Kem, please join us on stage." The audience began to applaud and the women, including Jasmine, were screaming. As the two soulful singers made their way to where Darius and Jasmine stood, she couldn't believe that two of her favorite singers gave her a hug and a kiss and were standing right next to her. Darius began to speak again.

"I would like to give out a life-time achievement award to a very special person."

"Hold up. You can't do that without, our other boy on stage with us." Brian McKnight interrupted, looking at Darius and Kem who co-signed on Brian's remark. Then Kem approached the microphone and asked Maxwell to join them. The room immediately erupted with screams and applauses as Maxwell began to sing, *"A Woman's Worth"* as he walked on stage. Brian and Kem joined in on the song as the three soulful singers surrounded Jasmine and serenaded her.

"Fellas, that's my woman, what are you all doing?" Darius blurted over the microphone. The audience giggled and laughed. Jasmine was laughing and blushing at the same time. She was on cloud nine, and enjoying every second of it.

Brooklen Borne

"Well Darius, what are you going to do brother?" Magic yelled out from the audience. Darius looked at Magic with a smirk and everyone began laughing again.

"Well, before I was interrupted...I was going to give out this award." Brian, Kem and Maxwell stopped singing and waved their hands jokingly at Darius as they walked to the back of the stage; the audience chuckled. Jasmine's attention was divided between looking at the singer's walk away and Darius by her side. You could still hear women giving their love calls to the three singers who were now standing and chillin' at the back of the stage.

The house lights went down as a bluish white spot light shown on Darius and Jasmine. She looked around, as if to say what is going on? The place became so quiet you could have heard a pin drop. Darius turned to Jasmine and said, as Kem started singing" in the background, *Back in My Life*.

"I would like to honor you with this token, for your hard work, dedication and sacrifice you've made since I've known you. We have collaborated on many projects so I would like to ask you a question...would you?"

"Would I what baby?" Jasmine asked, looking Darius in his eyes with such love.

"Would you marry me?" He sincerely asked, dropping down to one knee while opening a blue velvet box. The spotlight made the ring bling, as he removed it from the elegant casing.

Jasmine stood there speechless with her hand covering her mouth, as tears traveled down the cheeks of her flawless face. A female voice yelled out, "Honey if you don't, I will." The audience broke out in laughter. Jasmine frantically shook her head, indicating a yes answer. After putting the ring on her shaking finger, the house lights came back on and he stood up, giving her a loving embrace, accompanied with a passionate kiss. Magic Johnson smiled as he handed Jasmine two dozen long stemmed assorted roses. Kem continued to sing the song. Jasmine was still in shock, crying and clinging on Darius for dear life. When it came to Jasmine, there was no limit.

Three Months Later...

Their love for one another had survived the test of time. Now they were going to make it official. Only a few close friends and family were flown to Hawaii to witness the union of Darius Hamilton and Jasmine Deveraux.

When the guest and wedding party arrived at the Kahului Airport in Maui, they were greeted by big smiles; hugs and each person received a beautiful flower Lei before being escorted to an awaiting limousine. Each guest gasped for air when they arrived at the Four Seasons Resort Maui at Wailea. The resort and view was breathtaking; something right out of a romance novel or movie. The sun was setting and the place was lit up. A light breeze came off the Pacific Ocean to play with the palm trees before putting each guest in the island spirit. It was just a beautiful introduction to the couples' special occasion. Each guest suite had a big bowl of fresh fruit, two bottles of champagne, and a personal hand written note from Darius and Jasmine welcoming everyone to their special celebration.

The following evening, Darius and Jasmine had the most beautiful sunset wedding on the beach. He wore a white linen two piece, with the buttons open partially exposing his sexy hairless chest. She wore an off white wedding gown that had a sheer, see through top; except for the breast area. The rest of the front was laced with small off-white pearls and the back of the gown donned a semi long train. Her veil was from the same sheer material, that made up the shoulder and chest are of the gown, playing peek-a-boo, that covered her beautiful face; with a touch of make-up to enhance her already flawless beauty..

The ceremony and reception was held on one of the Four Seasons' private beach. While the couple was exchanging their wedding vows, they personally wrote to one another, Essence Magazine was snapping photos, capturing the couples' very special day. The back drop was indescribably breath taking with emerald mountains stretching into the cloudless sky and a picturesque waterfall singing its' naturally soothing song for all to enjoy. The guests were treated to a fabulous traditional Hawaiian luau and Polynesian show. The beautiful women and the handsome hulky dancers wowed the beautiful couple and special guests with their traditional native dance.

Once the dancers completed their show, the guests were treated to another special guest. Tank, came from behind a palm tree and serenaded the couple with," Amazing," off his CD, "Now or Never". Jasmine and Darius danced to the song, giving each other kisses while everyone watched the lovely couple.

"You've made me the happiest man alive." He whispered, as they slowed danced.

"I love you baby." She whispered back, resting her head against his chest.

"I love you too!" A few hours had passed, when Jasmine said.

The Write Lover

"Hun, I'm tired, and my feet hurt. I just want to get out of here and lay down. The baby's been kicking me all day."

"Alright honey." He gently placed his arm around her waist, walking over to the DJ table, asking him to lower the music and motioned the DJ to hand him the microphone.

"Hello, family and friends. Jasmine and I want to thank you all for sharing our special day. Everyone drink, eat, and be merry. My wife is understandably tired and we are going to retire for the night." Family and friends moaned in disappointment, then cheered and clapped, as the couple walked over to the table where Jasmine's sister Felecia and her two sons, Kyle and Kai, were comfortably sitting.

"Sis, you are the most beautiful pregnant bride I've ever seen." Felecia smiled wiping a tear from her eye, standing up giving her little sister a hug. "Take care of my sister." Felecia said to Darius as she hugged him."

"The best care there is." He replied.

"Hey boys, mommy's really tired. I'm going to go lay down. You mind your aunt and I'll see you in the morning."

"Okay mom." They both said in unison, giving Jasmine hugs and kisses.

"Darius are you still going to take us scuba diving tomorrow." Kyle asked, as Kai looked on; with excitement.

"Yep, just us guys; no girls allowed."

"Yeah!" The two boys cheered. Jasmine was relived her sons had warmed up to Darius so well. It filled her heart with joy. The newlyweds said their good-byes to the rest of the immediate family before disappearing back to the luxury beach house. Jasmine was just a little over six months, and her belly was poking out big time now. Sex was beginning to be a challenge and had to get more creative. She was often tired by the end of the day. Darius lifted Jasmine off her feet as they arrived at the door.

"Can you carry my fat butt?" She joked, laughing as she held onto his neck.

"You're not fat, you're pregnant and you're still light as a feather to me. You know your man is strong baby. I have to carry you over the threshold."

"Aww you're so sweet." He kissed her softly as they entered the fancy beach house filled with lit candles and rose petals covering the floors and bed as he requested. Jasmine was in awe of the ambience. She kicked off her shoes as he gently sat her down on the end of the bed, kneeling between her legs, lifting up her gown and removing her garter belt on her upper thigh.

"Oh, we were suppose to throw that to all the single men, huh?" She asked.

"Yeah, but it's mine now." He said smiling. Jasmine laughed, pushing him back.

"Hold up baby. I have to pee." She giggled. He helped her to her feet, assisting Jasmine with the clamps on the back of her gown as she slid out of it wearing only her white satin slip. She wobbled off to the bathroom while he admired her shaped plumped booty.

"Umm, look at all that ass."

"Shut up!" She shouted, just before entering the bathroom. Darius began to loosen his bow tie, removing his shirt. Stripping down to his boxers, he slid in the bed awaiting his bride. When she came out the bathroom, she had let her pretty, black hair down and washed off her make-up, letting her natural beauty show. Jasmine had decided to grow out her hair for the wedding and the birth of their baby. She looked just as stunning with long as she did with short hair.

"Come here baby." He whispered. Jasmine crawled into the bed next to him as their lips met and their warm bodies pressed against each others. Jasmine rested her head on Darius warm firm chest, yawning. He knew she was tired and had a long action packed day. Darius kissed her softly on her forehead.

"I love you baby. Rest and get some sleep."

"You don't want any on your wedding night?" She whispered.

"Baby, I know you're tired and laying here with you in the bed as my wife, is more than enough." She gave him a kiss before turning over on her other side.

"Well, since that dick is officially mine, I want some on this official day." They giggled. He kissed her between her shoulder blades, gently massaging her breast, belly and derriere; before entering her from the rear. She was wet and ready. "Ummm baby!" She moaned in a whisper.

The Next Morning...

Jasmine was still sleeping like a baby and Darius didn't bother her. He kissed her on the forehead and went to pick up Kai and Kyle as promised, to take them snorkeling. When he arrived at their hotel room, Kai and Kyle were already waiting at the door, anxious to get going. Darius informed Felecia that he'd have them back in a few hours.

Jasmine finally pulled herself out of the bed when the sun light peeked through the curtain, and forced her to get up. The baby was rolling around in her stomach, kicking the mess out of her insides. She was happy to see that Darius had already ordered room service and set up the table for her. He was so thoughtful, a plate of fruit with all her favorites: blueberry pancakes, orange juice, turkey bacon, and a handwritten note that read: *Enjoy breakfast Mrs. Hamilton. Love your husband. I love you baby.* Jasmine heart smiled as she read it, making a quick trip to the bathroom. She then sat down in front of all the delicious food and ate until the baby stopped kicking. She laughed; rubbing her belly knowing the baby was full and probably went to sleep. Jasmine silently prayed that she was having a girl. Darius decided that it would be best for them not to find out the sex of the baby, so they could be surprised on the day of delivery. She agreed with Darius because she found out the sex of both of her boys before they were born, so she was excited about this new experience of not knowing.

After showering, she took out her personal stationary from her computer bag and sat at the desk. She wanted to write Darius a letter, to express how much she loved him, and the blessing of this baby. She wasn't sure what had came over her to write him this letter, but something in her heart told her to put pen to paper.

When Darius and the boys finished snorkeling, he took them to get ice cream. He was having a blast with Kyle and Kai, enjoying playing the new "official" step daddy role. It was fun just as he thought it would be. The boys loved having him in their lives. Darius knew how important it was to Jasmine that they functioned as one unit. The first few months were hard when they started spending time together, the boys would always bring up their father and sit in between Darius and Jasmine. But now it had been over a year and those days were long gone.

The Write Lover

"So do you want us to call you dad now?" Kai asked Darius as they slurped ice cream heading back to the beach house.

"No Kai, you don't have to call me dad," Darius laughed.

"You make my mom really happy," Kai added.

"Do I?"

"Yeah," Kyle interjected, "She laughs and smiles all the time now."

"Well, I love your mother very much."

"Are you going to hurt my mother, like our daddy did?" Kyle asked looking over at Darius.

"No Kyle, I will never do anything to hurt your mother." As they approached the beach house, they saw Jasmine standing in the doorway, watching them walk up. He couldn't help but notice her stunning beauty and how the yellow sundress complimented her complexion. She was practically glowing. Her hair flowed and bounced off her shoulders. She greeted them with a big smile.

"Well, if it isn't my favorite three men." Jasmine said in a cheerful tone. She gave Darius a soft kiss on his lips and then turned her attention to her boys, kissing both of them. "Where's my ice cream?" She asked with her hands on her hips.

"We were gonna get you some, but it's so hot it would have melted before we got it home momma." Kai explained.

"I'm joking. I had ate a wonderful breakfast; thanks to my sweetie. So did you all have fun snorkeling?"

"Yeah, we saw a lot of tropical fish, starfish and seahorse's. It was fun ma!" Kyle said with excitement.

"You should go next time, momma." Kai added.

"Maybe I will baby."

"We had fun." Darius said, walking inside. "I'm going to take a shower baby."

"Okay honey." Jasmine showed the boys to their room. She had already had their clothes laid out on the bed. She instructed them to shower and get dressed so they all could meet up with family and friends. Jasmine's well-mannered sons followed her directions as she made her way back to the bedroom. Darius was full speed ahead in the shower. The hot steam filled the bathroom and fogged the mirror when Jasmine walked in.

"Thanks for taking the boys snorkeling baby."

"You don't have to thank me. I enjoyed it. You know Kai asked me if I wanted him to call me dad?"

"Wow he did?" Jasmine said surprised, watching him rinse the soap off his body.

"Yeah, I told him he didn't have to. I was surprised myself." Jasmine leaned against the counter watching Darius' every move, wishing she could hop in the shower and attack him.

"Ummm, I'm one lucky lady." She sighed, watching him dry off. Even though she was in the late stages of her pregnancy, she still wanted to jump Darius' bones, but she restrained herself knowing her boys were in the next room.

"It's on tonight." She whispered in his ear, grabbing his butt, like he always did to her. He laughed wrapping the towel around his waist.

"You are crazy girl."

"You love it daddy." She replied, winking her eye at him, as she turned leaving out the bathroom.

Chapter Nineteen
The Gift of Life

"Wake up baby." Jasmine franticly shook Darius.

"Yeah, what's wrong hun? What time is it?" He replied, trying to gather himself looking over at the clock.

"Its 2am, I think it's time baby. I've been having some serious pains for more than five hours now. I think the baby is ready to meet mommy and daddy." Realizing what Jasmine just said, he leaped out the bed like a jack-in-the box, running around the room and searching for his clothes to put on, while babbling about nothing.

"Honey! honey!" Jasmine yelled out to him laughing, at his silliness despite the pain she was having. She had never seen him so un-cool and panicky before. She continued laughing in between the pains.

"Okay baby I'm ready, let's go!"

"Baby, just as long as you don't get out the car." She replied.

"Shit!" Darius said looking at his attire; he had everything inside out. "Come on baby, let's go." He said, picking up Jasmine's hospital bag while taking a hold of her arm and helping her out the door to the car.

Brooklen Borne

Speeding down the 405 highway in their smoked grey, S63 AMG Mercedes Benz, humming to the hospital with his hazards flashing, Darius made his own fast lane, as if they were in Germany on the autobahn. Even though he was moving at a high rate of speed, he was still being a safe driver. He pressed the blue tooth button on the steering wheel to call her parents to inform them he and Jasmine were on their way to the hospital, but the answering machine picked up. He then called her father's cell, and to his surprise her father picked up on the first ring.

"We're on our way to the hospital. Jasmine's been having pains and we thinks it's time for the baby to come."

"We're already on the road coming down to see you all."

"You still have the information for the hospital we're going to and the doctor's name, right?"

"Yeah, we have everything. We'll see you at the hospital."

"I love you guys." Jasmine interjected

"We love you too baby."

"Okay, we'll see you all at the hospital." Darius disconnected and called his brother.

"What's up man?" Darnell answered, still half asleep.

"We're on our way to the hospital. I think Jasmine is going to have the baby."

"Okay little brother, I'll get mom up and we'll meet you at the hospital shortly."

"Mom?" Darius replied with a crinkle on his forehead, making sure he heard his brother right.

"Yeah, she flew in late last night, and she wanted to surprise you and Jasmine this morning. I guess she is going to get the surprise." Darnell laughed.

The Write Lover

"Alright little brother, we'll meet you at the hospital."

"Alright! See you there."

"Did you call my sister?" Jasmine asked blowing, trying to control the contraction pain

"Yeah baby, I left her a voicemail; remember she is out of town. I'll give her another call later."

"Alright sweetheart!"

"How are you doing?" Darius asked, alternating his attention between the road and Jasmine.

"The pains are still close and strong, but otherwise I'm fine." When they arrived at the emergency entrance Darius jumped out, leaving the drivers' door open while retrieving a wheel chair for Jasmine. He rushed her inside to the nurses' station.

"Ma'am, my wife is having a baby and the pain is coming often." Darius said in a semi-frantic state. A nurse's assistant who was standing by the desk, was directed by a heavy set black woman behind the desk, probably her boss, to put Jasmine in room 203B.

"Sir, you need to fill out some forms." The lady behind the desk yelled out to Darius. He stopped in his tracks from following Jasmine into the room and returned to retrieve the forms. When Darius walked over to the desk to get the forms, another assistant who appeared to be in her early thirties was sitting next to the heavy set woman. She noticed the famous author in front of her.

"Oh my God, it's Darius Hamilton, the famous author." The heavy set lady began to laugh when she took a good look at Darius' attire. Not caring what the two ladies said or did, Darius' concern was with Jasmine as he began filling out the forms. He quickly walked to the room were Jasmine was being cared for.

"Baby, I'm going to move the car. I'll be right back."

"Okay, hurry back." He kissed her on the lips and rushed out the door.

"How are you doing Mrs. Hamilton?" The doctor asked.

"Get this baby out of me and then I will answer that question truthfully. I'm not sure what to say feeling like this." She replied, as she wobbled from the bathroom wearing the traditional hospital gown.

The doctor laughed as Darius and a nurse's aide helped Jasmine onto the bed. The doctor held small talk with her, while Darius washed his hands and the nurse prepped Jasmine for an examination. She put her feet in the stirrups and the doctor began her initial examination.

"Hmm Mrs. Hamilton, you are about seven centimeters, so I'll be back in about an hour to check on you."

"Uhhhh!" Jasmine screamed as another contraction hit. "I need drugs, give me something for pain. I need an epidural."

"Ms. Hamilton, I'm afraid it's too late to give you an epidural."

"The hell it is! Ahhhh!" Darius came back in and walked over to the corner of the room and set up the video camera to record the beautiful birth of the child.

"Breathe baby, breathe come on." He coached her. "Remember like we learned in Lamaze class." Darius began demonstrating how to breathe, when Jasmine snatched her hand away from his giving him a look of death. After that look, he just kept his mouth shut and caressed the side of her face.

"I am so lucky to have you as my wife." Jasmine took a deep breath and then the pain passed, but she knew it wouldn't be long before the next one hit.

The Write Lover

"I know why I didn't want to do this shit again! Damn, this shit hurts. I know I must love your ass to be going through this shit again!" Darius grinned at Jasmine, bringing her hand to his mouth and giving it a tender kiss.

"I'm sorry baby." He said with sincerity.

"Don't be sorry baby. It's just the pain talking. Honey I would give my life to give you life." Not fully understanding what Jasmine meant by that, he answered back,

"I know honey."

"I love you." She whispered before the contraction kicked in again.

"I love you too." He held her hand, watching Jasmine take the pain like a champ.

An Hour Later . . .

"Okay, Mrs. Hamilton, let's see how far you've dilated." The doctor said, as he put on his sterile rubber gloves and lifted her gown. "How far apart are the contractions?" He asked, looking over her glasses.

"They are about thirty seconds to one minute apart."

"WOW! Nurse, prep Mrs. Hamilton. She has dilated ten centimeters and is ready for delivery." Darius was rushed away along with Jasmine's mother to another room to put on some sterile hospital clothing for participation in the delivery. A few minutes later, Darius and Jasmine's mother were back by her side.

"How are things looking, Doc?" Darius asked, very concerned.

"Well, sir, your wife is ready to give birth," the doctor replied as the medical staff took up their positions.

"That's great. How are you doing sweetheart?" Darius asked, kissing her gently on the forehead.

A few more nurses had entered the room and everything was set for the miracle baby arrival. Darius was holding Jasmine's hand while her mother was on the other side of the bed, moving Jasmine's hair from being in her face.

"Okay Mrs. Hamilton, let's get ready to push...push!"

"Ahhh!" Then Jasmine began her control breathing using the blowing technique.

"You're doing very well. Take a couple of more deep breaths and push!" Jasmine squeezed Darius's hand, as she gave another push.

"Ahhh!" She screamed out again. Darius patted her forehead to wipe away the perspiration. He noticed how Jasmine was looking at him. It was a look he never seen before from her. It was a look of fear. As tears left her eyes and traveled down the side of her face, Darius bent down to ask her if she was alright?

"I can see the crown. You're doing great Mrs. Hamilton. Okay, push." The doctor instructed.

"Ahhh!" She screamed out again, as she continued to breathe in rapid successions. Darius knew not to say anything to her, for fear of being cursed out.

"You're almost there. Give me a big push." Jasmine's mother was praying and saying out loud encouraging words to her daughter. "The baby shoulders are coming through. Give me another big push."

The Write Lover

"Ahhh!" Jasmine screamed out while clenching her teeth, as she pushed with all the energy her tired body could muster up. The baby came free from the safety of its mother's womb.

"IT'S A GIRL!" The doctor yelled out and everyone in the room cheered. Darius kissed Jasmine on her soft lips before going to the other side, hugging and kissing her mother. He then leaned down, kissing Jasmine again on the lips.

"Thank you for giving me the gift of life." Tears began to trickle down his cheeks. The nurse handed Darius the scissor, so he could cut the umbilical cord. The camcorder was catching every precious moment. The nurse quickly scurried the newborn to a nearby table to get cleaned and weighed before wrapping her in a blanket. She then took a picture and made a foot print of the baby before handing her to Jasmine.

"She's seven pounds and one ounce." The nurse informed Jasmine, as she placed the baby in her arms. Jasmine smiled and showered the newborn with kisses. "What's the baby name Ms. Hamilton?" The nurse asked smiling from ear to ear.

"Her name is Jasmine Marie; in honor of my mother and grandmother. Darius was the happiest man on earth, smiling and hugging everyone in the room. Her mother kissed her on the cheek before leaving the room to inform her husband and Darius' mother and brother about the good news.

Jasmine looked Darius in his eyes with pure joy and true contentment, when all of a sudden, she began having difficulty breathing. She began blinking rapidly and tears began to flow from her beautiful brown eyes. The machines that were attached to her went into alarm mode; signaling to everyone in the room that something had gone wrong. One of the many nurses quickly removed the baby from Jasmine's arm and passed her on to another nurse who quickly left the room; then placed an oxygen mask over Jasmine's nose and mouth.

"What's happening? What's going on?" Darius demanded as another nurse quickly took hold of his arm to escort him out the room. "Code Blue! Code Blue!" Blared over the intercom, notifying everyone on the floor, there was a serious emergency. More doctors and nurses rushed pass Darius and into the room. Both families hurried toward Darius when they heard the code blue alarm and saw the worried expressions on his face.

"What happened?" Jasmine's mother asked?

"When you walked out the room she was smiling and kissing the baby, then she looked at me with the biggest smile I ever saw. Then all of a sudden she started having problems breathing. The nurses escorted me out the room." Darius continued to explain as he paced and looked around confused.

"OH MY GOD!" Darius' mother blurted out as she raised her hand to cover her mouth. Jasmine's mother began to cry as she placed her face on her husband's chest. They all paced the hall waiting for the doctor to give them a status update. What seemed like hours, but in actuality were only a few minutes, when the head doctor appeared to deliver Jasmine's status.

"Are you the husband?" The doctor asked, looking at Darius.

"Yes I am."

"I'm sorry to inform you, that Mrs. Hamilton has passed away."

Darius stood there motionless, as if his feet were cemented to the floor. He just stared at the doctor as a flood of tears streamed down his cheeks. He could faintly hear the rest of the family members crying and consoling one another. He was numb, in shock and in disbelief. He felt like someone had reached into his chest and ripped out his heart. The moment seemed so surreal that for a few seconds he couldn't breathe. The love of his life was gone. Then all of a sudden…

"WHAT HAPENED? I THOUGHT SHE WAS FINE. EVERYTHING SEEMED TO BE FINE. WE HAD THE ENTIRE TESTS RUN BY THE BEST DOCTORS. HOW COULD THIS HAVE HAPPENED? THE DOCTOR'S ASSURED JASMINE AND I, IT WOULD BE SAFE; TO HAVE ANOTHER BABY!" Darius screamed at the doctor.

The doctor understood his pain and just stood there, taking the verbal beat down. Darius' mother put her arms around his waist. The doctor had a chance to get a word in, when Darius was trying to catch his breath.

"I think Mrs. Hamilton may have died from a pulmonary embolism. Due to her past history, as a high risk pregnancy patient; but we will not know until we do an autopsy. I'm very sorry, Mr. Hamilton."

"NO BODY IS CUTTIN' MY FUCKIN' WIFE OPEN! DO YOU HEAR ME?" Darius screamed walking towards the doctor. Darius father in-law, stepped in his path, restraining him; so he would not put hands on the doctor.

"I'm very sorry Mr. Hamilton, but its hospital policy to do an autopsy to find out why a patient died suddenly under these circumstances."

"Can we see her?" Jasmine mother asked.

"Yes ma'am. I'm so sorry." The doctor repeated, as he placed his hand on Darius' shoulder before walking away.

Brooklen Borne

Jasmine's body laid in the bed with a sheet pulled up to her shoulders. There was a light above shining down on her face. "She looked like an angel." Jasmine's mother said, as she gently caressed her daughter's face. Everyone continued to sniffle. The tears would not stop. Darius took a hold of Jasmine's hand and looked up and down her lifeless body. Unable to say anything, he just looked and cried.

A few minutes later, everyone left the room to give him some private time with her. He said in a whisper, "I can't go on without you Jasmine." Then he broke down crying. His brother, along with Jasmine's father came back into the room to retrieve him. Both grandmothers went to the nursery to check on the baby.

"Darius, you have to pull it together now. You have a daughter that is depending on you. Jasmine will always be by your side, living through the baby. His brother said, as he placed his arm around Darius's shoulder, pulling him in close. Darius pushed his brother away from him.

"SHUT UP. JASMINE WAS MY BEST FRIEND, MY LOVER, AND MY WIFE. YOU DON'T GET ALL THOSE QUALITIES IN A PERSON, BUT ONCE IN YOUR LIFE TIME. YOU KNOW THAT!" Darius yelled at his brother, with fire in his soul; along with a stare, that would have made a tough guy heart skip a beat. His father in-law walked over to Darius taking a firm grip on both arms and with a stern look, told him.

"Son I truly understand. Mourn your way; but don't take it out on your brother. Your brother is right. You have a daughter that is now depending on you." With tears streaming from his eyes, rolling down his face, like Niagara Falls and mucus from his nose like a kid on cold winter's day. Darius replied.

The Write Lover

"I don't know what to do…I'm lost without her."

*****

Jasmine's father kissed his daughter on the forehead, and then Darius kissed her gently on the lips, before pulling the sheet over her face. As the three men turned to walk out the room, Darius legs buckled and he dropped to one knee. His brother and father took a hold of each arm and helped him back to his feet. He looked back at Jasmine's covered body one last time before turning around and exiting the room. Darius' brother reached over and grabbed the camcorder that was in the corner where the whole ordeal, from birth to death, had been recorded.

Chapter Twenty
The Funeral

    A horse drawn, glass enclosed carriage, pulled by five white horses came to a stop in front of the church. It was like a scene from the movie, *"Imitation of Life."* After Jasmine's casket was taken inside, the immediate family filed inside and took their seats. The church was filled beyond capacity with thousands of mourners who came from near and far to show their respects to one of the best authors in the business.

    Darius was sitting in the front pew, holding baby Jasmine, trying to keep it together. Sitting next to him was Jasmine's mother, followed by Kyle and Kai, then his mother and Jasmine's father and sister.

    The pastor began the homecoming with a prayer. The chorus sang a few hymns and the reading of Psalms 23. Another church representative, an older lady, who seemed to be in her sixties walked over to the podium putting on her glasses, that was resting on her chest and began reading the condolences from people who couldn't attend, but wanted the family to know how much Jasmine meant to them.

    After all the condolence letters were read, the pastor asked Darius if he had any parting words. He stood up and handed baby daughter to Jasmine's mother, before making his way to the podium. He began to give his dedication of his wife and the mother of his child with such feeling that everyone was captivated by the words that were coming from his mouth. Behind him on a big screen was a slide show, showing Jasmine's life, from when she was a baby, to her book tours and accepting literary awards a few weeks before. When he finished his dedication, he signaled to the chorus director, for them to play Jasmine's favorite song. The song was *"Like You'll Never See Me Again"* by Alicia Keys.

Hearing that song, he became light headed, from the overwhelming of grief. His legs trembled and gave away. As he was falling to the ground, a hand came out of nowhere and caught him at the juncture of his armpit. He looked up to see who the Good Samaritan was; it was Eric, Jasmine's ex-husband. Standing next to Eric was Kai and Kyle. Darius quickly gathered himself, getting stable on his feet again, while looking Eric square in the eyes; and said.

"Thank you. I really appreciate that."

"We're family." Eric replied. He was right. Eric's sons and Darius' daughter were definitely tied together as family. Even through death, Jasmine was making things right with all the people that mattered. With that gesture, and what was said between the two, the pastor began to cry. He never witnessed anything like that before between an ex and present husband. The pastor tears began a domino effect and members of the congregation began to let tears escape their eyes; as well.

Once Jasmine's favorite song finished playing, the pastor made his way back to the podium and told everyone to take a moment and read Jasmine's obituary in silence.

Obituary

Jasmine Renee Deveraux-Hamilton
12/24/1973 – 3/21/2011
Los Angeles, CA.

Jasmine Deveraux-Hamilton, 37 of Los Angeles, CA. passed away on March 21, 2011. Mrs. Hamilton was born Jasmine Deveraux, on December 24, 1973 in Sacramento, California to Marie and Dallas Deveraux. She was a hard working mom, raising her children before embarking on her writing career. A career that earned her Four Essence Literary Awards, Best New Author, Two Oscar Nominations for best screenplay and two novels that were brought by HBO and Showtime for a miniseries.

Jasmine died in Los Angeles on March 21, 2011, at the age of 37, following the birth of her third child at the Cedars-Sinai Medical Center. She is survived by her husband, Darius R. Hamilton, two sons Kyle Kai, and one daughter Jasmine one sister, Felicia Deveraux of San Diego, her mother Lesley Deveraux and father, Dallas Deveraux both from Sacramento, CA. and a host of family and friends.

Mrs. Deveraux-Hamilton was a devoted mother, wife, creative and caring woman, who was cherished, loved and respected by many. She will be missed by all the lives she had touched and through them, she shall always live on.

*****

A minute later the ushers began escorting rows out for the final viewing of Jasmine's body, before closing the casket. Standing at the foot of Jasmine's casket was a violinist, playing a soft but

The Write Lover

powerful tune that made the whole church flood with tears. There was not one man or woman who left out that building with a dry eye.

At the gravesite, the pastor said a few more words before releasing a hundred white doves in Jasmine memory. All who came filed by the casket and laid a flower on top. Darius just sat there, not crying out loud, but tears were flowing freely from his eyes. His mother, Jasmine's parents, along with his brother Darnell and his family, sat with Darius until he was ready to leave.

"Come on little brother." Darnell said, putting his arm around Darius.

"What do I do now Darnell? Tell me, what do I do now?" He asked his brother, as if he was ten years old again.

"Look at who you are holding little brother. You know what to do. We all will always be here for you whenever you need us. But now, baby Jasmine needs you to be her father." Darius held his baby closer to him as they all walked to the awaiting limousines.

Later on that evening after Darius' mother put baby Jasmine in her crib; she sat down next to him on the couch.

"I wasn't meddling, but I found this on your nightstand when I went to put your bible in the drawer." She handed Darius a letter and kissed him on the forehead before going to bed. The letter was from Jasmine. He focused on the letter with a heavy heart. On the outside of the envelope the words *With Love from Hawaii* was written on it. He looked up to see his mother disappear down the hallway. Darius looked back at the letter, opening it. His eyes began to water; wiping them with the back of his sleeve, he began to read:

To My Dearest Darius,

If you are reading this letter, it means that I didn't make it through the delivery of our beautiful baby. Don't cry honey, for I'm in heaven with my Lord and Savior. I will have no more pain or any worries, for I'm free of any burdens. I wish I could have spent more time with our bundle of joy, but God knows what's best, even if we don't understand His decisions. You have made me a very happy woman and for that I'm very grateful, honey; I couldn't have asked God for a better man than you. So the love that you shared with me, continue that with our child and by doing so, our baby will be blessed with the love you have given me.

Also, I would like for our child to have a special relationship with his/her brother's Kyle and Kai. It's very important that family knows and stay close together. We as adults may have had problems with one another, but the children shouldn't suffer because of our inabilities to get along.

Besides spending time with my other two sons, you have been my joy. Along with that joy, you have given me a peace of mind; you have been my strength, best friend, supporter, lover and my rock when life was trying to be unfair. We have had special moments and spent quality time together that most people will never experience in all their lifetime. I don't think you will ever know how much your love and devotion has meant to me. Thank you Darius and I want to end this letter by saying, my love for you was so strong, that I have given my life, so that I could give you a life.

Love from heaven
Jasmine

Brooklen Borne

The letter slowly fell from his grasp, as he placed his face in his hands and silently wept. After losing Jasmine, his best friend, lover and wife, Darius had intensions on moving to London, but after reading the letter his wife left behind he decided to stay. He wanted to honor his wife's request, for baby Jasmine to
have a close relationship with her grandparent's, and most of all, her two half brothers. Darius was so distraught about Jasmine's death he never wrote another literary piece or did an interview. He had made millions off his books and movie deals so he and baby Jasmine didn't have to ever worry about anything financially, for the rest of their lives.

The End

Music For The Write Lover

1. **Like You'll Never See Me Again** by **Alicia Keys**
2. **Diary** by **Alicia Keys**
3. **Where Did it Go Wrong** by **Anthony Hamilton**
4. **Can't Let Go** by **Anthony Hamilton**
5. **Amazing** by **Tank**
6. **Your Sweetness Is My Weakness** by **Barry White**
7. **A Woman's Worth** by **Maxwell**
8. **Back In My Life** by **Kem**
9. **Tonight** by **Kem/Marissa Rose**
10. **Giving You All My Love** by **Carl Thomas/Kelly Price**
11. **She Got Her Own** by **Fabolous/Jamie Foxx/Ne-Yo**
12. **U Got That Love** by **Gerald Lavert**
13. **I'd Give Anything** by **Gerald Lavert**
14. **Baby I Love You** by **Jenifer Lopez/R. Kelly**
15. **Beautiful** by **Jim Brickman/Wayne Brady**
16. **Shoulda Let You Go** by **Keyshia Cole**
17. **Down And Dirty** by **Keyshia Cole**
18. **Secret Love** by **Kelly Price**

19. **Sorry Seems To Be The Hardest Word** by **Kenny G/Richard Marx**
20. **There's No Me Without You** by **Toni Braxton**
21. **Un-Break My Heart** by **Toni Braxton**

Book Club Discussions About The Write Lover

Q. Since Jasmine was having an affair with Darius, should she have been mad at Eric for staying over another woman's house, with their children?

Q. What made Chandra think Darius wanted her by his side at the hospital, since they were no longer married?

Q. Should Darius have gone to Jasmine's house to pick her up, knowing her children wasn't ready to meet him yet?

Q. Should Jasmine and Darius let their feelings for one another get so deep, before getting out of their unhappy marriages?

Q. Did Eric really think that his controlling ways and lack of attention in the bedroom wouldn't send Jasmine looking elsewhere for fulfillment?

Q. Should Jasmine have kept her tubes tied?

*Books by
Brooklen Borne
Along with
Other Upcoming Authors*

Brooklen Borne (Author)

"Savannah"

"In The Naked City"

"Being Homeless Is Not an Option"

Anetral Hall (Author/Model/ Poet/Spoken Word Artist)

"Revelations the Untold Truth"

"And Now I Am a Woman"

Karl "The Pathfinder" Anthony (Author)

"False Pretense"

"Fair Game"

"Deadly Consequences"

Beverly "Dimples" Rowley (Author/Songwriter)

"Relationship Contracts"

Katrina Gurl (Author/Publisher)

"The Balcony View"

Charlene A. Harvey (Author)

"The Adventures of the Tiger Club" (Book One of a series)

Kenyetta York (Author)

"The Girls"

Made in the USA
Charleston, SC
24 May 2012